INSPECTOR ANDERS AND
THE SHIP OF FOOLS

Also by Marshall Browne

The Wooden Leg of Inspector Anders

INSPECTOR ANDERS
AND
THE SHIP OF FOOLS

Marshall Browne

THOMAS DUNNE BOOKS
St. Martin's Minotaur
New York

THOMAS DUNNE BOOKS.
An imprint of St. Martin's Press.

INSPECTOR ANDERS AND THE SHIP OF FOOLS. Copyright © 2001 by
Marshall Browne. All rights reserved. Printed in the United States of
America. No part of this book may be used or reproduced in any manner whatsoever without written permission except in the case of brief
quotations embodied in critical articles or reviews. For information,
address St. Martin's Press, 175 Fifth Avenue, New York, N.Y. 10010.

www.minotaurbooks.com

ISBN 0-312-27821-7

First published in Australia by Duffy and Snellgrove

First U.S. Edition: July 2002

10 9 8 7 6 5 4 3 2 1

INSPECTOR ANDERS AND
THE SHIP OF FOOLS

I

THE EIGHTH OF OCTOBER

THE BOMB exploded at 3.00p.m. on the thirty-third floor of the Frankfurt office tower; more precisely, in the boardroom of Chemtex AG, a space known as the 'fish-tank', twelve metres by six, situated at the western end of the floor and enclosed in walls of toughened multiple-ply laminated glass. The designers of this state-of-the-art security hadn't considered an assault from within. The thirty-third floor, otherwise, was open space dotted by a few groups of leather and chrome sofas. Sixteen managing directors, the combined management boards of Chemtex and InterDrug AG, had been meeting to transact special business. Very special business.

The three witnesses, who'd been waiting outside that glass fortress at the eastern end, were thrown heavily to the floor. They were the head of strategic planning for Inter-Drug, Chemtex's chief of security, and the private secretary to the head of Chemtex. In shock, the two men later agreed that what they'd seen resembled sixteen buckets of red paint being hurled simultaneously against the unshattered glass walls of the fish-tank. The secretary wasn't able to say anything, and hasn't spoken since.

Within minutes, the streets of the Frankfurt CBD were swarming with emergency vehicles. The shrieking of sirens and the clattering of police helicopters above the office towers was deafening. Officers of the state Crime Investigation Office were quickly on the scene, hotlines were already open to the federal Criminal Investigation Department, and the federal Ministry of the Interior.

At 6.00p.m., arriving at his flat in Lyon, Inspector Anders saw the newscast on television. He'd taken off his hat and coat before switching on the set, and he stayed standing, watching the stark images from Frankfurt.

The network reporters were excited and apprehensive. The talk on the street was of other bombs. They were filming from a block away. A blond, long-haired taxi driver, who looked like an ex-player in *Jesus Christ Superstar* was being interviewed. He'd been sitting at a rank nearby and was volubly describing how, at the moment of the explosion, the upper section of the forty-storeyed Chemtex building had swayed towards its neighbour as though nodding a greeting. The cameras cut upwards to the towering building, which despite the paroxysm described, appeared inviolate.

Abruptly, a reporter's breeze-pinched face filled the screen. In staccato sentences he informed viewers across Europe that the two boards had been meeting to sign off on the merger of the pharmaceutical giants, which had been dominating the European financial news for the past two months. There were no survivors in the boardroom.

No survivors. Anders switched it off and walked into his bedroom. His flat, overlooking the Saone River, was long and narrow. His Interpol colleague, Matucci, called it 'the corridor'. The bedroom, the kitchen, and the bathroom were small enclaves off this corridor, which was actually the living room. A rearrangement of internal walls in the substantial nineteenth-century building had created this unusual accommodation. Anders kept it dim with a few side-lamps.

'Dark as a cave' – another Matucci verdict. And silent. His flat was always lit up as brightly as a supermarket and throbbing with music – often jazz. But Anders felt at home here, and sometimes at peace. Sometimes. On quiet nights, he could hear the gurgle and murmur of the river.

Boiling water for pasta, Anders considered the outrage. Terrorist bombs had been a big part of his career, of his life, and this looked – smelled – like one such. His thoughts came in an automatic sequence: Responsibility? Objectives? Thirty years ago in Germany, in the days of the Red Army Faction, the answers would've been obvious. Today, almost anything could arrive from left-field.

Regardless of this, the probability was that a claim for responsibility would come very soon. Doubtless, facts and background were already flowing in to their Lyon computers from the organisation's National Crime Bureau in Germany.

He'd have a look at it first thing tomorrow.

His kitchen was tiny, but his movements in it were slightly circumscribed for another reason: his artificial leg. It was the latest model, courtesy of the Italian government, which had been keeping him equipped since he'd lost his left leg high above the knee in a terrorist explosion in Rome in 1982. It was the third in line; the previous two had been destroyed in an incident in southern Italy eighteen months ago. Actually, something more than an incident. 'Sacrificed for the greater good,' said Matucci, who was much more talkative about this, and in general, than Anders.

Tonight, Anders' stump was tender, and after he'd eaten and tidied up he took his cup and the coffee pot into the bedroom and undressed, putting on a silk gown given him by a woman in Turin three years ago. Then he sat on the edge of the bed and removed the prosthesis. For several minutes he rubbed in the special lotion. The stump was red, but not chafed or bleeding as it sometimes was. He'd been on his feet throughout most of the day, which was unusual. At the Interpol General Secretariat, where he and Matucci had been seconded to a special section, it was mainly desk-work.

He'd brought home a report to read and, propped up by pillows, he lay on his bed, scanned it, and drank a second cup of coffee. The printed words blurred before his eyes, and presently he lifted them and gazed across the room at the wall. He didn't see that, either ...

The mafia had found him on a showery, late summer evening in the northern Italian mountain town. In a cafe, where he was having a celebratory grappa. Risking it. Fate. It'd played a disproportionate hand in his life. It was the day he'd written *finis* to his book on the poet Anton Anders, his long dead ancestor. Six months of hard daily labour, scanning his index-cards, pen in one hand, the Beretta, near enough, in the other ... The wall was in his head now, and the scene was rolling across it. He'd chosen a corner table, his face to the door. They'd entered. Two of them, blinking, to adjust their eyes. Closed, death-dealing faces. In the moment before those eyes found him the Beretta was in his lap, beneath the table, the safety off. They'd taken separate tables. Two metres apart. Abruptly, the three waiters and the barman had disappeared. The half-dozen patrons had, almost simultaneously, frozen. Still-life. Eh, what a country!

Their hands were in clear view. Then the right hand of each was moving. The Beretta came out from beneath the table, to the side, and he shot the one on the left in the face. Thunk! Crash! Facedown, scattering crockery and sugar-bowl. The one on the left had, for a fraction of a second, caught the barrel of his Uzi submachine-gun inside his coat. Then he shot the coffee cup, the glass, and everything

4

else off the top of Anders' table, but the inspector was slithering away, horizontal along the banquette, the bullets stitching it in pursuit, and two-handed now he fired his bracket at the man's torso. One in the sternum, one in the left side of the chest, one in the right. This man had been half on his feet and he went back in his chair and it went over. The last crash – though the bar still reverberated from the gunshots.

Putting his hat on, pistol still in hand, Anders walked past white, staring faces to the bar, laid the card with the ministry's special number on it. The barman's taut face had popped up like one on the stage of a *Punch and Judy* show. 'For the carabinieri,' Anders said. He left cautiously. Is there a third? But there wasn't. Why hadn't they waited till he'd come out? It would have been simpler. But they hadn't. In too much of a hurry. A lack of brain-power.

He'd walked up the hill. In his shock, he told himself: B grade marksman. But at that range, good enough.

Later that evening a plainclothes carabinieri colonel with two men had appeared at the house and had driven him, all night, back to Rome. He and his manuscript. To a safe house.

A week later, when they'd made the arrangements, they put him on a plane for Brussels. Looking back at the barrier, he'd the impression they were wiping their hands with relief. He'd been shown to his seat, and sat down beside a grinning Matucci.

The phone rang. He started, the report still open at page one on his chest. Had he been dreaming or thinking all that? Automatically he looked at the clock as he picked up the phone: 10.35. Imperatively, the Parisian accent, the voluble voice of his section chief was filling his ear.

'You've seen Frankfurt?'

Anders straightened himself up. 'Yes. The six o'clock news.'

'The NCB's[1] just phoned. The Germans want us in the field. You and Matucci are to go. You'd better take the earliest flight – report to Commissioner Erhardt at the state Crime Investigation Office for a briefing.'

'What information so far?' Anders' heart had begun to work harder.

'Just preliminaries. It's still coming through. No-one's claimed responsibility yet. That boardroom, apparently it's a slaughterhouse. Worse. Just mush, bits and pieces. Maybe that's better. Whatever, I guess it won't worry you. Phone me when you get to the terminal in Frankfurt. I'll let you know what's come through overnight before you see the Krauts. And the basis you'll be working on.'

Anders put down the phone, slowly exhaled. His section chief disliked Germans. Detested their murderous French accents, among other things. He picked up the receiver again and dialled a mobile number. It was no good trying to call Matucci at home at this hour. A long ring.

'Matucci.'

'Meet me at the airport at 6.30a.m. –'

'Is it Frankfurt?'

'It is. If you've seen the TV you know as much as me. We'll be going to the Crime Investigation Office for a briefing, and Fabre will give us what he has when we arrive.'

'The Germans'll call in the feds for this.'

Anders agreed. If it was a terrorist bomb, the German federal Ministry of the Interior, and the federal Criminal Investigation Department, would be quickly into the picture, one way or the other.

'Nonetheless, the state office is where we start,' Anders replied. 'See if you can get us on a 7.00a.m. flight.'

He hung up. The background noise: nightclub. And there had been two female voices speaking French close

1. Interpol's National Central Bureau

by. When they'd arrived at St Cloud twelve months ago, Matucci's performance at the one-month intensive French language course run by the organisation had been abysmal. Since they'd come to Lyon his social circle had expanded, and he was becoming fluent. Anders knew both French and English, and they'd get by somehow with the German police.

He set his alarm, switched off the light, threw away one pillow, and turned over. Fabre had said 'it won't worry you', which was incorrect, just conversation, and he thought the astute Frenchman had, months ago, guessed the reality.

In view of their duties in Lyon, the call was a surprise. Wheels within wheels. When he and Matucci had been quickly re-posted from the small anti-terrorist unit at St Cloud to the general secretariat, Matucci had said, cynically, 'What gives?' Anders had replied, 'Politics.' They hadn't been welcomed at St Cloud.

It appeared that someone was greasing those wheels a second time.

His heartbeats had settled down. But a strange, steely taste had come into his mouth, a slight constriction into his breathing. He'd been in a delicate state when he'd arrived in Lyon. He'd kept the lid on it. Pretty much. In the early days here there'd been chapters of lurid dreams, and on a couple of occasions the weirdness of hallucinations. Shell-shock, he'd self-diagnosed. Medicos hitherto had been useful for binding up wounds. So he'd taken himself to a French GP. Ativan, the man had prescribed. He'd not taken it. Instead, he'd become reclusive, and it'd all quietened down. Desk-work, as it had once before, had come to the rescue.

Now it appeared he was headed for the field again. A knight in rusty armour, with a creaking leg. He shifted his thoughts to the real world. Images from the past arose in his mind, grounded in the same territory as today's event.

7

It was solid food for thought. Though mush, the chief had said. What a prospect! Tonight, Inspector Anders could not even raise one of his slight, ironical smiles, and it was quite a while before he slept.

II

THE NINTH OF OCTOBER

A.M.

FROM THIRTY thousand feet Anders gazed down on the hazy heartland of the European Community. He squinted against sunlight, peered through the wavery, rainbow-hued vapour trail of excreted jet fuel. In his mind, a vision came: of tightly circumscribed geography. Of sixteen countries, of their millions, shoe-horned into this tiny patch of the Eurasia landmass. He imagined it overlaid with a collage: pasted down edifices – European Council, Council of Ministers, European Commission, Parliament, Court of Justice, Central Bank. Balloons emerged with labels: trade, fair competition, unified currency. Metal tubes appeared, linking prolific bureaucracies, compartments of regulations and directives. Like on one of those old navigator's maps a flag popped up, tagged 'the Euro', blown by a wind, depicted as 'the United States Dollar'. The big experiment. Twelve months in Brussels and he was feeling brainwashed by it. Yet, he'd read that an incoming meteorite the size of a municipal football field would wipe it all out; dust-clouds would blanket the sun for years. Quite sobering.

Ding-dong. He looked up, and the chart-vision vanished. He was back in the aircraft cabin. Turbulence ahead.

At the airport they waited for a taxi. On arrival at a destination, Anders was accustomed to absorbing the prevailing mood, and right now he was receiving a crackling tension; it was penetrating his system with cold precision. His lips tightened.

Anders was a fraction above medium height, a little over fifty. As they waited in the autumn chill he turned his blue eyes, his narrow, serious face on his colleague. They both were senior inspectors in Interpol, though Anders was the ranking man. Matucci was forty, big and blond, with a kind of amused, devil-may-care look, though, when he chose, the ice-blue eyes could go into you like steel skewers. He was a stylish and expensive dresser. Anders had decided that the bulk of his assets were either on his back or in his wardrobe.

Anders realised that Matucci was putting on weight. He'd never have said so. He was naturally polite, surprisingly so for a policeman of his experience, his wear and tear. It was a quality which attracted some women.

The taxi weaved through the traffic, the suburbs. Anders frowned. Sixteen influential men, stalwarts of the business world and, doubtless, of their communities, had ceased to exist in an eye-blink. Apparently, nothing that remotely defined a physical resemblance remained. In that calamitous mini-second, their life's achievements had been separated from their identifiable physicality. Their families had no bodies to bury or incinerate. That's how big bombs worked. And the business plans they'd been about to enact – the merger of two large corporations – were now ideas in limbo, words on paper.

For the moment, anyway. He leaned to the window and

gazed up at the sky: lightly varnished with pollution, an apology for blue. The taxi-driver began to punch buttons on his console. Might've punched one for his voice. He spoke in English, the language Anders had given his instructions in. 'Our government's crazy. They've been releasing those '70s and '80s terrorists. Drip feeding 'em back into the community. Locked up for twenty years or so, then turned loose. The bastards should've got life – *or* been put up against a wall and shot.' He hawked to spit, but didn't.

'Old men and women now,' Matucci said, catching the drift.

'In their forties and fifties – young enough to set a bomb. They wouldn't forget how to do that,' the driver replied curtly.

Though would they still have the anarchist inclinations of their youth? Anders wondered. He'd asked to be dropped a block away from police headquarters. An old habit: don't disclose destinations to strangers. A section of the city centre was blockaded by the traffic police, he noted.

'Have a safe stay,' the taxi-driver said meaningfully.

'Welcome, colleagues from Interpol.' Nine-fifteen a.m. Commissioner Erhardt, head of the state Crime Investigation Office, gripped their hands in turn. 'Wait!' He dived into a nearby room, had a brief conversation.

'Sorry, sorry.' He sat them down in his room. He was red-haired and freckled, of Matucci's age and size. Quickly he briefed them on what was known to date. It wasn't a lot. 'Our technicians are still at the site. That's going to take days,' he explained. 'A team from federal Crime Investigation's arriving within the hour. The state government's shitting itself over this one. All these prominent guys dead. They hate to call in the feds.'

They drove downtown to inspect the scene. The Chemtex tower was cordoned off. They were met by the corporation's deputy chief of security. 'My boss is still in hospital,' he said. Anders shook his hand. It was wet and trembling. They went up to the thirtieth floor in the lift, then had to take the stairs to thirty-three as the lift machinery was out of plumb higher up. A uniformed cop was stationed on the landing. The Germans watched the way Anders negotiated the stairs.

He paused on the landing as if to catch his breath, but it was more than that. A reluctance had risen in him to re-acquaint himself with such a scene. Perspiration had broken out on his brow. In his armpits. Why am I here? Still in this business, back on the chopping block? His hand on the balustrade, he wondered if it was inertia. Recently he'd been to Holland, tossing up whether that would be a place to retire to. He'd returned, irresolute and depressed.

From the distance, Erhardt warned, 'This isn't pretty.'

Anders came back, nodded. But it was about what he'd expected. The 76mm-thick glass walls of the boardroom were painted with gore and an encrustation of fragments: bone, tissue, skin, clothing, furnishings. Through patches in the obscene caking, Anders could see blurry figures in over-alls moving. It seemed an amazing arrangement for a boardroom. Fish-tank was an appropriate description. His stomach had turned over. Vomit ascended his throat, descended.

Matucci stared at the ghost-like figures, his hands in his pockets, his face blank.

'No point in going in,' Erhardt said with a glance at the clearly affected Italian, 'I'll call the chief tech out.'

12

The man appeared, removing a surgical mask. A portly, white-haired type, fifty, with the rosy complexion of a Bremen housewife.

'We're speaking English,' Erhardt told him.

'I'm having to change the shift every hour,' the man said. 'That's as long as my people can stick it.'

He grinned sourly. 'The average-sized adult male has about 5.5 litres of blood in his body. Multiply by sixteen, and you can paint a room.'

Erhardt grimaced and blew his nose disgustedly. '*Christ*. What have you got so far?'

'Plenty. But it'll all have to go back to the lab. Lots of tiny bits of metal. Not another thing to tell you except that the blast was intensified to a terrific degree by that bloody super-toughened glass.' He emitted a short, stressed laugh. 'Okay?' He hurried back.

'How did they plant it?' Anders asked tightly. 'And when?'

The deputy chief of security's pager was chattering away on his belt. He switched it off. He was blinking rapidly, and looked taut. Erhardt nodded to him to answer Anders. He cleared his throat. 'The tower was built in the 1970s. Because of what was going on in those days every piece of security technology that could be thought of went in. This floor, isolated behind armoured doors. Two entrances: the lifts and the stairs. Both needing codes to gain access. The boardroom, isolated within this, had its own code. Only six persons with the code to the boardroom. None of the directors had it. Four of the six are down at police headquarters being questioned. Two of them are in hospital – my boss, and the managing director's PA. The other man who was on the floor is also in hospital – the strategic planner.'

'None are critical except the PA. Mental with' her,' Erhardt interposed.

Understandable, Anders thought. Your boss is dictating to you, and, hey presto, an hour later you can't find enough of him to fill a soup can.

The deputy security chief said, 'Just to get in the building itself without the proper authority, or codes is –'

'Impossible?' Erhardt queried tersely. 'That's what you thought.'

'Perhaps the bomber or bombers had the correct authority, and the codes,' Anders suggested. The others exchanged glances which took them nowhere. Slowly they walked to the east side of the floor. Anders eyed a sofa. 'The security cameras?' he ventured.

Erhardt shrugged angrily. 'On floors 32 and 33 the records show they were switched off for ten minutes on the day before. Between about 4.30 and 4.40p.m.' He gave Anders a look. 'No reason's been forthcoming. The chief of security, who was controlling the panel, can't give one.'

Anders glanced at Matucci. He saw that his colleague was also surprised at this.

'All recent movements in and out of the building are being checked,' Erhardt said flatly. 'Especially the day before. There's a team burrowing into the terrorist archives. We've asked Interpol to do the same.' He took them downstairs. In the lift, he said, 'The day before yesterday Chemtex's headquarters was like Grand Central Station. Visitors coming and going.' He ticked them off on his fingers: 'A delegation from West Africa, the labour union, EC politicians, a task force from the EC competition directorate, legal advisers, directors' wives, et cetera.' He spread his hands. 'We're busy trying to sort it out.'

In the spacious ground-floor foyer, Anders and Matucci

examined the procedures for entering the building: X-ray machines, metal detectors, a holding-area with electronically operated doors as used in safe-depositaries. More survelliance cameras. Standard, for big German corporations. They spent fifteen minutes looking it over.

Erhardt was slapping his pockets as though he'd forgotten something. 'I've got to get across town. I've an appointment with the two West African government ministers heading that delegation. Then I've got to brief the feds.' He shook hands with the Interpol men. 'There's an office for you at headquarters ...' His mobile began to ring. '*Erhardt.*' He became alert, walked away, listening. He stopped at a bench, brought out a note-book and pen, and began to write down what he was being told. Obviously, there'd been a development. Anders and Matucci waited.

The commissioner closed off his phone, laid it down and continued to write for a moment more. He turned decisively to the Italians. 'There's been a contact,' he said grimly, passing the note to Anders.

THE EUROCHEM BOMBING IS THE
RESPONSIBILITY OF THE JUDGMENT DAY
GROUP OUR MANIFESTO AND DEMANDS
WILL BE ANNOUNCED

Erhardt gazed at Anders. 'Typewritten. Addressed to the state police commissioner. Received in the morning post. Posted in Munich.'

Ah, yes. The response had arisen in Anders like a sigh. Did their scriptwriters all come out of the same mould? 'Eurochem?' he asked.

'It's what they're calling the merged group.'

'Cranks?' Anders essayed. 'Is it legit or has some ratbag

15

jumped on the band-wagon?'

The German shrugged. 'Forensics have got the note. We'll know more a bit later. I must go –'

Anders walked across the foyer to shake hands with the deputy chief of security. Again, not a pleasant experience, but Anders believed in the niceties. The man had settled down, except his eyes were watering profusely.

They followed Commissioner Erhardt out. He turned back to them, 'I'm going the other way. Can you get back all right? What'll you do now?'

Anders stared at the street. 'We've got a roving brief at this point.' That's what Fabre had told him when he'd phoned the secretariat from the airport. 'We'll go and talk about it.' He passed their mobile numbers to the German.

Matucci said as they walked away, 'Eh, Anders! A new pack of anarchist bastards? Or rejuvenated ones? Or something more sophisticated?' His English was poor but he'd got enough of it.

'We'll go and eat and talk about it,' Anders said. He didn't feel like eating, but he'd had no breakfast. Matucci grinned at the prospect of lunch.

Erhardt's car stopped beside them, and he wound down the window. 'Let's hope this isn't the start of a *second* German Autumn,' the redhead said grimly, and sped away.

Anders stared after him, nodding to himself. 'German Autumn' was the name given to the period in 1977 when there had been a resurgence of terrorism after the Baader-Meinhof Faction. The commissioner's speculative remark fitted the mood that had come to him when he'd stepped off the plane.

Whatever their origins, these terrorists had engineered a smashing blow at capitalist big business, possibly the most successful – and brutal – ever. Inspector Anders could almost hear the clash of two sabre blades, each of tempered steel. On all sides, the ethics, the moralities of an amalgamating Europe, were a salad being continuously tossed. Hard duty, hard thinking – for a man of social-democratic convictions, sympathiser of the socially down-trodden, seeker of justice. Despite the pleasant sunshine, he felt an ominous and depressing chill.

III

THE NINTH OF OCTOBER

P.M.

'I T'S SO small I can't take my jacket off,' Matucci complained. He wasn't impressed with his room.
'Try harder,' Anders suggested equably. On a previous visit Anders had stayed at this small, inexpensive hotel near the old Opera House.

Matucci feigned indignation, then grinned. 'We aren't going to sit on our arses at state headquarters on a three-way liaison between Lyon, the NCB, and the Germans, are we?'

They were in the coffee shop. Anders was trying to eat a soup full of sausage, cabbage and dumplings. His stomach still felt slightly squeamish. He glanced at his colleague, who'd polished his plate off, and pushed his own away.

They *could* do that, and some of their colleagues might have. Interpol's main contribution in a case like this was its computerised International Criminal File. And its database of major crimes. The evolution of the European Community had meant that criminals crossed national borders at will, and the organisation was a key resource in keeping track of many such movements. Its NCB, located in each country, liaised with the federal police.

Anders' and Matucci's Lyon assignment had turned out to be gazing at computer screens, shifting paper: intelligence-gathering and communications. However, somewhere along the line, a decision had been taken for the directorate to move into an active investigatory role when so requested by a member country. 'Politics' wasn't much of an answer as to why they'd been put on this case, but it was the best one Anders had at present. He looked around the coffee shop

'Be patient,' he said. He was waiting for more information. It was early days, and their ignorance was profound. Doubtless, several of the tense conversations at nearby tables concerned yesterday's mass-murder. This morning the Frankfurt newspapers had printed head-and-shoulders photos of the dead on the front pages: lined-up like political candidates the morning after an election.

Anders' mobile rang. Commissioner Erhardt said, 'We've got something on the note. Same typewriter as the machine used twice in the late 1970s by a splinter gang which became active after Baader-Meinhof was broken up. The lab says no doubt about it. They started off with a few bank robberies, graduated to a couple of bombings of US bases, kidnapping and murder of an industrialist.'

Anders was amazed. He knew the group. 'Karl-Heinrich Stuckart.'

'That's the one.' Erhardt sounded surprised.

'Never apprehended – and the leader was reported dead in 1989.' Anders had been reading the database at Lyon for twelve months.

'Correct. The Munich police have located his ex-wife. They've been questioning her for the last hour ...' He gave more information on this, and Anders jotted down a few points.

'I'm back at headquarters,' Erhardt said. Suddenly he sounded angry. 'When I got to their hotel the West Africans wouldn't see me. One of our foreign ministry people was there. Told me not to push it. They'd given him a statement that they'd observed nothing untoward during their visit to Chemtex and had nothing to say. Do you believe it? My chief is calling the foreign ministry. We can't let it lie there.'

Anders made a sympathetic sound. He'd taken a decision. 'I'll go to Munich,' he said. 'Inspector Matucci will come into that room you offered.'

The commissioner was silent for a moment. 'You won't find her in a good mood, Inspector Anders. They say she's no shrinking violet ... The man to see at the Munich crime office is Lieb.' He tailed away. 'Got to go. Now we're drowning in the feds. My boss's tearing his hair out.' He paused. 'Is Stuckart alive, and kicking? That's what our people are asking.'

This was left echoing in Anders' ear. He put down the receiver, and returned to the table.

After lunch, Anders went up to his room, and Matucci, looking well-fed and ebullient, glad to be back on the street, strode from the hotel headed for police headquarters.

The rooms *were* on the small side. He called the hotel receptionist to book him a flight. He sighed and unstrapped his shoulder holster. Like the 9mm Beretta it held, it showed signs of its long service. Old acquaintances. He sat on the edge of the bed and removed his prosthesis, and his right shoe. He'd lie down for an hour, then take a plane to Munich. By the time he arrived he expected the Munich police would've finished with Frau Stuckart – though now she called herself Frau Huber. If he had to see her, he wanted her to himself. What fool would use an identifiable typewriter?

The businessmen's shuttle touched down at 6.20p.m. The nerves in Anders' stomach flared up as the plane's wheels bumped on the runway. Grimly he thought: despite everything, it seems that when Button A is pressed I lurch back into action, giving it my best shot. Depressing. In that mood, he took a cab into state police headquarters and found Detective Lieb in a room full of tension and cigarette smoke that you could've cut with the proverbial knife. She'd been released at 5.00p.m. She'd been adamant (more than that, the detective commented sardonically) that she knew nothing of the bombing, and that her ex had died in '89. She was unbelievable, but as far as possible they'd checked out her story. He shrugged, gave Anders a look as though to say 'over to you'. He hadn't had dealings with an Interpol man before.

The Munich streets were adorned with illuminated shop windows. Over kilometres of cobblestones, electric light rippled. A new city to Anders. Warily, from the rear seat of a cab, he watched it go by. At Frankfurt, he'd picked up the London *Economist* and found what he was looking for: an article on the Chemtex–InterDrug merger. It spelled out details which interested Anders. High above southern Germany, he'd learned that the sixteen directors of the managing boards had been unanimous in approving the merger; that an estimated 21,000 jobs would be lost in the EC. The cool, unadorned prose seemed unreal in the light of the horror unleashed on the merger's protagonists – just two days after the article's publication. He pondered this.

It was a ten-minute taxi ride. Tramtracks gleamed

coldly in the centre of the cobbled street. There was a minor amount of traffic, a few pedestrians, a sobering cool breeze.

An unmarked police car was parked fifty metres away from where Anders alighted from his cab. He picked that up at a glance: two plainclothes cops, watching. Presumably they'd been told about him. From the file in Lyon, he knew what Stuckart had looked like: a lot of black, unkempt hair, a large, unshaven jaw and big, zealot's eyes. His ex-wife had been a small fish – hardly even that – and he'd only a sketchy idea of her. Tall, stringy blonde, forty-three, in jeans and jumper, the Munich detective had said. That was a lot of women in Munich, or anywhere.

He went across the pavement. The apartment block had a metal security door but it was open. Behind him he heard them coming. 'Inspector Anders?' a voice said in German. He turned. The one in the leather jacket had spoken. About thirty, lean and blond. The other was dark, with a narrow, intense, face. They were both wound-up as tight as springs.

'Yes,' Anders said.

'Lieb called,' the blond one said in English. 'Watch yourself, Inspector. If that killer Stuckart's dead, my Aunt Rosie's a ballet dancer. This Huber woman's lying. All these ex-terrorist women are liars. Total liars. Watch your back. That's all.'

'Thank you,' Anders said. He turned away, and entered the foyer. He took the lift to the third floor, and pressed the buzzer beside the only door. He removed his hat while he stood patiently in the lens of the spy-hole.

The door opened on a chain. 'Yes?' A sharp inquiry from an unseen woman.

'Frau Huber?'

23

'Yes.'

'I'm sorry to disturb you, but I'm an officer of Interpol. I'd appreciate you answering some questions,' he said in English, and held his accreditation in the gap. 'Might I come in?'

A pause. 'Jesus Christ.' A low, despairing exclamation. But she unhooked the chain, swung the door wide open, swept him with a glance. He sighed to himself: a look at him, and nearly always the innocent granted him entry.

'Come in, why not? The whole Munich police department's 'been here. I've been eight hours answering questions at the police station, drinking their lousy coffee, while they turn my apartment into a slum.'

She *was* blonde and stringy, wore no cosmetics, and in Anders' judgment spoke edgy, but near perfect English. She turned her back and led the way into the living-room. It was plain the detectives had been thorough and not over-careful.

'Now I've got Interpol calling,' she tossed back. 'Jesus,' she said again, hands on hips, inspecting the room.

She turned blue eyes on him that reminded him of Matucci's. 'I won't give you coffee, or ask you to sit down. Make it quick, will you.'

'Your ex-husband –'

'Is dead. Seventh July, 1989. I saw him in the coffin. Before that I hadn't set eyes on him for five years. He hadn't changed much. Though thinner. I had a lot of bad memories at that moment. But I was the nearest and dearest.'

She laughed, almost choked on her breath. Coughing, she pulled cigarettes out of her jeans, stuck one in her lips, and lit up. Anders could see her hand shaking. 'I had him cremated.' She whirled around and went to a cupboard,

24

pulled out a flask from a low shelf. She opened the lid. 'Take a look. Everyone has.' Anders glanced down at the fine ash. 'Here's all that's left of Karl-Heinrich. I was going to throw it in the garbage. But I didn't. He was a human being of sorts. Aren't we all?' She put it back.

What she'd just said and done proved nothing. Except that she was hyper. Anders thought for a moment. 'Why don't we have our little talk over a drink. Is there a bar nearby?'

'No!' she said emphatically.

Then she came a little out of her world and stared at him – this Italian Interpol investigator with his serious face and polite manner issuing a social invitation. A difference from the shouting and cajoling detectives she'd had in her life earlier in the day.

She brushed back the short blonde hair with a nervous gesture. 'All right. I could do with a drink. There's a bar around the corner.'

★

Frankfurt airport: 7.00p.m. Commissioner Erhardt, three of his men, and Matucci, stood with their backs to Rhineland posters on the departure hall's wall. It was busy. PA announcements continuously fractured the upper air. Trolleys were clashing. Kids were squealing. The police party had eyes only for the group at the Air France first-class check-in counter: the two Africans who stood on the red carpet, expensive raincoats draped over their shoulders, smoking cigarettes, while their bulky minders did the check-in, manhandled the luggage. They'd come across the hall like a royal procession. A small party of press were there, and the minders had shoved some aside. The

25

government ministers weren't talking. Until this week the West Africans' mission to the German pharmaceutical giants hadn't been much of a story. But it was emerging. And now with the bombing ... The foreign minister and the health minister. Erhardt didn't know which was which.

Erhardt had come out to the airport in the hope that he might secure a last minute interview with the Africans. But it he now saw that wasn't going to happen. He felt tired. Two Germans walked across from the check-in and stood beside Erhardt. 'Thanks for your help,' the commissioner said. 'It's been wonderful.'

The senior man from the foreign ministry said, 'This is very political. Very delicate. They've got a case. German companies have been up there with the other multinationals blocking the cheap new AIDS drugs. It's a big problem. A sensitive one for the government. We don't want to bring any more focus on it than can be avoided. Not at this moment.'

Erhardt grunted. The Africans had cut short their visit; were leaving a day early. Already he had witnesses to the acrimonious meeting with Chemtex directors the day before the bombing. He didn't like it, and he was furious. Give him one more day to get the government sorted, but now these bastards were minutes away from departure.

'Anyway,' the foreign ministry official said soothingly, 'haven't you got our home-grown terrorists to go after? These fellows say they've nothing that'd help your inquiries.'

'Thanks for your thoughts,' Erhardt muttered.

A belated journalist and photographer were running across the hall. The camera flashed in the ministers' surprised faces. One gestured and said something. An African minder swung the photographer into a headlock, another grabbed the camera and peeled out the film.

The German foreign ministry men tensed. Erhardt's detectives looked at him for a lead. The big redhead stood there stolidly, glowering, but gave no signs. The photographer was released, thrown his camera. The West Africans swept away to go on board.

Matucci, leaning against the wall, smoking, was surprised that the visitors wouldn't welcome all the publicity they could get for their mission. But he had an imperfect understanding of politics, and he did have the impression that the mission had gone sour.

*

Her name was Renata and she'd been picked up in Stuttgart in '79, convicted and sentenced to two years imprisonment for being a member of a terrorist organi-sation. What a laugh, she said bitterly. Even then I was separated from him. I'd left that gang of mad people two months before they went underground, started their violent phase. I was lucky to get out. If I'd stayed longer it wouldn't have been possible. He said they should let me go, and they did. So I'm alive, or not serving twenty years. Then they began the bank hold-ups, and the killings. But the court didn't care. The government, everyone, was paranoid about the terrorism. The time in prison was just lovely. I had a state lawyer who was sympathetic, and, finally, he got the case reviewed. The Stuttgart court released me in December '81, just in time to get my butt frozen off that winter.'

He listened. She smoked, drank pilsener, and talked gesturing nervously – as though she hadn't had a conversation for years. Her fingernails were bitten ragged. What had the detectives in the unmarked car thought when he'd walked

27

past them with her? He crinkled his eyes against the smoke. She drank the pilsener down like a man. She said that one night in '85 Stuckart had turned up here. He had a new name. For God's sake give me a break, she'd told him. He left a bag. To get him out of the place, she'd had to let him leave it. She'd opened it pretty quick, nothing but clothes, books, camera, and his old portable typewriter. Her eyes flicked to Anders, away. Seeing how he was taking it? A liar? Possibly.

'And that was that.' She shook her head in disbelief, stubbed out a cigarette. 'Now here I am, unemployed, on welfare, with a new name and apparently anyone who wants to can find me when they like.'

One of the detectives from the car had entered and was having a beer. Anders ignored him. 'What about the typewriter?' That was why they'd descended on her, why he was here.

'Stolen three months ago with his suitcase. The fools this morning couldn't believe it. Had I reported it? No. Why? I don't want to see policemen.' She was sincere, or she was glib. Anders hadn't taken his eyes off her face.

'"He's alive," one prick starts shouting. "The bastard's still with us, back at his old tricks."

'"You are a frigging idiot," I told him.'

Anders smiled slightly. He could picture it.

'"The imprint of a particular machine is like a fingerprint," another one says. Jesus, so what? That's nothing to me.'

He saw that she'd become a little drunk. Careless, if she were lying. Was she a great actress, or was her story true? He couldn't tell, and he took her out into the cold and back home.

She sat in a chair, her hands on her knees, her head down. He sat opposite, poised to leave. What a strange one, she was thinking. She could feel his sympathy on her like a balm.

Unsteadily, she said, 'I've never had an Italian dick in me. Haven't had anyone's in a long, long time. *Oh, Jesus!* Fancy saying that!' She slapped the back of one hand with the other. 'Skinny, forty-three-year-old blondes with sagging tits aren't in much demand around here. How's it where you come from?'

Tears began to roll down her face, drip on her spread hands. Her shoulders had begun to shake.

She wasn't crying about that, or today, she was crying about her life, Anders understood.

'Let's get you to bed,' he said.

She allowed him to lead her into the bedroom. He folded back the covers, took off her sneakers, helped her lie down, pulled up the covers. She closed her eyes, and left this 'frigging' day behind. As he went out, she murmured 'Your English accent's terrible, and what is wrong with your leg?'

In the living-room, after a moment's thought he placed his card on the coffee table, pulled the front door closed, rode the lift down, shut the security door, stepped into the street, and walked away from the police car.

Looking for a taxi he brooded on his own day. His instinct told him that the German police – and he, himself – had spent it in a fog. Maybe up a blind-alley. That old typewriter hadn't been used carelessly or accidentally. Persons who could assemble and put in place a bomb like that weren't fools. Either they had a great contempt for the intelligence of the police agencies, or ...?

He shrugged in the near-empty, pristine Munich street.

29

Street-cleaning here was clearly an art-form. Routinely, he checked the environs. He felt detached – as though he was a thousand kilometres away. Much more solid was the instinctive feeling emerging, that he'd stepped into tortuous territory. Whether it had anything to do with the 1970s epoch of terrorism was an open question.

Renata Huber may or may not have been lying. But she was holding something back. He was certain about that.

He caught the last flight to Frankfurt and arrived back at the hotel before midnight. He knocked on Matucci's door. Light and jazz music were coming from under it. The big detective opened up and stood there in shirt-sleeves. His hair was brushed back smoothly and he still looked dapper. He'd managed to get his jacket off. He ran his eyes over a weary Anders.

'Late for you. I thought you'd call.'

'I'm going to take a shower, then I'd like to talk.'

Anders took his shower, and changed into a light linen jacket he kept for evenings. Wearing it somehow made him feel that he was having a respite from his work. But not tonight. His ablutions took him longer than most: the leg. Always the leg. And his nerves were back; no doubt about it. And the resentment.

They sat in lounge chairs in the small, deserted lobby, in the shadow of a potted palm. Matucci had bought a brandy miniature for Anders, beer for himself.

Briefly, Anders described Munich, and the conclusions he'd reached. He was more interested to hear his colleague's news – and he asked two specific questions.

Matucci responded: 'They've pretty much cleared and sifted that glass tank. They say it was Semtex-H. One thing – they're rebuilding from metal fragments what they

30

think'll turn out to be the circuit board. If they can get enough it might be a lead. But it'll take time. Also, they've found some magnetic material.'

The desk-clerk, across the room, spruce and alert, pushed computer buttons efficiently.

'As to how the bombers got in,' Matucci shrugged. 'We had a nice little trip to the airport.' He explained that. 'Then we went to the labour union office. Ten of their leadership sitting around a big table. Jesus, you should've seen 'em. Hard as nails. The way they told it there must have been blood on the carpet at their meeting with the Chemtex directors. Chemtex people were talking redundancy payments, the union fellows were talking rolling strikes. The union boss said: these lousy directors are putting 21,000 of our brothers and sisters out on the street so they can unload more dough on themselves and the shareholders. He wouldn't answer any questions Erhardt wanted to know the answers to. Just wanted to spout the politics. They finished up shouting at each other. Bottom line is that the union and Chemtex reached no decisions. It was just opening shots.'

Anders' eyes were drooping. He jerked himself awake. He was back on the thirty-third floor. According to the deputy security chief, no-one had been on that floor since the day before when it was cleaned, as usual, by two old employees under the supervision of his boss. 'On the day, what about flowers, food?' Anders asked.

'Neither on that floor. They ate in the dining-room on thirty-two.'

'That gap in the camera surveillance?'

Matucci shrugged. 'Nothing more.'

'Mmm,' Anders said. He sipped the brandy.

'The German feds have taken over. They're pulling out

31

all stops. Going after people from all the old terrorist groups. Dragging 'em in for questioning. Using our database and their own. Stuckart's mug will be in papers across the EC in the morning. They've aged it, given him a human haircut. There are check-points up. Extra men at airports.'

Too late for that, Anders thought.

The phone at reception rang and the desk-clerk answered it. Brooding on the man's late-night brightness, Anders recalled that in the late 'seventies it'd been estimated that 1,200 highly dangerous persons were undercover in Germany, with another 6,000 active sympathisers. Today they were fewer but more variegated in their missions. He sipped the last of the brandy, and Matucci tipped the bottle and swallowed his beer.

They agreed to meet at 7.00a.m.

Matucci said, 'Maybe there'll be a glimmer of light, if and when this manifesto's released.'

'It will be and soon,' Anders replied as they walked to their rooms. He thought: that's what happens next. Otherwise what's the point? As for any light …

He lay awake. It was a phoney war at present. But the fish-tank wasn't phoney. It stood as solid and indestructible in his mind's eye as it still did on Chemtex's thirty-third floor, and its red hue glowed and glowed on the back of his eyelids. He realised he was sweating profusely. Mao's classic words wafted into his mind: 'Punish one and educate one thousand.'

IV

THE TENTH OF OCTOBER

A.M.

GEOGRAPHY WAS a problem when Anders opened his eyes. Then he remembered: Frankfurt, and heard the low steady sound of early commuter traffic beyond the double-glazing. He sighed. Munich, Renata Huber, and Karl-Heinrich Stuckart, dead – or alive? His stump was hurting, and he didn't feel refreshed. 6.20. He turned on the television, and began his ablutions.

The self-important newscast music brought him out of the bathroom. The French news had commenced. He'd caught something about a sensational overnight development. The pretty blonde newsreader, looking both excited and scared, was saying:

'*6.00p.m. last night in Brussels a Belgian freelance journalist was kidnapped by the group identifying themselves as the Judgment Day group, which yesterday claimed responsibility for the mass-murder of the sixteen directors of the giant German chemical companies Chemtex AG and InterDrug AG. In his parked car, a gun held to the back of his head, the journalist, Monsieur Philippe Dupont, was forced to take down its manifesto which stated that the terrorist group would strike at any corporate*

33

merger that damaged European workers ...'

Anders switched off the set, harnessed up, pulled on his suit-coat and hurried down to the coffee shop. Matucci was there, absorbed in the Italian papers. The detective looked up. He spread his hands, and continued his scanning.

Anders took *Le Figaro* from a rack, and sat down.

TERRORIST MANIFESTO RELEASED

The Frankfurt bombing is a warning to giant corporations and multi-nationals whose activities, be they mergers or down-sizing, sacrifice the lives of European workers and their families on the obscene altar of directors' salaries, bonuses, and share options. These amoral persons, ripe with greed, are going to be called·to account. Our eyes will range the corporate world searching for such abuses. We will show no mercy. Our reach will go into EC government and its agencies. The EC competition directorate is put on notice. Now our eyes turn to the proposed Supermarkets (France)–Country Fresh merger which will decimate communities in France as upwards of 17,000 jobs are eliminated. Let the boards of those companies swiftly re-think their position, or beware of the consequences.

'Ah,' Anders said.

'Now France,' Matucci growled.

Anders leaned back in his chair, read that the Belgian journalist had sold his report to Reuters and the German and French TV networks. Quick work, all done in a few hours. His photograph was on the left-hand side of the front-page. Beneath it, Anders read: 'Monsieur Dupont said that the final words spoken to him, the gun still at the back of his head, were: "Who cuffs and beats his human brother/That nothing did to harm another/Offends the sense of many another."'

Anders read this twice. He gazed across the room. What was this? The terrorist had carefully repeated it, Dupont said.

Abruptly Anders pushed the paper to Matucci, tapping the place.

'Bloody-handed poets,' his colleague commented after a moment. The words meant nothing to either of them.

'Erhardt,' Anders said folding up the paper.

Matucci tossed aside his. 'Ten minutes to put something in my stomach?'

Anders sipped coffee and watched the other detective wolf down ham and eggs while newspaper pages and businessmen's pre-meeting nerves rustled all around them. He thought about this craziness. The terrorist mind took no prisoners. That's what he'd always hated. It could be said that the capitalist mind didn't, either. His communist trade union father had said that. Bloody murder on the one hand, corrupted ethics and cynical manipulation on the other. What a world! All he could do was practise his trade. If he was still up to it.

Commissioner Erhardt was in the operations room with fifty senior uniformed state police, federal and state detectives. A deputy commissioner from the federal Crime Investigation Office slapped a rostrum with the flat of his hand for quiet.

'Our Belgian colleagues are running an interrogation of this journalist, Dupont, at 2.00p.m. We'll have people there −'

'I hope they'll kick his arse,' a high-ranking state officer interrupted. The German police hadn't been advised of

Dupont's filing until 4.30a.m., when a Frankfurt editor had phoned as the papers were coming off the presses.

'How would you expect one of those freelancers to act?' the deputy commissioner said sarcastically. They were all on edge. He launched into a summary of yesterday's activities. He finished: 'A task-force's presently being assembled to go to the Ministry of the Interior in Paris.'

In the corridor outside, Erhardt, who looked like he hadn't slept for two nights, said to Anders and Matucci, 'The feds are shifting the focus to Paris. The Chancellor's going on television at 5.00p.m. We're assuming Stuckart's alive, that the bastard's feeling his oats again after laying low all these years.'

Anders nodded. 'We'll sit in on Brussels.'

'Frau Huber?' Erhardt said. 'What did you think?'

'I think she might be holding back on something.' Anders shook his head slightly.

Erhardt gave him a look, and strode away.

Out front, there was a traffic jam of departing vehicles. To an accompaniment of slamming doors and revving engines, Anders said to Matucci, 'Go to Brussels. Hear what Dupont has to say. Try to get him alone afterwards. You never know, he might hold something back from the session which a persuasive fellow like you can extract.' He shook his colleague by the hand. 'I want to talk to a banker I know.'

Banca Internazionali Di Roma announced the brass plate on the modern four-storeyed building in the quiet, leafy West End street. Anders entered its foyer, nothing as sordid as tellers or well-used bank notes here. A fragrant smell, and no street sounds. This was an investment bank working in the capital markets. Anders smiled at the dark-haired

36

receptionist. For looks and grooming, the women employed by private banks were in a class of their own.

The short, mid-forties banker from Rome came out to greet Anders, and they shook hands. His name was Dottore Romano Zanotti. 'It's been some time,' Anders said politely, 'but you're looking fit and well.'

The other smiled. 'And you, Inspector. Despite everything.' Their association went back six years to a banking scam in Rome. An old unsolved case which Anders had been instructed to re-open, and which had gone nowhere.

'With Interpol now?'

'Yes. A section dealing with terrorists, sad to say.' It was a relief to speak Italian.

'Ah.' The investment banker managed to make it both a commiseration and an acknowledgment of the outrage. They entered a room and sat down.

'How can I help?' Zanotti asked.

Anders told him. Could he supply a list of major corporate mergers in the EC already announced or currently under negotiation? The banker nodded quickly. This morning, like every man of commerce in the EC he'd studied that turgid manifesto. The bank specialised in merger advice, though the smaller-scale deals. He asked Anders to wait, and left the room. He was back within five minutes, a computer printout in hand. He laid it before the detective. 'Four big-ticket mergers are on the go.'

Anders read the names. Chemex AG and InterDrug AG, Frankfurt. Supermarkets (France) SA, and Country Fresh SA, Paris, two big Dutch oil groups, and finally, Agribank France SA, Paris, and Deutsche Rural-Credit Bank DG, Frankfurt. His finger, his eyes rested on the last. He'd heard the names but knew nothing about them.

'That's an interesting one,' the banker said. 'The French

bank's got strong roots in the French agricultural sector.' He smiled at his pun. 'The other's a comparable institution in Germany. They're in negotiations, nothing decided yet. There's a rumour the merged entity would have its headquarters in Strasbourg. That's where the talks are being held. Given Strasbourg's past, a symbolic unification.'

'Any estimate of job losses announced?' Anders asked.

'Nothing on that. But you could count on a lot going. Though, if it went ahead this would be different from the others in that respect.'

'Oh?'

'They're vast organisations, each has two to three thousand branches spread across regional cities, large and small towns in the respective countries. There's no duplication of branch network. What you can bet on is that they'll be looking at rationalisation in other ways: the wholesale closure of branches to be replaced by centralised district offices, automatic telling machines, telephone banking, the internet. Getting their customers out of bricks and mortar branches, or making them travel a bit further.'

Zanotti swivelled his chair to stare at a framed map of France and Germany. 'Let's say they converted branches into district offices at a ratio of around 4:1 – that's maybe 1500 branch closures – which gives an idea on the personnel cuts.'

'Do you think it might go ahead?'

The Rome banker smiled and shrugged. 'The fact that it's out in the open, in the media, says it might – if they can get the EC competition directorate's approval. Crossborder mergers have an extra layer of complexity.'

Anders was politely effusive with his thanks as they shook hands.

'Good luck,' the banker said.

Three men were entering a conference room, attended by one of the banker's colleagues. Zanotti looked surprised. He hesitated, then turned to Anders. 'Those three are the gentlemen from the competition directorate who dealt with the Eurochem merger.'

Anders showed his interest. 'The merger task force that was at Chemtex the day before the bombing?'

'I guess so.'

Anders thought for a second. 'I wonder if they'd have a few minutes to see me?'

Zanotti hesitated again. 'Why not? I can ask my colleague. Wait here.'

Hat in hand, Anders entered the conference room with his usual politeness. He shook hands with the three men. They had five minutes before their meeting started, and were pleased to talk with him. They regarded him curiously, aware of his famous exploits in Italy. Two of them, tall, Frenchmen, one fair, one dark, early forties, wore charcoal grey pinstripe suits and white button-down collared shirts. Bayard and Fouralt. Senior bureaucrats to their fingertips. The boss, a Belgian, Arminjon, was short and paunchy, wore a flashy tie and a red rose in his buttonhole. He was smoking a cigar, had the appearance of a bon vivant. Zanotti did the introductions, and left them alone. They sat down.

'It's an honour to meet you, Inspector,' Arminjon said. 'We're still in shock. A terrible business. And now this manifesto. We had a conference call with Commissioner Erhardt yesterday. Told him all we could. But it was a routine visit – for us. We met Herr Bosch.' He frowned. 'The late Herr Bosch and three of his ... late colleagues. A few matters had to be settled between us on the merger approval – and were. The meeting lasted less than an hour. We came, we talked, we left.'

Anders nodded slowly. 'This was on the thirty-second floor?'

'Yes. The corporate headquarters.'

'There were several meetings going on. Did you observe any of the others?'

'The union was in. We certainly heard that going on in the background,' Fouralt said. 'It was torrid. Herr Bosch said he felt sorry for his colleagues who were meeting with the union leaders. He made a joke about it. But he looked a bit worried.'

'Did you see the West Africans?' Anders asked.

'No,' Bayard responded. He looked at his colleagues. 'I think they'd left before we arrived.' The others nodded.

Arminjon glanced at his watch. 'That's about all we could tell Commissioner Erhardt.'

Anders took the cue. 'Thank you for seeing me. It's most useful to have a first-hand report.' They shook hands and Anders went out. Zanotti's colleague hurried past Anders into the room carrying a stack of papers. The door closed.

Dottore Zanotti had vanished, and Anders left. He wondered if the three men he'd just seen would be working on the Strasbourg merger. If it came off. He liked Zanotti, but his bank had a Temple of Mammon atmosphere that left him cold. He'd never had money himself.

He stood in the leafy, sweet-breezed street. Here, the world seemed quiet and harmless: the promise of a better place. But the city's priests and pastors were working to capacity. The names on that printout ... Were the clergy of Europe looking at a boom-time, and the undertakers, if anything was ever left for them to deal with? He smiled grimly. You're turning into a black humorist – or a glib cynic, he upbraided himself. But deep in his heart there wasn't any humour.

V

THE TENTH OF OCTOBER

P.M.

ERHARDT WAS locked up in a meeting. Anders sat in the office and waited. Stuckart's face – twenty years back but doctored by the experts – stared up at him from a paper's front-page. Moodiness personified. Psycho. Looked like he'd slit his grandmother's throat for the right cause. Zealot and terrorist. All of that, the guts and the crisis-points of Anders' life. In the semi-bedlam of the state police headquarters, *Banca Internazionali Di Roma's* temple-like silence seemed like another planet. But behind that aura such banks were operating in their own cut-throat world. Dealing with those suave bankers, you should know that ... Did anyone answer telephones around here? Anders winced at the latest shrilling outbreak. He thought about the list of mergers. He felt at a remove from the events in progress. A spectator.

Erhardt came in, looking slightly more relaxed: the feds were taking some of the strain. 'Inspector Anders, you think the Huber woman's not coming clean?'

Anders nodded. The red-headed German stared at him. 'She was a bit-player. Served time, and that clams 'em up.

The Munich boys say she's lying. Probably is. But about what? *Is* Stuckart back in the land of the living? If not, who used his typewriting machine? And *why* use it when it's bound to be identified?' He shook his head. 'We'll watch her, maybe pull her in again.'

Anders had an idea about the 'why'. He paused, thinking how much to say. 'It smells of new blood to me. A new group that *wants* the search directed back into the past.'

'We're always going to start with our databases.'

'True.' In Lyon, Anders had the history of European terrorism at his fingertips. He'd been closely involved in the rise and fall of the Italian terrorist-anarchist cells in the 1970s–1980s. For a while, new groups had been hard to get a fix on; they'd learned from the mistakes of their predecessors. They'd come out of the universities, the student world – mainly unknown faces. Until they'd made *their* mistakes.

The commissioner scowled. 'The West Africans are home and dried. Off our screen. Though they've got people here we're looking into. Did Inspector Matucci tell you about our pleasant interlude at the union office? And now we have this journalist prick, Dupont.'

Anders nodded, said, 'The manifesto sets a topical agenda.'

'Holding a gun to a journo's head in a parked car's inviting trouble. Hell of a way to get the word out. They could've just mailed it to Reuters.'

'Precisely,' Anders agreed.

The Frankfurt crime chief gave him a look. He sucked at his teeth, then said expansively, 'But listen to this: scholars have been calling in about that verse. It's a translation of lines from a book called *The Ship of Fools*. Written by a Strasbourg man, Sebastian Brant, in the fifteenth century.' He rolled his eyes. 'God Almighty! Does it mean something? Or are these madmen just dressing up their mayhem with colourful, roughly relevant words?' He shook his head. In his mind, poetry and mass murder were as compatible as wine and axle-grease.

'Strasbourg?' Again. Anders gazed at the wall where a large-scale map was tacked up. His eyes found the old city on the Franco–German border, now home to the European Parliament and the European Court of Human Rights.

The phone rang and Erhardt picked it up, listened, and covered the mouthpiece with his hand. He looked more harassed than ever. 'Well, what are you going to do?'

Anders shrugged. 'Inspector Matucci will be back tonight, then I'll decide.'

★

Matucci had hired a car at the airport. At five-twenty p.m. he was parked in a street near Brussels' police headquarters watching the journalist Philippe Dupont getting into his Volvo. Dupont was short and overweight. Matucci had studied him at the police interrogation, watched his brown eyes flick here and there.

The journalist steered out into the traffic, abruptly turned right into a narrow street and accelerated. Matucci saw why. An unmarked police car had also been waiting and had swerved onto the Volvo's tail, cutting off Matucci's Renault. The Italian detective braked, swore softly.

If the journalist was trying to lose them, he quickly gave it up. He stopped at a post-office, parked, went in and came back with a handful of letters. Sedately he drove to a suburban Chinese restaurant, set in a garden festooned with coloured lanterns swinging in a breeze. Matucci

43

parked in the street a hundred metres away and walked back. The two cops sitting in their car gave him a look as he sauntered by.

Dupont was alone at a table slitting letters open with the blade of a pocket-knife. It looked like he hadn't collected his mail recently. Matucci smiled at the hostess in her cheongsam, pointed at Dupont and went to the table. He stood looking down at the journalist. The brown eyes flicked up, and then stared. Dupont's lips were full, and petulant. Matucci held out his accreditation. 'Interpol,' he said laconically. 'Could you give me a few minutes.' He was pulling out a chair as he spoke.

'Jesus – weren't you at that road-show?'

'I was.'

'So?' The tilt of his head was arrogant, self-important.

Matucci took out his cigarettes and lit up. 'I wanted to get better acquainted.'

Dupont, his hand held over the opened mail as though guarding some great secret, received a whiff of Matucci's pungent tobacco. 'What is this?'

'Interpol is maybe on a different road from the Belgian cops. I was hoping for a one-on-one.'

The journalist leaned back, breathed out – a long sigh. He scanned Matucci's face. The detective's broken nose somehow made him look even more handsome. 'Do you want some dinner?'

'Chinese is my favourite,' Matucci grinned. That was true this year.

Dupont, his finger slithering down the shiny menu on a familiar journey, ordered stewed duck with black mushrooms, Yin Yang shrimp, sweet and sour cabbage with dry red pepper. Matucci grinned approvingly. At the meeting, what had interested him wasn't Dupont's regurgitation of

44

an ideologue's political claptrap, or the self-dramatising telling of the verse (which the emissary had spoken twice) but the details of what had actually happened during the encounter. He'd found Dupont unimpressive.

But he concealed that behind his ready grin. 'How about telling me the real story?'

Dupont reddened with anger. Then shot the detective a sly look. 'What d'you mean?'

Matucci shrugged. 'You journalists are good at keeping some things secret 'till you're ready to use them.'

Dupont's look turned calculating. He nodded slowly. 'What's in it for me?'

'Maybe yours truly, or Interpol, can help you out one day.'

Dupont analysed the answer, surveyed Matucci. 'Okay. I'll give you a private run through. Not that there's much difference.'

This was the way he told it: at 6.30p.m. last night he'd left his house and got into his car parked beneath one hundred-year old plane trees. It was dark. The street was empty. He was going to a reception at a hotel in town. He was about to put the key in the ignition when –

'Don't panic. Don't move.' A distorted voice, and cold steel had pressed into the back of his neck. He froze. Quite understandably. 'Above all do not turn your head. If you see me I will have to kill you. Please take care not to see me.'

(Afterwards, he'd found the rear-vision mirror twisted up.)

'I have a scoop for you. The biggest you will ever have in your life. I suggest you take out your pad and your pen and record what I'm about to say.'

Dupont said that it'd come to him that if he did what he was told he'd survive. Then he'd been plunged into

45

Thursday's bomb horror. Again he'd gathered his wits together. Five or six minutes and it was done. *'You will cancel your engagement, go back inside and write the story. Then you will phone your contact at Reuters, and negotiate a deal ... Which should be lucrative. Do not go to the police before you file the story.*

'Now, look at the floor ... remain like that for two minutes.'

The cold steel had vanished from his neck, the rear door had opened, and he'd been left with the sounds of the breeze in the plane trees.

A slight twist in the thick lips, he stared at Matucci.

The detective exhaled a gust of smoke. 'Well, well, that's a *bit* more than you told the road-show.'

But not much, and, in any case, was it true? Matucci looked at his hands. He couldn't find it in himself to trust this man. His street-cop's instinct was vibrating. He'd the feeling that Dupont was holding something back. He felt pretty sure the fellow would manipulate the truth when it suited him. Was he planning a second big story, another big pay day?

The thought hit Matucci: the journalist might be one of them. Not impossible. One of their devious, though weaker, links. If it wasn't, why choose him?

Dupont was perspiring. He glanced impatiently towards the kitchen. As if in response, the steaming dishes arrived.

The food was excellent, and Dupont had ordered two bottles of Tsingtao beer. The assessing eyes flicked afresh over Matucci. Over his gold watch, gold tie clasp, superior tailoring. His wide shoulders. 'I don't talk while I'm eating,' he said, and it seemed non-negotiable. Clearly he wanted to taste every nuance of flavour, to take in every detail of the handsome Italian from Interpol.

When they were drinking the red tea, he said, 'You want to go on to a club?' He went to work with a toothpick.

Matucci grinned. 'Love to, but ...' Abruptly, the big detective beat out a rythmn, Caribbean-style, on the tabletop like it was bongo drums. '... but no go – this time man – gotta rush down – the old autobahn.'

Dupont's eyes widened in amazement. Matucci desisted. Still grinning, he wiped his mouth very deliberately with the napkin. 'I'll be back.' He took out his card and laid it by the journalist's plump hand. 'You can get me on this number – day or night. Maybe the truth will come back to you.'

'What?' Dupont didn't know how to take it. A cop-humorist? He frowned, then shrugged. 'Here's mine.'

'About the voice?' Matucci asked.

The journalist's eyelashes fluttered. 'As I said at the conference – some kind of synthesiser was in use. Similar to the sound of someone who's got an artificial voicebox after cancer. I do have the feeling that the voice is going to turn up again – with more news.'

Dupont was getting tired. A few moments before the evening had looked interesting, now it'd turned dull and bureaucratic. The bill arrived, and arrogantly he pushed it across to the Italian. 'Interpol's paying, I take it.'

★

Anders saw the speedometer needle flickering on 190 kph, and felt pushed back in the rear seat by their speed. Erhardt hadn't put on his seatbelt. Illuminated autobahn signage shot out of the dark, and in an eye-blink flicked behind them. On its outsize puss-in-boots' tyres the big Mercedes

47

was as steady as a rock. All around them, home-running traffic was doing a similar speed.

The call had come in thirty minutes ago. An ex-member of Stuckart's old faction had been tracked down. Released from prison three years ago he'd been successful in disappearing – until now. Living in a nice house in Bad Homburg, they said. Two families.

'This dragnet's got him. At one stage the guy was Stuckart's right-hand. An animal. Killed an officer in cold blood in a bank holdup. They should've thrown away the key.'

'Five minutes, Commissioner,' the driver said.

Frau Huber said her ex-husband was dead. The records certainly showed that a Karl-Heinrich Stuckart had died in Munich in 1989 and had been cremated. The police didn't believe the records. They'd had experience of the supposedly dead. Anders hadn't made up his mind one way or the other on that point. Renata Huber had something on her mind, though. About that, he was fairly sure.

The Bad Homburg street was quiet as an evening prayer. Good-looking houses, most of them lit-up. After this, the residents would be doing some heart-searching about the neighbourhood, Anders thought. He stood in the soft breeze watching the preparations. The three cars from Frankfurt were parked around the corner with a local police car. The local inspector said he'd men in the alley at the back of Number 44.

Number 44 showed no lights.

'Okay,' Erhardt said to his men, 'let's do it.'

Quietly, the local inspector with a sergeant carrying a mobile battering-ram moved to the front door. Four of Erhardt's men followed them closely. Pistols were drawn. Erhardt and Anders brought up the rear. Anders thought he heard voices inside.

The sergeant moved into position. His inspector stood back leaving clear passage for the detectives. WHAM! The front door crashed open. The detectives streamed in.

The dozen faces, all ages, in a half-moon around the huge TV, suppers on their laps, snapped around. Big eyes, open mouths. Then food was flying everywhere. Women were screaming, kids squealing. The detectives dived at the two men. A big fellow with a goatee beard got as far as a door before they hauled him back. He was fighting hard. The other sat tight, his eyes darting around. They dragged him out of the chair, forced handcuffs on. A woman was clawing at one detective's face, screaming abuse as he swatted her away. A black cat launched itself at Anders' shoulders, used them as a bridge to the door. Kids were scuttering underfoot. Deftly Anders grabbed a couple of toddlers by the arms and lifted them into a corner out of harm's way. A woman came from nowhere and tore them from him.

They had the cuffs on goatee beard. He was still struggling. They'd stood the small, dark fellow against a wall. His eyes were looking everywhere.

'*Where's Stuckart?*' Erhardt's inspector yelled into his face. He shook his head, shook off the spray.

'Dead, you idiot.'

Crack! Flesh on flesh. The inspector's hand – man's face. Ceramic clatter. Dentures on floorboards. All the kids began howling vociferously.

'Same answer, *arsehole.*' A jet of saliva spurted into the detective's eyes.

'Okay!' Erhardt seized his man's arm, arrested the next blow. 'Take him, and him, and her and her, into headquarters. Now!' His finger jabbed at the ones.

Anders was glad to be out of it. He'd a headache. Half the street were standing in their gardens, gawking. Sirens approaching. 'The big blond with the little beard's the one. We'll work on him,' Erhardt said to Anders as they drove back to Frankfurt.

Anders returned to his hotel at nine. About a dozen interview rooms at headquarters had been engaged. They'd been bringing people in from all quarters. The goatee-bearded fellow hadn't said anything except to ask for a lawyer.

The Chancellor was speaking to Germany, the European Community, on French cable television; voiceover in French.

'The government and the people of Germany will not sacrifice their democratic values in the face of *any* threat. The cowardly perpetrators of the outrage in Frankfurt have deprived the nation of sixteen of its leading business-men, and their families of loving husbands and fathers. They will be relentlessly hunted down and brought to justice. The German people can rest assured, that no revival of the terrorism of the past era will be permitted. Above all, these terrorists should note that the march forward of the European Community is irreversible. They are deluded in thinking that their objectives can be attained. The clock cannot be turned back. In this hour of distress, we all stand together ...'

For a long moment, he stared into the camera's eye.

Staring into the eye of the storm, Anders thought. Worthy sentiments, but not that simple. Some of the words had sounded like Helmut Schmidt's in '77. He switched off the set.

Paris was in the spotlight now. Why didn't he just go

50

there? Or, better still, stay here. Do the liaison job. Keep out of everyone's way. Keep out of harm's way.

He sighed and felt his heart beat faster. He'd decided otherwise. God knew if he could handle it. He picked up the phone and called Lyon. His section chief had gone off to a four-day conference in Amsterdam, so he was put through to the deputy. The man was a bureaucrat to his boot-straps; not a supporter of the organisation's field investigations.

'*Anders,*' he said. The intonation was that of a hunter who'd found something good in his trap. 'Let's hear it.'

However, first he made a meal of emphasising the NCB's valuable liaison activities with the German federal Criminal Investigation Department. Thanks to this, the German authorities now had the form and status of every known terrorist and anarchist group in Europe.

'*Now* what progress are *you* making?' he demanded.

'Tomorrow, we'll be moving to Strasbourg.'

'What! ... *Why?* Paris is where –'

'I've some experience in these matters,' Anders interposed.

'I can't take responsibility for this.'

'No-one is asking you to. The chief gave me a free hand. Are you revoking that?'

Silence. Condemnation and distrust were coming down the line. 'Very well. Report tomorrow – without fail.'

Anders put down the phone. 'Every *known* terrorist group' was the operative phrase in the man's diatribe. All the current frenetic police activity might be headed in the wrong direction. Going to Paris in accord with the ideas of a fool like that, suddenly seemed like a fishbone stuck in the throat. The big merger being negotiated in Strasbourg was a beacon in his mind, and the verses from that city

51

flickered in it like fireflies. And, the more he thought about it, the more the Stuckart–Munich situation seemed like a subterfuge to confuse the police. He'd take a look at Strasbourg. No one else was.

'Eh! What a day.' It was nearly 11.00p.m. Matucci was standing there, grinning wearily. He sat down on the bed and told Anders about Brussels. Anders listened. Erhardt was right to be puzzled by the method chosen to release the manifesto. What about this Dupont's credibility? He asked that question.

Matucci sucked his teeth. 'A Belgian cop I sounded out claimed he's no terrorist. They reckon his record's clean. But my hunch is it didn't happen the way he's telling it.' He shrugged. 'He might've been sucked in, for the dough, or something else. Or maybe it's just that he's held back something to dole out for a second pay-day. I've called a man to look into his past. We'll see.'

Anders nodded. The possible Agribank–Deutsche Rural-Credit merger in Strasbourg was on his mental screen, demanding attention. He told Matucci about his day – and evening. About the Strasbourg connections. He got up and took the few paces the room allowed. Back and forth. 'We'll shift our base to Strasbourg tomorrow.'

Matucci gazed at him. His instinct was to go to where the action was. Always. The Krauts were taking Germany apart. Especially the terrorist and ex-terrorist world. But their high-flying team was off to Paris. 'Are you sure about that?'

'Absolutely. We'll look into this giant merger, but keep options open on Paris.'

Matucci still showed his doubt. 'They won't like it in Lyon.'

'They don't. I've talked to Roget.'

Matucci groaned. The ace bureaucrat. His personal name for the deputy chief.

'We're going, Matucci.' Anders stared at his colleague, felt the outbreak of spasms under his left eye.

Matucci nodded, turned, and left. Anders closed the door behind him.

In the corridor, Matucci lit a cigarette and inhaled. The hotel was dead quiet. A great place for Inspector Anders to think in – though wherever they were, he was hardly ever not immersed in his thoughts. Even when he was asking you to pass the salt. Obviously, this assignment was about as welcome as a diagnosis of cancer. In recent months that nervous eye-flicker had gone, but tonight it was back. He was fragile again.

The blond detective shook his head. He hoped Anders' nerve wasn't going to crack. Courage was like a bank account. Gradually you used up the deposit, and went into overdraft. He'd have to keep a close watch on his compatriot. The signs were he was on the brink of 'over-drawn'. And going to Strasbourg might be a bad mistake.

'Shit,' he told the corridor.

VI

THE ELEVENTH OF OCTOBER

A.M.

STRASBOURG WAS dreaming in an azure morning when Anders and Matucci came to it. A heritage city, a university town. Anders had been looking through a guidebook during the flight. He was an addict of guide-books, the older the better. City of the Romans, of pâté de foie gras and the 'Marseillaise', of Luther, Gutenberg and the first printed Bible, of the cathedral spire (1439); historically, exchanging its nationality between Germany and France, and now permanent seat of the European Parliament. She waited pure and open-faced in the mellow sunlight, like the city's ancient seal: a virgin with outstretched arms. He brooded on the new scene, on his notion. He'd never known much about virgins.

They'd touched down at 8.35a.m. Before departing Frankfurt, they'd called at police headquarters. A senior detective had briefed them on activity overnight. The Stuckart situation remained a mystery. The interrogation of the ex-terrorists hadn't turned up a thing. At 7.00a.m. the German cop had said, 'The Chief Commissioner of the fed's Criminal Investigation Office's flying to Paris to confer.' From today, German investigators would be attached to the French Police Nationale, and Gendarmie; Interpol was continuously relaying updated profiles on all known terrorist and anarchist groups, et cetera. Grimly he'd advised that more memorial services were taking place today; tomorrow the Chancellor was to attend a combined service.

On the short flight south, Anders had had a look at the French papers. The front pages concentrated on the manhunt, and the feared *next target*: the Supermarkets (France) and Country Fresh merger. The principal of an economic think-tank, Felix Servais, was profiled. In *France Soir*, a slab of print beneath the man's rather doleful, bearded face lauded him as the architect of the merger, told how he'd sold his idea to each corporation, and steered the deal through the EC's competition directorate. Servais hadn't been available for comment on the present situation.

Understandable, Anders had thought. If he'd any brains, he'd be off for a long visit to New Zealand.

On inside pages: grief-haunted faces of people in cavernous Frankfurt churches.

At the taxi-rank, Matucci, lighting a cigarette, said, 'What d'you think about that circuit-board?'

That was the other news. Frankfurt forensics had already sifted out and pieced together this scrap of evidence: a fragment of an electronic timer. They were trying to decipher the maker's name.

'Keep tabs on it,' Anders replied. Like the Munich typewriter, he wondered if it would lead into a dead-end.

Anders put down his suitcase with obvious relief. Matucci had a smart suit-carrier slung over his shoulder. He used his looks and charm with stewardesses to have it hung correctly, even in jam-packed aircraft. He'd given up trying to get hold of, and carry, Anders' leather case, which had travelled the length and breadth of Italy, and looked it. He was annoyed. Anders had hardly spoken a word on the flight.

Their taxi skirted the city's ancient centre, an island enclosed within the languorous arms of the river Ill. It reminded Anders of Amsterdam's watery world where a month ago he'd been, partly on a sentimental mission, partly trying to make up his mind about quitting this life.

They registered at a small hotel in a side-street which ran back from the river's southern arm. Matucci's eyes sparkled as he chatted up the slim brunette who checked them in. 'Christine, is it?' he said.

'Right on. I'm dayshift, free at night.'

'Are you ready?' Anders said insistently from the front door.

Matucci muttered under his breath.

★

The low-rise office building in the outer suburb which was the regional headquarters of Agribank France SA was already, as usual, buzzing with the energy of its staff. But today there was more in the air – a current of excitement, mingled with fear. In the boardroom four people sat, two either side of the long table.

A short, powerfully built man with black, crinkly hair watched a secretary pour coffee into white cups, and then place a Meissen basket-weave plate of airy pastries on the table. He nodded, and smiled at her. 'No interruptions, Louise.' His voice was deep.

Henri Bosson was chairman of the management board

of Agribank. Beside him, a tall woman with a mass of blonde hair swirled in a perfect, if rigid, arrangement, smiled slightly to herself. With a sideways flick, her head assumed an arrogant tilt. As well as being his wife she was one of the bank's managing directors. Ten years ago she'd been on the stage.

Bosson stared across the table at his opposite number at Deutsche Rural-Credit Bank, Klaus Hofmann. The German was six foot four, in his mid-forties, a steely, handsome man. On his forehead was a birthmark, the size of a one franc coin. He was a crack skier who'd represented Germany.

'May I say again, how delighted we are at the prospect of the union of our institutions.' Bosson's wide lips moved in a gratified smile, the somnolent eyes opened a fraction wider.

Hofmann said, 'We needed to move fast and we have.'

Almost everything was settled, though the announcements had been perfunctory as yet. In principle, the merger had been agreed by the two men after meetings with board committees, and the sign-off on the deal, subject to shareholders' approvals, was to take place at a joint meeting here in Strasbourg.

It had been fast all right. Had to be. One of the big Frankfurt banks had been sniffing around Deutsche Rural-Credit. Everyone knew about that, as they did about Henri Bosson's ambition. Within a tight circle in the German rural giant, a very few knew of another factor germane to the merger: in its mortgage portfolio, a financial time-bomb was ticking away.

Henri had wanted speed, but he'd sensed that Klaus had wanted it even more. That gave him an itch of concern. Unresolved issues still existed, including the approval by the EC competition directorate. Also, several directors on each board had announced their opposition. But Bosson and Hofmann were confident that the merger could be sold to all the parties.

For half an hour, they talked.

Bosson cleared his throat. 'The Chemtex–InterDrug atrocity gives pause for thought.' He looked at Hofmann. 'We both knew several of those who were so foully murdered. What should our reaction be? *Should* we have a reaction?'

'The Chancellor's determined to find the terrorists,' said Hofmann. 'The enforcement agencies are much better prepared than in the seventies. We should take adequate precautions.' His eyes travelled methodically over their faces. 'However, it seems the Supermarkets–Country Fresh deal's the focal point now.'

Bosson nodded. 'Yesterday, the chief of the local Police Nationale called on me. The Interior Ministry's concerned, and they propose attaching three officers to you and me, Klaus. For our other directors, they suggest our security consultants.'

'It should be done.'

Dominique Bosson appeared irritated at the digression. She said, 'The Competition Directorate's not yet declared its hand.' Her teeth were a tribute to the orthodontic profession. She flashed them at Hofmann. Her smile had a force which disarmed most recipients, but Hofmann stared back stonily. Undeterred, she went on, 'When Herr Kramer and I laid the proposal before them last month in Brussels the response was reticent.' She glanced across the table at the thin, pale-faced man opposite. On the white shirtfront revealed by his opened suitcoat, she'd detected a faint red smear.

In puzzlement, her husband, who missed very little, was also looking at Kramer's shirt. He said, 'Cross-border. They're cautious. That's predictable. In the final analysis, I expect their approval.'

'Yes,' Hofmann agreed. 'Our networks are in different countries. The anti-competitive aspect is minimal.'

Bosson seized a second pastry – as if it might escape. He wolfed it down. His weakness for anything sweet showed at his waistline. Hofmann's stomach resembled a flat piece of steel.

Those Brussels bureaucrats were expanding their empire, Bosson thought. They might start ferreting into what effect the *rationalisation* of networks would have on both banks' customers. Maybe. He switched his thoughts to Hofmann.

Sunlight glinted on the German's steel-rimmed spectacles. His blue eyes met Henri's. The merged entity would have joint chief executives until the end of the financial year. The new board of managing directors would then elect their chairman, and deputy. Probably Klaus was as confident of attaining the pre-eminent appointment as he was himself. That couldn't be permitted.

But Hofmann selected neutral ground. 'Congratulations to Madame Bosson, and to our own Herr Kramer. They've joined their intellects with an admirable result.'

The two executives, each the head strategic planner in their institution, had evolved the concept. It amused Kramer, who had more of a sense of humour than Dominique Bosson, that the grand design had emerged from pillow-talk. This morning her red fingernails had raked his chest as she reached orgasm. He smiled secretively.

Hofmann gave a slight, formal bow to each. Madame Bosson resisted an inclination to look at her lover. Hofmann thought: not only their intellects have been put together.

Henri Bosson's mind had circled back. 'The Frankfurt terrorists' manifesto – those verses from *The Ship of Fools* struck me as intriguing. I do hope its use by these anarchists is merely a coincidence.' Again Dominique looked irritated.

★

The headquarters of the Police Nationale was bleak and unwelcoming. Anders and Matucci took no notice. They'd spent a good part of their lives in such buildings. The police chief – a central commissaire – was expecting them. 'Rolland,' he announced. A grey-haired, grave-faced veteran. Anders' first impression was that he'd absorbed the old university city's aura. He had a prominent nose upon which capillaries had exploded in red confusion. On the left side of his face was a constellation of moles. A handkerchief was stuck in his sleeve.

Anders lowered his gaze. He was continuing to expand his gallery of examples of the police chief genus.

'A welcome to Interpol and its representatives,' Rolland said, with formal handshakes. He'd come around from behind his desk. Anders blinked. Counterparts in Italy might have raised their bums a centimetre from their chairs.

'Congratulations on your fine record, Inspector Anders, against the Red Brigades, and the mafia. It's widely known in the EC.' Anders nodded politely. They stood there. The police chief appeared puzzled. Maybe curious. He said,

'*Our* police, and the Germans, are focusing on Paris as the next likely flashpoint. And Interpol comes to Strasbourg?' His serious eyes moved over the Italians. 'Is there a message in that, Inspector?'

Anders' leg creaked softly as he sat down in the chair indicated. He arranged himself into a comfortable position. 'All one's eggs shouldn't be in a single basket, should they, sir? And you have two big banks talking merger in your city.'

It was an incomplete response, but he felt dull. He'd hardly slept. In the 'seventies and 'eighties in Rome, he'd launched himself at the terrorist crisis with passion and energy. But he'd been younger – and uncrippled. And not prey to mental aberrations.

Matucci brooded on trophies in a case, on the commissaire's compliments, on Anders' mood. He began to reach for cigarettes but changed his mind.

The police chief was back in his chair. His eyes hadn't left Anders'. 'May I inquire what you are proposing to do here, Inspector?'

Anders' mobile shrilled. He reached for it, glanced at the police chief. The commissaire nodded.

'Erhardt here, Inspector. You'll be interested in this. Chemtex's deputy chief of security's gone missing. He and his car about 7.00 last night.' The Frankfurt crime chief gave a few details. 'Takes us in another direction! Things are fluid aren't they? ... Why Strasbourg, Inspector?'

'I'm in a meeting, Commissioner.'

'Okay we'll talk again.'

Anders put his phone away. The badly shaken security man was clear in his mind's eye. Commissaire Rolland was waiting. Anders reported the development. 'Aha,' Rolland said softly. 'The bomb ... an inside job?'

62

Anders spread his hands. 'Commissaire, would you arrange for me to speak to Monsieur Bosson? At the earliest opportunity.' He added politely, 'That is my starting point.' He'd plucked it out of the air.

The Strasbourg police chief frowned. He pushed a buzzer, and a short, powerful man, dark as to face and hair, mid-thirties, promptly stepped into the room. Apart from his dour face, he brought whiffs of garlic and tobacco.

'This is Inspector Ferrand of our urban detectives. He's at your service. He'll make the necessary arrangements.'

Anders and Matucci rose briefly and shook hands with the detective, who after a few words from his boss, ambled out again. Anders, in turn, was curious about something. 'Are you a native of Strasbourg, sir?' he inquired.

The commissaire studied the Italian's politeness with the degree of attention he devoted to the daily log-book. He was considering whether he was being out-manoeuvred on his own ground. 'No. I've been here twenty years.'

'Doubtless, you've good contacts in the university community?'

'I'm not unknown in that circle. I took a degree here.'

'Congratulations! How interesting.' Anders could see the commissaire sipping Alsace muscat at the university. Abruptly, he stood up. Matucci followed his lead.

'I won't take up more of your time. May I be in touch?'

'I hope you will be,' Rolland said succinctly. He'd become thoughtful. Suddenly, he declaimed: '"Who cuffs and beats his human brother/That nothing did to harm or bother/Offends the sense of many another."'

From under thicket-like eyebrows he gave Anders a stare. 'Perhaps *that* is one reason why you're in Strasbourg, and not Paris, Inspector?'

In the anteroom, while they waited for Inspector

Ferrand, Matucci said, 'I bet it's a degree in literature. Good basic training for catching terrorists, eh!'

Anders smiled. His colleague's mood seemed to have improved. 'It could be helpful to us,' he said.

VII

THE ELEVENTH OF OCTOBER

P.M.

'INTERPOL?' HENRI Bosson drawled. 'Why in Strasbourg? I understood the main action's now in Paris.'

Anders smiled disarmingly. 'I'd be grateful, Monsieur, if you'd listen carefully to what I have to say. It concerns your personal security, and that of your colleagues.'

The chairman of the management board of Agribank frowned. Did he know anyone high up in Interpol?

Matucci cast a discerning eye over Bosson's suit. Then over his consort. A small white dog was sniffing at his knee. Madame's pet.

Ferrand sat quietly, careful with his eye-contacts. These people had influence. Tons of it.

'You've not answered the question, Inspector,' Madame Bosson intervened.

Anders turned to her. 'Madame, we're here because of the merger negotiations. We're cautious, and wish to cover all possibilities.' His blue eyes drifted over the tall blonde. Here was a woman who'd gone through the so-called glass-ceiling like a laser beam, picking up Bosson on the way, he supposed. Strikingly beautiful. Perfect complexion.

He turned back to Bosson. 'Sir, I recommend the cancellation of all board meetings. Any meetings should be held by conference calls, television hook-up –'

Dominique Bosson clicked her tongue. '*None* of that'll be convenient.'

Anders paused. He was rather leaping above the heads of the local police. However –

Bosson gave his wife a look and said, 'I think we *can* manage that – at least until the shareholders' meetings, which are still a way off.'

'Good,' Anders said. 'It is important.'

Madame's face flushed deeply. Her shapely legs were crossed and Anders could see the distinct tracery of a varicose vein in one calf. Not quite perfect, he thought, and recalled the writer Sciascia's reference to the worm eating the perfectly painted Sicilian apple from within. Suddenly, he'd that strong feeling about her.

'I suggest, also, that you're scrupulous with your personal security.' He went on for a minute or so telling them the precautions they should take. 'Doubtless you're conferring with your in-house and external security –'

'This is *tedious*.' She slashed her red-tipped hands through the air. 'I am not frightened of these people, Henri.' She stared at Anders with dislike. 'And I don't believe they'll come *here*.'

How can she know that? Anders wondered.

'We know you're not frightened,' her husband said patiently. 'That's not the issue.'

He ignored her furious look, and nodded at Anders.

As they departed, Anders thought: she *should* be frightened witless – that these terrorists might come knocking on her door. Arrogance was a frequent handmaiden to

66

wealth and power. But this woman appeared to be running an agenda, and the chairman was watching her maybe closer than she knew. He stared ahead. He would've preferred to have never set eyes on either of them, but this institution, these people, might be the terrorists' principal target. His stump was hurting. And the flickering under his left eye was back. Indisputably. He sighed with disgust.

Anders' room was on the top floor of the old hotel, wedged under the roof. Mini-sized windows looked out over undulating vistas of orange-tiled roofs, impregnated with similar windows that reminded him of the apertures in old dovecotes.

He washed his hands and face, removed his trousers, unharnessed prosthesis and pistol, took off his right shoe, loosened his tie and lay down on the bed, putting his hands under his head. The room was large but dotted with six rough-hewn timber pillars. He surveyed it: hazardous for a man hopping to the bathroom in the small hours, still enmeshed in bad dreams.

A breeze wafted into the room. Daylight was softening to evening light. He was an addict of new cities, towns. A sizeable part of his life had been spent arriving and departing from them. On duty. Architecture, history, local customs, food – all the overlays. *And* the underlays: crimes and secrets – in abundance. Corruption and abused power – super-abundance. Dark and strange streets. Hopeless cases. Fearful danger. It came with the duty. And sometimes there were women, waiting in their lives. But not for a long time now.

Roget the ace bureaucrat, Commissioner Erhardt, Commissaire Rolland were in his dream. The banging was inside his head. Then on the door. He awoke to Matucci's voice sounding anxious.

Matucci had been talking about dinner when they'd parted earlier. Anders' own preference was for Italian regional cooking, and in a modest way throughout his career he'd been tracking down rare dishes in odd corners of Italy, as he'd tracked down criminals. Diet-wise, it'd been a thin time in France.

Italy seemed very distant these days and yet too close. But he didn't want to think about that.

Now Matucci wanted Chinese food again. Anders tried to remember when and where he'd first heard his colleague enthusing about the oriental cuisine ... six months ago in Lisbon. A Macanese restaurant specialising in Cantonese food. Portugal's colonies seemed to have consolidated to a collection of African and Asian restaurants in the capital.

They walked into the heart of the Grande Ile. Matucci hadn't put on his overcoat.

Why the verses from *The Ship of Fools*? Why force Dupont to relay their demands to the media? Or was he one of them? Why apparently steal and use an old identifiable typewriter? *And how was the bomb set?*

He stopped dead. And how had the thief known of that typewriter? What was the connection? *If* Frau Huber wasn't lying about it ... Matucci had stopped too, impassively staring at him. Impassiveness edged with impatience.

They walked on. Anders turned his thoughts to tomorrow: they'd head for the university, tap Rolland's contacts. Forty thousand students, he mused. Doubtless a hotbed of leftist politics.

All his working life he'd tried to take logical steps into an investigation's unknown future, applying his complicated mind, and instincts. But with this one a button had been pressed, and the motor had just started automatically. And he'd dropped into his most reticent mood. Matucci was peeved. Anders was fully aware that he was getting on his colleague's nerves.

'Are we on the right track?' Matucci asked, trying to put more of the Shanghai duck on Anders' plate. The man needed building up. Would that help his mental state? *His* inclination was still to go to Paris. To him, the gravitational pull was that way. The Frogs and Krauts thought so. Which was why, he guessed, Anders was here. The man's too-subtle mind. *And* his hard-won instincts. Blown-up twice, the first time he'd lost his leg, the second he'd taken out forty-odd top mafia bosses, in a way which had mesmerised the nation. He'd had luck when he'd killed the two mafioso in that mountain town. And a cool head. Thus far, his nerves hadn't let him down at crisis-points. But what did the future hold? Eh, eh! he said to himself, but can *I* stand much more of his bloody silence?

Anders smiled at last. Earlier, Roget had phoned from Lyon. 'Matucci, what could we do in Paris, anyway? The local police and the German feds are crowding the field – as thick as a ragu from Bologna. Here, we've a clear run – any direction.' He looked at the slick oriental decor. Into a bunker if I choose. He was ingesting cynicism with the Shanghai duck. 'We await the next move, the next message from this Judgment Day group.' He left the grandiose phrase, and the subject, in the air.

'I hope it's not another bomb,' Matucci said. He glanced at his watch, took out his mobile, and went to a quiet corner. Anders pushed his plate away, and gazed into space. Where were the terrorists now? What evil act would occur next? Tension coiled in his belly. Across the room, Matucci was listening intently, then talking.

At last Matucci returned, grinning-serious, sat down. In a low voice, he said: 'Wow! Dupont! The bastard's sex-life! And other stuff. But listen to this. He was an exchange-student at Stuttgart University in '78. *Stuckart's* old stamping ground, and the same time. He was in touch with an anarchist faction. Just a fat boy ingratiating himself with the hard people, my contact says. Doing a bit of hairy stuff, but basically going along for the ride. Is he still doing that – playing around with fire?' He sat back, and lit a cigarette. 'That's more than the Belgian cops know about him. Maybe I should go back to Brussels. Lean on fat boy.' He gazed at Anders through smoke. 'Okay?'

Anders frowned. 'No. Sit on it for the moment.'

Matucci shrugged, looked away. Shit, he thought, it's a real lead. He'd been about to impart something else to Anders, but now he clamped his mouth shut.

Anders glanced at him. 'I'd be very grateful, Matucci, if you could find us an Italian restaurant.'

There had been a dramatic change in the city's character. With nightfall, it had become dark and moody. What he might have here was schizophrenia. Urban variety. So thought Anders, standing outside the restaurant. A virgin's simplicity, the fragrance and sweet breath, seemed to have moved aside for the old odours of history. The misdeeds and the mayhem. There had been showers during the afternoon, and he sniffed the sourness of wet leaves. It was the season. It was his mood. Maybe ... the Shanghai duck felt like lead in his stomach. An ultra-modern tram, nearly empty, slid past. At that moment, droplets of rain flicked coldly into his face. He lifted his head, taking it as a warning signal. Be alert! he instructed himself.

VIII

THE TWELFTH OF OCTOBER

A.M.

ANDERS OPENED one eye, the other was glued up with sleep. He lifted his head. He seemed to be lying in a be-nighted forest: the pillars in the room ranged away like dark tree-trunks. A forest of silence. There was a dull pain behind his left eye, the blurry one. The phone rang. Instantly, Anders felt he'd awoken in anticipation of it. 12.05a.m.

'Inspector Anders. Ferrand. There's been a development.' Anders was absorbing one of *those* pauses. 'Felix Servais has been murdered at his Paris residence. Found in his study after 11.00p.m. Single shot to the forehead.'

Anders was up, sitting on the edge of the bed. The Supermarkets (France) strategic guru … dead! In Paris. Bad news in more ways than one. He said, 'The security?'

'They didn't see or hear a thing. Nor did the housekeeper, until she came in from her quarters with his nightcap.'

'*Where* were they?' Anders was standing now, holding onto the bedhead.

'One on the gate, one in the apartment lobby.'

'Access?'

'Not known.'

Good God, Anders thought. Were they all asleep? Then: this isn't right. He rubbed his jaw thoughtfully. The next move *had* come in Paris. Assuming this murder was part of it. Where did that leave him? Ferrand was waiting.

'No message from the perpetrators?'

'Nothing.'

'Very well, Inspector, we'll meet at 7.30 as arranged.'

★

Matucci awoke. Dupont's voice was babbling in his ear. Somehow the mobile had moved from the bedside table into his hand. 'It's happened again, half an hour ago, Christ, I'm half-dead with fright. I'd spent the evening downtown with a few fellows got home late and –'

'Hold on,' Matucci said. 'Tell it to me slowly.'

And the journalist did.

He'd parked his car under the plane trees and got out. He'd glanced nervously up and down the deep-shadowed street. A hundred metres away car-lights had faded out. The Belgian police sticking close, he'd thought. He walked up the path to his door. He inserted the key, and paused. A car started up its engine. Without lights, it crept closer. The police …

He went in, switched on a lamp in the hall, put his keys on the table there, took off his overcoat, entered his living-room and reached for –

'Don't move. Don't panic.'

Ice-cold metal jammed hard against a vertebra in his neck. The voice sliced his guts to pieces, froze his heart. *That* voice. The whirring sound was inside his head.

'*Stay calm. Don't look around. Keep your head and eyes down. Don't see me. Stay alive.*' The synthesised tones whined and echoed in his ear. '*Move to your desk … Very carefully … sit … Take down what I tell you. Last time you did well. Here's more easy money.*'

He edged across the room to the chair, drew it out, sat. Took up a pencil. Was shaking like a leaf. The ironhard pressure on that vertebra, unrelenting. Now – his body felt like a lump of soft mud.Then, the voice said its piece, the staccato utterances echoing in the room. Sweet Jesus, his brain whispered to him: *Felix Servais*. But somehow the pencil formed the shorthand symbols. The voice stopped. His hand poised, trembling, waiting for what he knew would be next: Brant's verse. He wrote it down.

He sat at the desk. His legs felt dead. Weren't attached to him. Had it been one minute or ten since the pressure at the base of his neck had gone, and the front door had clicked shut? The page of scrawls lay before him. He found himself at the drinks cabinet, pouring Scotch, drinking it, no taste, but feeling its descending heat in his gullet, the wallop in his gut.

The voice in Matucci's ear stopped dead, but the fat man's heavy breathing kept coming down the line. Then the voice came alive again, and slowly, he gave the message he'd transcribed. The detective got it down. 'Okay,' he said. 'Okay.'

A quiet knocking at Anders' door. Three-seven a.m. After Ferrand's call, the inspector had showered, shaved, fitted on Mark III and put on a dark-blue suit. There would be no more sleep tonight. Autumn and its weather were in the air, and in his mind. Together with much else. He was sitting in a chair facing the wide-open windows. He turned

75

his head to the unexpected sound, then went to the door.

'Who is it?'

'Matucci.'

The big detective, a yellow silk dressing-gown tightly belted, entered. 'Servais. Have you heard?'

'Ferrand phoned.'

Matucci grunted. 'Yes – and this.' He passed the sheet of paper. 'Dupont. Another nocturnal visit. This time, waiting in his apartment, he says. He's filed it with Reuters. It'll be front-page across Europe soon. He's rattled. Maybe he's in it, maybe he isn't.'

Anders took the note to a reading light.

Felix Servais the callous architect-instigator of the Supermarkets (France)/Country Fresh merger has been executed. This is the final warning to the two boards of directors. They claim that the clock cannot be turned back on the evolution of the global village under any circumstances. That the die is cast – the merger will proceed. Each one should now ask him or herself: Am I so eager to die for such a begrimed principle? For this year's catchcry of the economic pundits? To sacrifice 17,000 livelihoods? Time has almost run out.

"Deceivers many, cheats I see,
They join the dunce's revelry.
False counsel, love, false friends, false gold,
The world is full of lies untold."

The Judgment Day group

Anders was speechless, but thinking deeply. Matucci was shivering in the cold air. He looked at the open window and at his colleague's authoritative face lit by the shaded light. He seemed calm enough, except for that twitch being back. The narrow head inclined to one side as the page was re-read. The short hair, a mixture of grey and white. A man in his fifty-first year, but looking younger, despite everything.

Matucci said, 'I didn't tell you last night. *One* of the reasons Dupont might be shitting himself is that he did a laudatory piece on Servais last year for *Paris-Match*. A · mover and shaker in the new European economic paradise. A master of the global village. That kind of stuff. And wait for it, in July, he did a matching piece on Boris Bosch, Chemtex's chief.'

Anders looked up quickly. Then, down at his hands, spread open. Irrevocably, he was being sucked in. He said, 'Maybe your journalist's on the level. Maybe *that's* why he's being used as a conduit.'

Roget called Anders from Lyon – at 3.20a.m. '*Paris*,' the Frenchman said. Then he let it out in one burst. 'That's where its happening. Where Servais's been murdered. Where the French and German police are putting their maximum effort. *And Interpol's field team sits in Strasbourg!* Anders, this might be the way you operate in Italy, but I want your fresh proposals *now* and –'

'We are leaving for Paris this morning,' Anders interrupted concisely, and hung up.

Matucci grinned sourly and went to shower and shave. His colleague was sparking up. Those long silences might be on the wane.

The airport terminal smelt of hot coffee, fresh-baked rolls, and the scents of flowers. Jet engines growled. Anders and Matucci made the 7.00a.m. flight. Got the last seats right up the back. As the 737 climbed away Anders was already scanning the French edition of *Les Dernieres Nouvelles d'Alsace*. A black headline said: *Architect of French Merger*

Assassinated/ Terrorists' New Edict. He ran his eyes over the words he'd had a preview of a few hours ago. Took in that doleful photograph of Servais, and one of the zipped-up sheath being carried out of his apartment. Then below:

JOURNALIST LINKED TO MURDERED BUSINESS LEADERS.

Last night Belgian journalist Philippe Dupont was again held at gun-point and given a message from the Judgment Day group announcing Servais's murder, and threatening the directors of the French corporations. Police are questioning Dupont. Earlier this year he wrote three major articles for Paris-Match *— on Boris Bosch, chairman of Chemtex, Felix Servais, and Henri Bosson, chairman of Agribank France, the bank currently engaged in merger talks with the German bank Deutsche Rural-Credit. Sources advise that French police have stepped-up Monsieur Bosson's security.*

'Ah, yes. *Three* of them,' Anders murmured. He drew Matucci's attention to Bosson's name.

The Judgment Day group – leapt out of the columns of print, here and there. The manhunt going on throughout Europe was summarised. Stuckart, and the Chemtex security man, were prominent. The German police still believed Stuckart's resurrection was on the cards. Ex-terrorists pulled in for questioning were listed. Half-forgotten names like The Baader-Meinhof Group, Brigade Rosse, Action Directe, were being bandied about. Anders knew the police would be holding back information. He shook his head, and turned the page.

A stewardness was pouring coffee into Matucci's upheld cup.

'Damn,' Anders said. *Famous Italian Anti-Terrorist Investigator in Strasbourg.* He was looking at an eleven-year-old photograph of himself. Beside it was a mini-gallery of the main figures in the local merger negotiations. Side by side, Henri Bosson and his wife gazed at the camera, super-affluent, amused, and superbly prepared for whatever would come next in their lives.

'Damn,' Anders said again. *Senior Inspector DP Anders of Interpol's General Secretariat has been sent to Strasbourg.* He sighed, and passed it to Matucci. The reader had merely to glance from his box to the other photos, and the Servais headline, to make the connection the editor intended.

'Somebody's talking,' Matucci growled. 'Would it be our literary-minded chief, by any chance? Or maybe that woman?' His big finger traced over newsprint and came to rest on Dominique Bosson's jutting bosom. The 737 shook violently in turbulence.

They had a man called Jean Daire in a room at the central directorate of criminal investigation; the security man who Lefebvre said had been in Servais' foyer. In shifts, they'd been grilling him for seven hours straight. About 6.30a.m. his colleague had collapsed and been taken to hospital, an inspector told Anders and Matucci. The inspector said, 'It's an inside job – no other answer. Their pistols weren't fired, but they must've let the killer in.'

'Anything known about them?' Anders asked.

'Nothing,' the inspector grunted. 'It's a case of money talking. Big money.'

Anders took in the room: filthy with cigarette smoke and stinking of it. And of body odour. And of fear. And hot under the big lights. Two detectives, tieless, coatless, seated on hardbacks were confronting the guard. A third was pacing the room like a caged big cat. Everyone needed a shave. And a sleep. Anders, the inspector, and Matucci entered and stood along a wall at the back. The interrogators shot them looks. One grinned wearily.

The security guard sat half-slumped over a table. From a private company. He lifted his eyes briefly to the newcomers. Sullen and confused, Anders thought. A detective with a shaven head banged knuckles on the table. 'Look at me you bastard,' he snarled. Suddenly he shouted: 'Who paid you off? Who – you shitkicker?'

'Look at *me* Daire,' his colleague screamed. 'How much did you get?'

'We know you let the killer in. Maybe you pulled the trigger yourself,' the pacing man shouted. 'Man, are you in the shit.'

They went on and on. Over and over. Thumping and shouting. Sometimes they extracted a mumbled response. They kept their hands off him. Maybe they hadn't before.

'Like a cigarette?' one of them said.

'Get fucked.' That was audible.

Anders caught the eye of the bald detective. 'Be our guest,' the Frenchman said.

Two large spots of blood plonked on the tabletop. Everyone stared at them in surprise. Anders thought they were from the man's nose. He stepped up to the table. 'Monsieur Daire, my name is Anders, from Interpol. Would you answer one or two questions for me?'

The man didn't speak, but he lifted his head, and looked at the Italian. 'I'm sorry you and your colleague are being put through this, but it's a very difficult situation. Is there *anything* you can tell us which might throw some light?'

A solitary tear trickled down the man's cheek. Anders walked to a water-cooler and filled a paper cup. The only sound was his footsteps, and the cops inhaling nicotine. Anders put the cup into the man's hand, and he downed it in a gulp.

He spoke, thickly, unexpectedly. 'All I can tell you is … I've got nothing to tell. All I remember is that police inspector talking to me … Asking me what in the hell'd happened … didn't know what. I'd seen nothing, but he was dead.'

'Jesus,' the bald cop said. 'And there you were standing in the apartment's hall. Why don't you change the record.'

'Thank you,' Anders said. He walked out. The inspector and Matucci followed. In the passage he said to the inspector, 'You're wasting time with him. I think he's telling it straight.'

The man reddened, and stared at the Interpol man. 'You amaze me. You just walk in, and know it like that. Well, what's your theory?'

'I wish I had one,' Anders said. He turned away and led Matucci out of the hell-hole. The French policeman was right: they'd only caught the tail-end of the interrogation, but it was enough for Anders. They took a cab to Orly Airport.

Matucci said, 'We're not going to take a look at Servais's place?'

'No,' Anders said. 'There's a muddying of the waters going on, Matucci. Or at least, several things are in play. Strasbourg's got its place on the agenda. Its turn hasn't come yet.' He stared grimly out the cab window. 'Don't ask me how I know it.'

Glumly, Matucci shook his head, put a cigarette between his lips, but didn't light it. It had been a quick visit to Paris, to say the least.

They arrived back at Strasbourg and Ferrand was waiting. They were going to the university. Late yesterday afternoon Anders had spoken to Commissaire Rolland, who'd arranged an appointment for them. As they drove through the streets beside the river, Anders' eyes followed the curves of the large island on their left: the historic heart of the city jammed with elegant eighteenth-century houses. The cathedral's mighty spire soared above this concentration of architects' inspiration and builders' sweat, 'a giant and delicate marvel' Victor Hugo pronounced in the guidebook. The solid residue of men who were dust. Hopefully, they'd had a more natural exit than the Frankfurt sixteen.

Matucci and Ferrand discussed the Servais killing, the terrorists' communication, and the Paris interrogation. Matucci glanced at Anders. His colleague had been sunk in his thoughts on the flight back.

Ferrand briefed them on what was known of leftist activity at the university. 'It's frightening,' Matucci said, 'all those Hanss and Louises talking politics, and screwing each other cross-eyed.'

Anders stirred himself, and asked several questions, but Ferrand was confirming it as a milk-and-water environment. His intentions for the coming interview had turned, quite forcibly, in another direction.

Professor Lestang was forty, tall, fair, vigorous – and curious. His brown eyes held Anders'. An intense contact. His skin was warm and smooth as they shook hands. Professor of Economics, Rolland had said to Anders. A frequent commentator *against* neoclassical economics on television, in the press. 'With his out-of-fashion Keynesian social democratic economics, it's quite remarkable he continues to hold onto his job,' the chief of police had suggested. 'He also has a doctorate in psychology.'

Anders studied him.

'I'm delighted to meet someone at the cutting edge of the fight against extremism,' the professor said. 'The article in our morning paper was intriguing for what it did *not* say about you, Inspector. However –' He whirled, and with a theatrical gesture indicated chairs. At the last moment, he seemed to restrain himself from assisting Anders. Matucci was watching him with interest, Ferrand, with his dour respect.

'Now what can I do for you? The Commissaire said our leftists?' He explained about this. Five minutes. Politely Anders asked two questions, heard out the answers. He dropped the subject.

'Professor, Sebastian Brant's *The Ship of Fools*. Could you direct me to an authority –'

'*Ah!*' Lestang made a quick exhalation. He leaned back imperceptibly, gave Anders another penetrating look. 'Of course, the *Narrenschiff*. The terrorists. The messages. You've come to the right place for that, Inspector. What a paradox it is, for a text at the forefront of early sixteenth-century German humanism, to be appropriated in the name of such inhuman ends.'

Anders was listening closely. The console on the professor's desk buzzed. He answered it, listened, frowning. He laid down the receiver, looked at Anders. 'I must apologise, this is very rude of me. I'm afraid something urgent has come up. But first –' He sat down at his desk and wrote quickly on a letterheaded sheet. He folded it, and came to Anders.

'Here's an introduction to a woman who's the authority you require.'

The three policemen stood. 'Call me at any time, Inspector,' Lestang said. 'I really would like to have a conversation on the terrorist mentality.'

As Anders followed the others out the door, the professor put a hand on his arm. 'The perpetrators of these acts have great intellectual arrogance.' He smiled. 'Doubtless this has occurred to you. Of course, one thing they're saying is, "We are omnipotent." Maybe, they see themselves as *the* pre-eminent jokers, in a world of fools.'

Jokers, Anders thought, wandering out through the halls of academe. Lestang hadn't seen the blood-painted fish-tank. Perhaps that horror was the ultimate in satirical comment. Yes, omnipotence was always present in the terrorist. And gut-pains, and an aching head, were the lot of the terrorist-hunter.

He brooded with this out into the cool, sunny noon. It occurred to him that the professor's brand of economics must be close to the terrorists' beliefs. Matucci didn't give much away at meetings like this, but he could tell his colleague had disliked the academic. His own reaction? Neutral. He glanced at sun-bathed buildings.

Something quite extraordinary was in play. In connection with the access to kill Servais. That was the conclusion he'd reached during the flight back. He could understand the French police's feelings – bewilderment. And similar – the Germans' – with the planting of the bomb in Frankfurt. Both mysteries – and no progress.

But maybe, on the last, there was. As they drove to police headquarters a message was phoned through that the car of Chemtex's deputy security chief had been discovered in a ditch outside a small town near Heidelberg.

IX

THE TWELFTH OF OCTOBER

P.M.

*D*R MARGUERITE *Dauban, Chief Librarian, Libraire Kleber,* Lestang had written. Anders entered a stone building. Concave steps. Automatically he wondered at the number of human journeys that'd worn them down. The building looked about three hundred years old. In Italy, a good part of his life had been spent walking into places like it. Probably, mathematicians could devise a formula to calculate how many persons had trodden these steps. Who might've done so fairly recently was his interest. Among other things.

A tarnished brass-plate: second floor. He clanked upwards caged in iron and brass, and entered a huge room which appeared to take up most of the second floor – a mezzanine overlooked it. Aisles of bookshelves ranged away, creaking with book-weight, smelling of old leather. Under-funded and municipal. So thought Anders. He fancied he'd inherited a feeling for these places from his poet ancestor, Anton Anders. Largely devoid of human beings. Though scores could've been beavering silently away in the maze-like aisles.

Hat in hand, he surveyed this. A young woman emerged, with an inquiring look. 'Doctor Dauban?' he asked.

'Do you have an appointment, monsieur?'

'I've a letter of introduction from Professor Lestang.' He gave her his card.

A nod. 'Follow me, please.' She led the way to a corner, knocked on the door of a room obviously built there as an afterthought, and went in. She re-appeared. 'You may go in.'

A woman came around the desk, her black, shoulder-length hair seeming wind-blown, to Anders. Her eyes were brown and interested. Immediately he guessed she'd been following the terrorists' sign-off verses – remarkable if she hadn't been – and that she'd read the piece about him in the morning paper. The news had moved from the front-page to her door-step.

'It's good of you to see me. Professor Lestang's kindly given me a letter.' With a slight bow, he proffered it.

She took and glanced at it. Her mouth flickered at the edges, became compressed. Amusement at his manners? Anders sighed to himself: he supposed he was a relic of an old-fashioned world.

About thirty-seven. A face the creamy hue of gar-denias, devoid of cosmetics. Yes, careless hair, nonetheless a faint perfume emanating from it. Her mouth was as straight-forward, humanitarian, and commonsense as Anders had ever seen.

She laid the note on her desk, and offered her hand. She turned a chair. 'Please sit down, Inspector.' Everyone's initial thought was for him to sit down. 'This is a first for me. No previous dealings with the police.' She gave him a reserved smile. 'But I can guess why you're here.'

Anders dropped his gaze to the carpet, faded and flattened with age. It had come to him: the small jolt like electricity. Of instinctive recognition. When a certain kind of woman stepped into his ambit. Or he, into hers. For the moment he brushed it off. He looked up with new eyes.

'I'm following an investigation which is parallel to that of the national police forces. One could say, free-ranging. These verses of Brant's are a factor for consideration.' He leaned forward. 'For instance, are they coded warnings, messages – or, are they merely the turgid appendages of jokers or ironists? Dressing on the salad. A play for extra public attention? What type of person would be familiar with this literature? What type of person would be attracted to such display?' He raised his hands slightly. 'Can a lead be found in that?'

She'd not taken a chair. She leaned back against her desk, crossed her arms and appraised him. 'It's a travesty – such a masterpiece appropriated for evil ends. Brant was deeply religious, from what we know a highly moral man. He sought in his book to improve the political situation of his generation by moral rebirth.' Her voice was quiet, even, yet very distinct.

Anders said, 'The terrorists believe they've their own moral dimension. To them criminal acts become political acts.' Blood-stained ones, he thought.

'Who would be familiar with it? Scholars and students throughout Europe – certainly. Not a great number, though a surprising number do turn up here to examine the Kleber's copy, a 1499 edition.' Her voice had faded away.

They were gazing at each other. Arms still crossed, she lifted her shoulders, as though to break out of a trance. 'Perhaps *you* should do that.'

He followed her down a short flight of stairs. She waited at the bottom, watching his adroit but careful descent. From above he noted how sharply sloping her shoulders were. How well-fleshed her hips. How erect she held herself. No undulations in that walk.

They entered a large vault with tables and chairs, and low-hanging shaded lights. Shelves behind decorative brass screen doors plainly held the collection's rarest books. She produced white cotton gloves. 'Please put these on.' She brought out a second pair for herself.

The book reeked of antiquity. Anders stared down at it and fancied Brant's voice whispering the verses printed on the thick pages. She opened it at the frontispiece. 'This is the third edition, printed in Basel during Brant's lifetime.' She turned pages slowly and Anders examined the German text, the woodcuts at each chapter-beginning. He'd dropped into the world of five hundred years ago. No trouble at all.

'Enough?' she asked after ten minutes.

He nodded. Back in her room Anders said, 'Do you keep records of who sees it?'

'Yes. A viewing is always supervised by me or one of my assistants.'

'How many have come, in say the past twelve months?'

She frowned. 'Perhaps forty or fifty.' She went to a high desk, retrieved a heavy ledger, and opened it at a section. 'Yes.'

'In your recollection, does any one of these stand out – as different in some way?'

Her eyes were moving down the page. She looked up. 'I couldn't say so. I can ask my assistants. Editions of the book are held in various cities. And translations in a number of languages are available.' She stared at her hands.

'The verse these people used after Frankfurt was taken from Chapter 10 – True Friendship. The one in this morning's paper, from Chapter 102 – Of Falsity and Deception.'

He considered this. He should go. Would she advise him what her assistants reported? She would. He would've liked to have stayed in this room listening to her and looking at her. But beyond these walls another world waited. Reluctantly, he stood up. 'May I contact you again if necessary?' He might ask for a list of those names on another visit. He didn't wish to invest time in that direction right now.

'Of course.' They shook hands. He was staring again. Her eyes dilated in surprise. He went down in the cranky lift. Mild sunshine in the street. A coldness in him. On a case, that coldness was rarely absent. And his mind was never at rest. There had to be a flaw in the security at the Chemtex building, at Servais' apartment. If he could find it in either case, a pathway to the perpetrators could open up.

Monsieur Henri Bosson's face came into his head: as sharp as an image in the cross-hairs of a telescopic sight. In contrast, *The Ship of Fools* suddenly seemed nebulous and obscure.

He continued to gaze at the street. His mind had dropped into a familiar rut. The case was taking him over. The reluctance, obdurate, was being pushed to the background. Creaking and groaning. The inertia had been sloughed away. But not the nerves. He sighed.

Five minutes later he was walking across Place Kleber. Flags fluttered languidly from a plantation of poles. The massive statue of the curly-headed French Revolutionary general stood in its oxidisation and pigeon shit. The many statues of the city's historic sons, all comparably tarnished and shitted on as though it was a badge of membership of some statues' union, gazed at the twenty-first century. Anders took in such detail.

Difficulties in his head, he was travelling the cobbled streets with some discomfort. The city of the fractured ankle. Decidedly unfriendly to artificial legs. There were smooth pathways through the dangerous tracts, and he was learning them. He caught a tram to police head-quarters.

Matucci was finishing a phone conversation. Anders sat down while his colleague gestured with his right hand as though he was an orator whipping up applause. He crashed down the receiver. 'Seibert – Lyon archives. We're really in the shit now. The ace's been telling everyone he's got us to Paris – and now, hey presto, we're back here. I guess St Cloud's been in his ear. However, fuck that, this is interesting. Guess who *Paris-Match* consulted in selecting the three EC captains of industry for those articles?'

Anders gazed at his colleague. 'Just tell me.'

Matucci shrugged. 'None other than Professor Marc Lestang. Mr Personality-plus.'

Anders waited.

'Lestang was commissioned to do an article on his kind of economics. Point out what those three guys were doing wrong.'

Anders nodded slowly.

'Bosson's still with us. Eh-eh! I wouldn't take a bet on that lasting.' He grinned at Anders.

Anders frowned. What *did* it mean? 'The articles are a side-issue,' he decided. 'Interesting, but only one thread in the pattern that's being woven. They're adding fuel to the publicity fire.' He thought, the manifesto sets out the main game.

Matucci shrugged, and lit a cigarette. 'In Paris they've put both corporate headquarters into a siege situation. The directors are being nurse-maided round the clock. And they're still scouring Europe. The President's going on TV tonight.'

Anders flinched at a gust of Matucci's blend. Henri Bosson must be giving his appearance in the *Paris-Match* series deep thought. It'd certainly look like a main game to him — and to the French police. They'd increased his bodyguards.

'What about the library?' Matucci asked with a curious glance.

Anders stroked his jaw. What could he say about that? Except that maybe one of these killers had gone poking around there after Brant's book. Out of a weird, obscure, motivation. Maybe. More probably the proposition was one of his flights of fancy. Given that the quotes could've been got from a book bought at a bookshop. As the delicious Dr Dauban had said, they hadn't needed the Kleber's copy. *Delicious.* The one definite conclusion he'd reached today.

He felt like he was swimming a good way offshore somewhere, treading water, trying to pick up movement and detail on the beach. Ten years since he'd been in the briny.

Inspector Ferrand came in, looked at the two Interpol men with his dark eyes, summed up their mood. 'It's time for coffee. There's a place nearby.'

★

Dominique Bosson and Paul Kramer were having their own coffee in the tiny, cobbled, leafy Place du Marche Neuf. Nearby a small fountain played. They were sitting outside for privacy.

'Henri must be worried,' Kramer said. 'First, Boris Bosch, then Felix Servais, his co-stars in *Paris-Match*. It's ominous.'

Dominique Bosson's face, her hair, had an enamelled lustre. When she smiled her teeth were brilliant, her skin seemingly undisturbed by the economical movement. She had on a pearl-grey suit, cut miraculously, which hadn't featured on this year's Parisian fashion catwalks; much more exclusive than that.

'With him who can tell – either way?' she said to her lover. 'He's maximised security.' She shrugged towards the two men from a Strasbourg security company.

Kramer gazed into space. 'Is he still making love to you?'

'Darling!' She laughed softly. 'He lumbers into action now and then. It never lasts long. Inside, one minute.'

He grinned at the double entendre. In bed-matters, he'd discovered she had a precise vocabulary.

She gazed across the leafy place, thinking how to put the correct amount of pressure on the man opposite her, her latest lover in a long line. As always, she had an agenda.

He said, 'What about that hacker?' Overnight, they'd had a hacker in their computer system.

She gazed at him over the rim of the cup held in her shapely, capable hands. 'Hackers are always popping in, roaming around like thieves inside a house. The bastards. They get into any room they can. We've found it doesn't mean much.'

She smiled, said off-handedly, 'Who's going to be chairman of the managing board of our new wonder-bank?'

He sipped his coffee, wasn't deceived. Henri's powerful ambition was nearly matched by Klaus's. And the German had something else pressing his buttons: the deep credit problems in his bank's mortgage portfolio. He smiled to himself. Something Dominique didn't know about. Should he tell her one night as she reached orgasm? It'd shoot her into orbit.

Her pink, pointed tongue flicked foam from her lips. She thought, What's the skinny fellow smiling at now? She said, 'Henri has the greater public standing – isn't tainted by Klaus's problem.' She was referring to Hofmann's homosexuality.

'Problem? Tainted, Dominique? I thought we lived in a modern world. Especially you.'

She studied him through her blonde eyelashes. 'Darling, you know what I mean. What our shareholders, that galaxy of rural mums and dads, thinks.' She leaned forward, embracing him with her breath, her perfume. 'How much do you really love me?'

Despite himself, he was startled. Not a gram of coquettishness in the remark. It had the deadweight tone of business.

'Enough to vote with the Agribank directors, and put Henri into the job?'

She watched him narrowly. His hair was as black and shiny as lacquer. She'd studied how he brushed it. An artisan at work. It impressed and amused her.

'That'd make life hard.'

She guessed he was wondering whether Henri had put her up to this. Whether their affair had been brought into the open. And, of course, who would be director for strategic planning in the merged entity, who deputy? 'You'd be reporting to Henri. No-one else.'

He looked down at his hands spread on the table. Then at her blood-red-tipped fingers almost docking with his. His chest still stung.

'Or, if you were absent from the meeting when the vote was taken. Same result.'

'Absent?' he said, looking up quickly.

'Think about it, darling.'

'You're assuming that the joint boards approve –'

'It's a fait accompli and you know it.'

He looked at his watch. It was 3.15p.m. 'I'll think about it, Dominique. Now – we should be getting back.'

'Oh yes, the Takeover Trinity from Brussels.' Her voice was tinged with contempt as she visualised the three bureaucrats of the Merger Task Force of the competition secretariat. 'Leave them to me.'

★

'I agree with you, Inspector Anders, I think *something* is going to happen in Strasbourg.' Ferrand turned to stare at this Italian. The three stood at the bar. He and Matucci were smoking. Different brands. Was it a competition for maximum pungency? Anders, reformed smoker, seemed to have merely exchanged active for passive smoking. He stared back at the French policeman, and sensed Matucci's sudden alertness.

Anders put down his cup. 'I'm glad to hear it. But what brings you to that conclusion? Have you information?'

The dour, dark detective inspected the counter, sucked at his teeth. 'This past week there's been much talk about the Agribank–Deutsche Rural-Credit merger here – and in other provinces. Articles in the press. Union meetings. The top brass have been silent about the job losses. But figures have been leaked. And they're huge. Far ahead of the numbers in the Frankfurt and Paris mergers. I've a brother in Metz who says the locals – customers and staff – are worried stiff. *Our* merger hasn't hit the Frankfurt and Paris papers in a big way. They're preoccupied with events in their cities … as are the national police. And Frankfurt's always watching what Munich's up to, and vice versa.'

He exhaled a stream of smoke. 'Commissaire Rolland has similar thoughts. He's been ringing Paris twice a day. Why *not* here – if that manifesto means anything?'

Anders and Matucci stared at the local cop with new eyes. He was no talker, but he made words count.

Anders said, 'I'm glad you're of that opinion, Inspector Ferrand, the trouble is, I don't think we'll know for certain, until something rather nasty happens.'

Anders returned to the hotel about 4.00p.m. He wanted to unharness and lie down for a half hour. On their return to police headquarters, he'd sought a meeting with Commissaire Rolland. Ferrand's remark had given him an idea. In a short conversation, it became clear that the Strasbourg police chief was indeed concerned about what he termed 'this blind spot' in the national investigation, overwhelmingly focused on Paris.

He agreed to phone Lyon, and suggest that the Interpol team was 'valuably employed' in his city. Anders was momentarily embarrassed at having to seek such an intervention, but once it was done, put it out of mind.

'No messages,' Matucci's sleek Mademoiselle Dayshift informed him. Did she have a message for Matucci, Anders wondered, as he rode the lift to the top floor.

He'd only divested himself of the Beretta when his mobile rang. 'Inspector Anders? It is Frau Huber ... in Munich.'

A silence, edged with static.

'Ah yes,' Anders said. He visualised the recumbent blonde woman murmuring to him as he'd walked out of her bedroom – four days ago. Tipsy with beer or despair he'd thought then – or had it been artifice?

'I have additional information. To tell you face to face.' It came into his ear in her excellent English.

'Surely the telephone –'

'Impossible.'

He had her tension now. He glanced at his watch. About three hours door to door – if he could get a flight. 'Very well, I'll be there this evening.'

The disconnection was immediate. In case I changed my mind, he thought.

What is this? Was a revelation coming on Stuckart? He went into the bathroom to wash his face and hands, and then he phoned the brunette below. He waited for a flight confirmation. Through the four open windows set into the steep-pitched roof came the cooing of doves. Today the sound seemed to have a mocking, even sinister tone. The thought came: was Renata Huber enticing him back – into danger? Stuckart had been adept at grabbing hostages. Extracting a ransom, or executing them as 'examples'.

A battle-weary knight riding steel steeds around the sky on his quests. So thought Anders, raising a shadow of a smile. The myriad lights of southern Germany pricked out sprawling patterns below. He made out lazily winding rivers: dark slugs inching towards a meal. He'd a notion of the giant corporations of Europe stalking each other across the EC.

Like a slow fuse, questions continued to sizzle in his mind. He'd phoned Frankfurt. The Germans were widening the search for the Chemtex security man around his abandoned car. Forensics had turned up nothing in it. It was just in a ditch. They'd finished interviewing all the visitors to Chemtex's thirty-second floor the day before the bomb. Except the West Africans, who safely home, were firing broadsides at multinational drug manufacturers. No real leads had been turned up. Stuckart's ex-faction members had stuck to their story: he was dead. The German drag-nets had yielded nothing. Reports had come in of Stuckart sightings. One in Munich. But you know what's it's like, one of Erhardt's men had told him. Nonetheless.

The Paris interrogation of Servais's security guard was the sharpest thing in his mind. There *was* something there. A new dimension. He felt it – like a sensitive tooth. But he didn't have a clue what it might be.

The aeroplane bumped down in Munich at 9.20p.m. Remembering other days, he was amazed at this free and easy movement across national borders – no passport or customs checks. One big, happy family, the welcome mat was always out. The crooks of Europe were in clover. Interpol's computers were almost surfeited with keeping track of them.

The suburban street hadn't changed, except the police weren't there. Or not in view. The apartment building showed a patchwork of lighted windows – solitary evidence of human habitation. Minimal traffic, and no pedestrians. A neighbourhood with perfect street-cleaning and zero vivacity. One day, he might settle down in one like it.

Tonight the security door was shut. He pressed the buzzer. Its sharp sound plucked at his nerves.

'Yes?'

'Inspector Anders.'

She opened her front door as he left the lift. He removed his hat, and they shook hands. Tonight, sober, and light-pink lipstick. The assessing blue eyes he was looking into seemed more inclined to pose questions than provide information. She'd rolled the blonde hair around the side of her head, and fixed it with a tortoiseshell pin.

A cigarette was burning in an ashtray. She nodded to an armchair. Her eyes kept going to his face, flicking away. She wore an almost summery dress; flower-print.

He stood there, tense and cautious.

'Can I offer you coffee? Where have you come from?'

'Strasbourg.'

'Ah ... not Paris.'

He nodded to the interior. She shrugged, and went into the kitchen. Without further ceremony, he walked through the flat.

They returned to the living-room at the same moment. She had a tray of cups, pot, biscuits. She set it down and sat opposite him. She leaned forward, her hands spread on her knees. 'Satisfied? He's dead and gone. Believe me.' Wearily, she added, 'I wonder can they get DNA out of ash-dust. I suppose not, otherwise the bastards would've.

'Well. What I've to tell you is quite short and sweet.'

Anders waited, sitting quietly, narrow head inclined.

'I saw the man who took Karl-Heinrich's typewriter that night. He came out of the lift just as I entered the main lobby. I said "Good evening." He nodded. Then I saw he was carrying *the* suitcase.

'Instantly he saw I'd recognised it, and paused. I walked

past him and got into the lift.'

Probably that had saved her life, Anders thought. From the look she gave him, she knew that, too.

'I did not know who, or what, I was dealing with. It all happened in a flash. And I just wanted to get into my flat.'

'A good decision. This man?'

She selected a fresh cigarette, and lit it with a cheap lighter. 'Very tall, thin. A kind of slump in his shoulders. His face was long and white – and his eyes were very dark. Perhaps black. He had long black hair. A black overcoat, belted at the waist, and a soft black hat. A wide brim.'

In those few moments Renata had seen a lot.

'Everything about him seemed black.' Her thin body was frozen with the memory. Abruptly, she broke free of the image, began to pour the coffee. Anders sipped his. He hadn't removed his overcoat, and the flat was warm.

She hadn't reported the theft before the Munich police had descended on her. Why hadn't she told them about this man? Anders sipped more coffee. She seemed to be following his thoughts.

'Twenty-three months in prison. One does not automatically tell everything one sees, or knows, to the authority. Keeping the mouth shut becomes second nature. Also – why didn't I tell you this on the phone?' Her hands were crossed under her chin, her eyes lowered. 'I could've, but I've been thinking about you, and I wanted to see you again.'

Anders breathed in deeply and quietly. She was gazing directly at him now with raw honesty. Four nights ago, in this room, she'd absorbed that he knew her life: an immigrant in this city, no friends, pension night, pink-lipstick night, bar-around-the-corner-night, drinking beer, watching that bit of life, ruined by her past, by the decisions of a twenty-year-old, loneliest of the lonely, paying forever. And the sympathy, if not a balm – something.

It had come down on him around his thirtieth birthday. Almost as if God had said: this is what your nature qualifies you for. Except, not God, himself. These life-weary women, with their quiet fortitude, quickened his blood, satisfied his intellectual and physical appetites. These trashed lives. It was as natural as breathing, and over the length and breadth of Italy he'd found many. Was always on the lookout for them, not as a predator but as a human being. They were his heart's desire. He supposed he was as damaged as any one of them.

Ten seconds had gone by. Anders stood up and removed his overcoat, not taking his eyes off hers. Then he did. He went into the kitchen, looked it over, came back. She shook her head, crossed to the cupboard, took out the urn, and carried it through to the bedroom. 'I'll put him where you can keep your eye on him.'

A moment later, she muttered, 'Not a good idea.' She took the urn to the window, opened it. 'Goodbye, Karl-Heinrich.' She dropped it into the light-well and way below he heard the smash.

For the second time, they made love. Anders moved his truncated body over her long, pale nakedness, his mouth tasting that sweet lipstick, their tongues together. Her arms were thin, the bones of her shoulders stark. But her hips and thighs were sumptuous. This was more peaceful than an hour ago when she'd bitten his shoulder and breathily babbled to him: *'Oh, so long. It's been so long.'* Later, lying side by side, she smoking, she said, 'Sometimes men at the bar try to pick me up. "Come on sweetheart." Trousers down, trousers up, and out the door with not a memory of it the next day. God, spare me from that! Karl-Heinrich liked to take me unawares. Once I was naked, bending over the basin cleaning my teeth when he got me from behind. I nearly swallowed the frigging toothbrush. Men are crazy.' She giggled at the memory. 'And the cops can't decide whether he's dead or not.'

Anders had. Now.

'No future. What about you?' she said. 'Are you a person with a future?'

Where did such post-coital questions come from, he wondered. 'I don't think of the future,' he said, which was nearly true.

She'd taken no notice of his stump. Some wanted to bring it into play. And then, for the second time, he'd rolled onto her and she drew him in. The air swished with moisture, flicked off their skin. Afterwards, she slept. In the dark, the Munich breeze floated white nylon curtains. Last night he'd been sitting in a chair while a Strasbourg breeze sighed into his face. Then he slept.

It became clear where he was: he was standing in the middle of the fish-tank trying to see outside, but the red-painted walls were impenetrable. On each side the red liquids streamed continuously down like a water-wall. Blender-smooth. He was trying to work out how the liquid was being re-cycled from bottom to top; there was no sign of plumbing ... It started. Faces. The front-page photos. Cut-outs. Diving, whirling, side-slipping around him, emitting the shrill little cries of bats, bringers of nightmares, murderers of sleep.

He jack-knifed upright. His heart was pounding, his body hot and streaming. The room was full of too much breeze. The curtains were rioting. Slowly he lay back beside Renata, whose breathing was regular and private in the deepest of sleeps. In the mid-distance a siren traversed the city, bip-bipping frenetically at intersections. It faded little by little, became dribs and drabs. Going to an emergency in the unknown distance. He felt empathy.

X

THE THIRTEENTH OF OCTOBER

A.M.

'JESUS, THIS guy's crazy.' The security man behind the wheel blinked, and nudged his dozing colleague.

'The Night Jogger jogs again,' the other said, sitting erect. He shook his head, and rinsed his mouth from a flask.

A man in a black sweat-shirt and pants and white runners had left the apartment building, and was loping away up the deserted street.

The driver checked his watch: 12.45a.m. He started the engine. The fellow had done this to them about the same time last night and had quickly lost them. They'd scoured the streets in their patrol vehicle, not reported it to base. It'd been panic stations until he'd turned up again at his apartment four hours later.

'These brain merchants are fools,' the driver said bitterly, making a sharp U-turn and accelerating. The running figure had a hundred metres on them now. 'Up to his same tricks. Bet my arse he ducks down one of these side-streets. Then you're going to have to put on *your* runners.'

The brakes squealed. They bounced around in the front seat. Last night he'd clearly kept a rendezvous he didn't want publicised. Tonight?

'There goes the bastard,' the man in the passenger seat said in deep disgust. The figure had turned into an alley where their vehicle couldn't follow. The driver screeched to a stop. 'I'll circle around to the other side. *On your bike,*' he said.

'Wish I had one.' The other leapt out, slamming the door.

Paul Kramer was grinning, cocksure, as he ran down the alley. He was enjoying the game. Last night he'd lost them in minutes, and had laughed at their faces when he'd returned home just before dawn. The senior man had accosted him. 'Sir, this is not in your best interests. If you don't co-operate we can't provide protection.' Normally, he would've been happy to co-operate. But Paris was where the danger was, not this sleepy place … A breeze cooled his warming face. His shadow ran jumpily ahead along the building façades.

The small flat Dominique had taken under an assumed name was a secret they didn't want blown. They'd had a lot of opportunities for private time when they'd been putting the merger plan together. Which had come first: the merger, or the screwing? It wasn't so easy now.

He was jogging quite fast through side-streets in a tri-angular sector near Place Saint-Etienne. They'd try to follow him on foot this time but he was super-fit, and only five minutes away from the flat. A cat darted away under his feet, startled and startling. He pounded on. The pale gleam of a TV screen shot across his path. Insomniac … No trouble in shaking off her own security last night. The way she drove they didn't stand a chance. Her red Porsche would be tucked away in its garage by now. He was breathing harder, but running nicely, a great fuck in prospect. He grinned: never let anything stand in the way of one of those … Henri was in Frankfurt overnight. Was he getting suspicious? Perhaps the soft-pricked bastard knew already? Perhaps these men were surveillance, not protection as far as Dominique and himself were concerned. *No.* All the directors had their security pair. Henri and Klaus each had their police team … Last night his sweaty body had really turned her on. Those red-tipped hands had grabbed his balls … Henri for chairman. Yours truly to vote for it. He'd keep *those* balls up in the air. He didn't know what move he'd make. Yet.

His runners thudded dully and rhythmically on the cobbles. Ahead a darkened vehicle loomed up, parked half on the narrow pavement. A long car with a misshapen rear roof. He registered that automatically: for wheelchair-bound passengers. He changed to the centre of the one-track street and accelerated, the breath spurting out of him now. The winning post in sight!

Right in his path the driver's door sprang open. BANG! With a terrific concussion he collided with it, bouncing back. Instantly, his breath was locked in his chest – *agonising*.

Shit! He was on his bum – his front teeth broken, blood spurting out. Gasping. Dazed. Vaguely he was aware of a figure standing over him.

The security man's breathing was raucous. It sawed at the silence in the deserted alley, made white steam around his head. He hadn't sighted the smart-arse. He pulled up and grabbed at an iron railing for support, bent over. Which way? Thirty metres ahead a strange-looking vehicle was moving away from him, its rear-lights aglow. It disappeared around a bend.

The bearded young man had his back to the wall of the old inn formerly called The Stallion, now The Raven. The girl had her tongue in his mouth and was breathing gustily. He was in her, moving slowly and with some difficulty because of their height disparity. She'd removed her panties and stuck them in his pocket. She worked in a foreign exchange bureau by day, and played around the bars at night: short and plump and avidly scented. It was their first encounter. He'd been teasing her, calling her Mademoiselle Rates of Exchange.

It was cold out here. In the inn's courtyard behind them the old fountain tinkled away. He could see over her shoulder across the deserted Quai des Pecheurs to the Pont du Corbeau lit quite brightly and similarly deserted. 'I'm getting there,' she breathed urgently, whipping her tongue out of his mouth, feverishly probing its tip into his ear.

A vehicle had come onto the bridge and stopped. Immediately it backed its rear-end hard against the low parapet. Fifty metres away, the young man saw that it looked like one of those ugly-shaped taxis for the incapacitated. A man had alighted from it, was moving to its rear.

He kept moving. 'Oh God,' she groaned. He slowed the movements of his hips, then stopped at the new sound. *Whirr-whirr-whirr.* Hydraulic equipment. The sound came across the river. Now he made out a mini-gantry with something unusual suspended from it. He peered across the fifty metres. A *metal cage* –

The girl's voice was shrill in his ear: *'Don't stop! Are*

you trying to kill me?'

He began to push in her again. The gantry had swung the cage just clear of the low parapet. There was a dark shape in the cage, moving slightly. What in hell was going on? The cage was dropping away –

'Bing-go!' the girl cried.

Splash! He heard it and then he was coming, too.

*

At 5.10a.m. Anders rose and felt through the darkness to the bathroom. He showered, harnessed up, and dressed in the dark. After knotting his tie, he fitted on the Beretta – the old pre-dawn routine in anonymous bedrooms. She was lying on her back, he leaned over and kissed her gently. Feeling, not seeing, the pale, sensitive lips, recalling her edgy, brash utterances. Camouflage for her damaged life. When he was at the door she murmured sleepily, 'Don't leave it like this.'

He walked for fifteen minutes, his breath misty, before spotting a taxi. Then he was on his way to the airport. He arrived at Strasbourg at 8.15a.m., one thing now very clear in his mind. *Vale* Stuckart.

Matucci's sharp blue eyes surveyed him. 'Kramer, the strategy chief of the Kraut bank's gone missing. Gave his minders the slip about 12.45 last night and hasn't been sighted since. Did the same the night before. But then he came home just before dawn.'

Anders stood looking down at his colleague. 'Mmm. I've been to Munich to interview Frau Huber again. She had more information.' He explained that.

Matucci grinned. 'I got your message. Did you have

some beer and white sausage before leaving?' Anders had missed out on the pre-noon Munich specialty, and breakfast hadn't been served on the brief flight. Hadn't had supper either. He hadn't taken in Matucci's remark. 'We can forget Stuckart. I'm satisfied he's dead. He and his typewriter have been a diversion – to send the Germans rushing back into the past – all the wrong directions.' He stared at his colleague, and slowly nodded his head as if confirming that to himself. 'To clear the deck here.'

Matucci gazed back, his cigarette forgotten. 'Diversion?'

'Matucci, this is a very muddy pool we're wading about in. Cunningly muddied. Stuckart's just one bit of mud. There're several elements –'

Abruptly Inspector Ferrand appeared in the door. 'The security company's in a sweat. Monsieur Bosson's been barking down the line to the Commissaire ... there's something else interesting going on downstairs. I want to catch it.'

He disappeared. Anders had dropped back into his thoughts. 'I need a shave,' he said. He used Matucci's Philoshave, and drank coffee and ate a roll and butter that Matucci fetched from the canteen. Watching him Matucci thought: he hands me out bits and pieces like candy out of a slot-machine. Apparently, no definitive reasons were to be forthcoming as to *why* Stuckart was off the screen. He sighed to himself. It was the way Anders' brain was.

Ferrand reappeared. 'A young fellow's just come in who witnessed a bit of strange business last night at the Raven Bridge.' He explained the details. 'Grappling and lifting gear is on its way. Maybe?'

'A cage?' Anders drank up his coffee. As if he'd been programmed to, he suddenly remembered something he'd read in the guidebook.

'A tall fellow, in a hat and a long, dark coat.'

'Let's go,' Anders said.

It was spitting rain when they alighted from Ferrand's car and walked onto the bridge, which had been half closed off to motor traffic. At the quay near the Palais Rohan the glass-topped boats were moored, and a long queue of tourists waited, white faces gazing towards the bridge. The river voyages should've commenced by now. On the downstream side of the bridge a police boat, propellers just turning, was nosed up against the current. As they reached the parapet a wet-suited diver fell backwards into the river, and a truck with a mounted crane, was backing into position.

Anders stared down into the murky water, saw a few reeds drifting by on the surface. The diver surfaced in a rush of displaced water, gave a thumbs up to those on the bridge, called something.

'He's found the cage, but can't see what's in it,' Ferrand growled. A cable with a heavy hook was being wound out from the truck; swinging wildly, it dropped into the water. The diver splashed after it.

Anders stared at the metal top as it emerged. A *cage*. They lifted it clear of the water: *the imprisoned corpse of a man*. Black clothes. Runners. It was swung over the parapet and deposited with a clang on the roadway.

'It's Kramer all right,' Ferrand said. The director of strategy for Deutsche Rural-Credit was curled up against the bars. His features were pale and water-softened. The eyes half-open. The front teeth had been badly damaged, lips cut, but all traces of blood had been washed away. The black hair was plastered tightly in place against the skull.

'Christ,' Matucci said. 'What a way to go.'

With difficulty, Anders bent down, and gazed through the bars at the body, centimetre by centimetre. He thought: must've had urgent business on hand last night. Or he was just careless, and didn't take sufficient account of the way his world had changed.

Anders straightened up. 'This is a cruel thing. A black-hearted thing.' He'd spoken half to himself.

Ferrand looked at him, lit a cigarette, said in his gravelly voice, 'It seems you are indeed at the right place, Inspector.' His mobile rang. He answered it, and listened. He said aside, 'They've found the vehicle.'

Walking back to the car, the French detective was thoughtful. He said in a meditative voice: 'In the Middle Ages, prisoners condemned to death were lowered into the river in cages from Raven Bridge.'

It was what Anders had remembered.

The vehicle had been found at the airport. It had been hired from a Strasbourg firm yesterday at 5.00p.m., and in half an hour the trio of detectives was at the company's office talking to the man who had done the transaction: an overweight fellow in a crumpled suit, with watery blue, surprised eyes. A man had taken it, he informed them. Paid in cash. Just for the night to transport a crippled relative. Had given his name as Sebastian Sag. Paris address; for identification, a French driver's licence. They examined the details on the form he showed them. Ferrand asked for a copy.

'What was his description?' Ferrand asked.

The leasing man looked blank. 'A man ...' he muttered. He tugged at an ear, and Anders read the mortification in his eyes.

'You don't remember more than that?' Ferrand asked, incredulous.

'No.'

'This was last night. Were you half asleep, monsieur?'

The man in the crumpled suit dropped his hand on the desk – a gesture of frustration, and amazement.

Anders said, quietly. 'Not a tall, thin man with quite long black hair, black or dark eyes, a pronounced stoop?'

The watery blue eyes conveyed the leasing man's brain's unavailing effort. 'Monsieur, I cannot remember a damned thing.'

Outside in the street, Ferrand looked glummer than usual. 'What an idiot,' he commented, as if embarrassed at this failure of local intellect.

Anders looked at the Frenchman. 'Sometimes the brain blocks out quite crucial matters.' Again – that strangeness. A point of departure? Did it fit with what had happened elsewhere? He stopped walking. Kramer didn't fit the *Paris-Match* scenario precisely. Nonetheless … he turned his head and stared at Matucci.

The big, blond detective stared back. 'Brussels?'

'Exactly. Your friend, Dupont, may be about to receive another message. So –'

'I'm on my way.' Matucci shook hands with Ferrand, nodded to Anders, and abruptly projected his finger like an aimed pistol at the heart of a passing taxi-driver. He was smiling as he got in. Here was the opportunity, if necessary, to lean on the Belgian journalist, in pursuit of the truth. What Anders didn't know, wouldn't hurt.

He'd wanted to have a look at Dr Dauban out of her drab and dusty archive; motivations both professional and personal. A lunch invitation had seemed the way. He'd not eaten a proper meal yesterday, and Matucci's research had located this Italian restaurant – the dark and alluring

Mademoiselle Dayshift, Christine, had been the source.

Grimly, he smiled to himself. He'd been celibate in Lyon. His sexual desire had died. In the early months there he'd seemed in a kind of convalescence – from what had happened in southern Italy eighteen months before, and in the mountain town when the mafia had tracked him down. From *all* that had happened in his life.

He waved away the waiter and the menu. He wished to speak with the proprietor who seemed busy in the kitchen …

The dreams and fits had come down on him. Crushingly. After he'd seen the doctor he'd become reclusive; in a stand-off with it. In the careful way that he had, he'd gone to the public library and found books. His brain circuits were being 'jammed' bringing on 'dissociative experiences'. Anxiety, stress, mental exhaustion, take your pick for a trigger. Overload = hallucinations. Full-blown delirium was the next phase. He'd still resisted taking the Ativan, gradually he'd been improving. Desk-work.

A waiter poured water into a glass …

He'd told Renata he didn't address *the future*. Dealing with the overlapping past and the present had him fully engaged. In one way though, he was functioning again.

It was only just noon, an early hour for him to eat, but he'd had to fit in with the librarian.

She came threading her way through the outside tables and stepped into the interior. Erect and hip-heavy. A precise walk. Arriving, her long, unrestrained hair had flicked back and forth across her shoulders. The romantic in him was thinking of old quarters in eastern European cities. Maybe Jewish.

Her face was serious and doubting in the moment before her eyes adjusted to the dimmer light and found him. Anders rose to his feet, and with what Matucci would have thought of as old-world politeness, pulled out a chair and settled her in it. Immediately, she produced a gold-tipped cigarette. 'Do you mind?' With the lighter that he kept for sentimental reasons, and for ladies, which was practically the same thing, he lit it. Had she heard about Herr Kramer's murder?

The owner came out. He was from Verona, and excusing himself to her, Anders briefly discussed that city and its gastronomic specialties. The man said his chef could make a good *risotto alla veronese*, with the regional mushroom sauce. They discussed the latter; how it would be like a mushroom stew and served separately. Anders selected a bottle of white wine – Soave from east of Verona; it was a good traveller.

Anders raised his hands and smiled at the man. It was now in the lap of the Gods – or the chef.

Her brown eyes were considering this Italian policeman, who had stepped into her world with his slightly dislocated walk. Who had come to her to talk about *The Ship of Fools*. Who had looked at her in a way which she couldn't quite fathom. Who was now engaged in gastronomic seriousness. Her experience of men had been surprisingly limited. Of policemen: zero. And now he'd invited her to lunch, when the telephone would have sufficed to hear what she had to report.

She put down her cigarette. 'I've just heard about the bank director. That is shocking.'

His face remained neutral.

'Professor Lestang phoned half an hour ago to tell me. He'd heard it on the radio.'

He imagined the claustrophobia in this small city. He wondered if the relationship with the ebullient professor

113

was closer than he'd thought. 'It is shocking. Even to me. He was overpowered and placed in a metal cage and lowered into the river from Raven Bridge.' He shrugged, indicating the outcome. She shuddered and gave him a distressed look.

'It is also called Bridge of the Condemned. It has a sinister history.'

'Obviously well-known to the murderer.'

'Yes.' She was watching him intently. 'Is it connected to the horrors in Frankfurt, Paris? The use of *The Ship of Fools*?'

The wine was being poured. Anders watched the pale yellow liquid splashing into the glasses. 'It's possible that it's not related, but my guess is that it is.'

'Then there'll be another message?'

'I'm expecting one.' He raised his glass to her. Where *did* a woman with a broad face, high cheekbones, and those eyes come from?

The meal arrived. Anders hadn't been to Verona in many years but he remembered the food. And he recalled the case that he'd been on, which had been connected to the university: a leftist economics lecturer had expanded his syllabus to bomb-making. He tasted the mushroom sauce, found it satisfactory, turned and raised his glass to the hovering proprietor: at that moment, to Anders, he became Signor Cantini.

This early there were no other patrons. She said, 'I've asked my staff about visitors who've come to see our copy. No-one stood out.'

Anders thought: ah, I suppose such a person would be endeavouring not to. He said, 'A man who looked like this …' He gave the description he'd had from Renata. 'It's only a possibility.' A remote one, he thought.

'Black, shining eyes. So much black. It means nothing to me. I will ask my staff.' She'd only drunk a little of the wine, but had eaten most of the meal. She opened her bag. 'I've brought this for you. Do you read English?'

'Better than I speak it.'

She passed him a book. He turned it over in his hands. *The Ship of Fools*. The publisher was Dover Publications Inc., New York. 1962. She said, 'It has the original 114 woodcuts. I think the two quotes that've come through the Belgian journalist are based on this English version by Professor Zeydel.'

He turned it over, read the back, then put it aside. He'd intended to tell her about Anton Anders – and his book. Building a bridge. And he did. Sitting here, far away, it seemed made up of smoky fires, hot casseroles, the sound of wind howling around the high-set house, low clouds, slanting rain, the Beretta within reach; always within reach. The widow … and that final blood-fest … an abridged version. She listened, her lips motionless and admirable to his eyes.

When he'd finished she nodded to herself, thoughtful. Then she flashed him a new look. 'I'm sorry, I must get back.' He stood. At the door, she said, 'Perhaps the Ship is meant as a metaphor – for our present-day corporate Europe.'

He spread his hands slightly, and shrugged. Maybe.

She said, 'The banker, the bridge, that's out of the darkest annals of our history. Black-hearted.'

That word again. Then she was gone, back to her world, leaving Anders in his.

And where were *they?* What next move was obsessing them?

He considered the man Renata had described. He'd

have an identikit done. What was his connection to the deceased Stuckart? How had he known about that suitcase? Renata had said so far as Stuckart valued any possessions they were in that case. Not much for a life.

He turned out of this. 'Excellent. For the kitchen,' he said to the proprietor, pointing to the remaining half-bottle of Soave as he paid.

'Arrivederci,' Signor Cantini said as they shook hands.

Ferrand was waiting outside. He leaned across and opened the car door. Anders saw instantly that the dour detective was suppressing excitement. He burst out: 'The chairman of Country Fresh has been blown up. In his car. Half an hour ago in a Paris suburb. He's dead.'

Anders froze. He felt like something had smacked him in the belly – and it wasn't the *salsa di funghi alla veronese*. That had tasted as country fresh as tomorrow.

XI

THE THIRTEENTH OF OCTOBER

P.M.

'THIS IS tragic and very serious,' Henri Bosson said, his eyes flicking to his wife, to Klaus Hofmann. He cleared his throat. 'No-one's claimed responsibility, but the commissaire fears it's the Judgment Day group.' His large, pudgy fists were pushed together under his chin. 'We must assume our merger's come into the sights of these madpersons. It seems this Inspector Anders, from Interpol, is on their wavelength.'

His eyes widened with emotion. 'We should be praying to God he can get them.'

Dominique Bosson's face was set and vacant. Was she hearing him? Bosson wondered. She'd screamed without knowing it when the commissaire had rung him with the news. The whole building had frozen. She'd rushed into her room, swept up her little dog, and buried her face in its white fluff.

Hofmann's birthmark stood out against its pale background. Despite his tension, the German was very much in control of himself. 'Paul will be greatly missed,' he said. 'I don't know what the poor fellow was thinking of.'

Hofmann's assistant had already collected and sealed the deceased executive's papers. In and out, before the police arrived.

Bosson frowned. 'It was stupid.'

The German gazed down at his strong hands. He did have an idea of what had sent Paul running in the night streets. His blue eyes lifted and fixed Bosson with a back-bone-building look. He feared nothing in business, and nothing where his athletic body could be brought into play. Henri mustn't waver now. He looked at Dominique.

'He's gone. We must go on. With even stronger resolve.'

From beneath his somnolent eyelids, Henri examined him. 'I remind you, Klaus, our boards have not yet given approval. A few of our colleagues aren't in favour and now, others may waver.'

'It *will* be approved. We *will* merge,' Hofmann pronounced with cold certainty. 'The directors on our side will toe the line. I will see to it. My dear Henri, I trust you will do the same.'

Bosson's face crinkled into a smile. He'd begun to re-think an aspect of the merger. One that had become worrying. He'd insert a tinge of doubt; put a bit of fear into Klaus. Perhaps unmask that worry – which related to the health of the German bank's mortgage portfolio. He was aware that Dominique had come out of her trance and was staring at him. Into her, as well. He said, 'Your confidence is impressive, Klaus.'

The German was silent, wondering at Bosson's tone; at where his mind had travelled to now.

When Hofmann drove home for lunch there was an extra police car. André, his partner of four years, a slim Moroccan in his early twenties, was driving, having slipped out from the apartment where he'd already fixed the lunch.

Hofmann's apartment was in the Petite France quarter, in an old building facing a navigation canal. He'd taken it four weeks ago. When the merger was finalised he'd commission an interior designer to do the place over. He and André would then commute twice a week between Strasbourg and Frankfurt.

Having parked the Mercedes in the courtyard garage the two men walked upstairs. More than a century ago the building had been an old tannery. Two of the police followed and stationed themselves outside the door.

Hofmann placed his arm around André's shoulders and they entered a front room whose windows looked down on the canal. A tourist boat, foam boiling around it, was entering the lock. A table was set with a cold collation and a decanter of riesling beaded with icy moisture.

Hofmann dieted rigorously. He was forty-eight but boasted that he didn't have a gram of excess flesh on his body. He worked out twice a week on the latest machines. He released the Moroccan and poured wine for them both. Surely Kramer wouldn't have revealed the mortgage portfolio imbroglio to Madame? No – he decided. But something unpleasant was working away in Henri's brain.

'I'm going to really miss Paul,' he said. 'He was a slippery bastard in many ways, but he always came through for me. The merger was a special achievement.' It was a bonus that he'd fallen for Dominique Bosson. Hofmann's people had contacts at hotels in Brussels and Frankfurt where she and Paul had stayed when they'd been working on the merger. They'd been careful, but anyone who thought they could avoid scrutiny when professionals were on the job was crazy. He'd some bitter personal experience of

119

that. Henri, ponderously moving through his life, hadn't suspected anything. He was pretty sure about that. Though now?

He'd been considering a little coercion at the right moment: in six months, when the new managing board met to elect a chairman. He'd some good photographs of the pair, with Dominique on top, clearly her preferred position. He might have to bring them forward.

He raised his glass and smiled at André. 'The lunch is delicious. Let's enjoy it then have a little siesta for an hour.'

★

Philippe Dupont was driving through central Brussels in his car, the Belgian police on his tail, which had become routine, when his phone rang.

'Matucci. What are you doing tonight?'

Dupont laughed. 'You're here?'

'On my way. I'm at Strasbourg airport.'

Dupont's laugh went up an octave. 'Where can we meet?'

'What about that Chinese restaurant for starters? Take one of those small private rooms at the back.'

'Good thinking,' Dupont said. '7.00p.m.?'

'Right. I might be held up. Wait for me.'

'Don't worry … Matucci, that killing in Strasbourg? What's going on? Is it connected?'

'You haven't had a visit? —'

'No. I hope to Christ I don't. And it's not quite like the others is it? I didn't write about him.' His voice had cracked.

'Maybe it's *not* connected,' Matucci said, but it wasn't what he thought.

'I want out. The money's terrific. But too dangerous. I'm going to take off. Exit. I'd like to talk about it tonight.'

The connection was breaking up.

'Let's do that. You've been busy. Boris Bosch, Felix Servais, and Henri Bosson all in *Paris-Match*. Anyone else coming up?'

Matucci was talking to himself. Behind him, on the TV screens the first French reports of the assassination were being shown. The Country Fresh chairman's wrecked car, the destroyed culvert. The trees, fifty metres away, where the bomb had been detonated. The witness who had seen a man take off on a red motor-bike. Matucci missed it all.

He went to board his plane. He'd set things up as well as he could. On the previous occasions, according to Dupont, the night visitor had waited in his car, and his flat. *If* that was so, those locations wouldn't be repeated; the element of surprise was needed. The Belgian police would be watching both apartment and car. Putting Dupont into a controlled situation for say four hours might facilitate a contact. *If* he was bona fide. Unless the plan had already been made. And if the perpetrator didn't smell a rat. Anyway, he'd have Dupont under observation. Nothing happens, and I'll take him somewhere and get bongo-drum practice.

Matucci shook his head. Maybe he was on the wrong track doubting the journalist's sincerity. Otherwise, what he'd just heard on the phone had been a terrific acting performance.

In Brussels, Matucci picked up his pistol from the airline's special desk. He'd time to kill so he went to a bar and ordered a beer and bought Belgian and French newspapers. At this point, he caught up on the Paris outrage.

His face expressionless, he watched the TV news.

This morning Paul Kramer's death had seemed a vindi-cation of Anders' decision to go to Strasbourg, seemingly ignoring the threat spelt out by the terrorists to the French merger. Now, he thought, Paris has come back in the frame with a bang. He grinned sourly. You could bet the ace was shitting razor blades in Lyon. The newspapers had nothing fresh on Servais' assassination, or the Frankfurt bombing. Or the missing Chemtex employee. And according to Anders, Stuckart was off the radar. If the police had any leads, they were keeping the lid on them. He thought: no. These fanatics have got us going in circles.

Anders hadn't taken him fully into his confidence. His senior colleague's reticence had plunged to new depths. That Anders had his own idiosyncratic, albeit nebulous view, of the Judgment Day group and related events, could be taken as a given. He lit one of his cigarettes, exhaled luxuriously. A couple at the next table got up and moved away. If another message was to be released, concerning Kramer's macabre murder, it'd happen tonight. *If* the killing was down to the group, and *if* Dupont was still in the game. As he'd said, he'd written no story about Kramer for *Paris-Match*. As for this new outrage in Paris ... Matucci shrugged. None of it made sense.

What kind of trick would be employed this time? Above everything, they needed this terrorist with the disguised voice, alive. If he could be grabbed he'd be made to talk. Hopefully, it'd open up the Judgment Day group like a can of sardines. French TV News flashed back: a new group calling themselves Daughters of Europe had claimed responsibility for the Paris bombing, announcing that they'd moved to support their Judgment Day brothers/sisters.

This time Matucci showed his surprise.

122

The Chinese restaurant was different tonight. Breezy and shadowy. Beset by heavy-handed hints of winter. *Not* looking like a place to yield answers. The front garden was frigid, and the swinging lanterns had a forlorn rather than a festive air. Then a tourist bus arrived and disgorged a party of Norwegians.

Parked under a tree, Matucci watched them arrive at 6.45p.m. At 6.55, Philippe Dupont's Volvo turned into the carpark, and he watched the plump journalist hasten up the path and pass between two red masonry lions into the restaurant. Dupont's body language exuded expectation of delights in store. Matucci grinned coldly.

An unmarked police car had drifted to a stop a hundred metres from where Matucci was. He wondered if a cop would go inside this time. He loosened his pistol in its holster, got out, and walked up the path. He didn't enter, but detoured to the side, treading quietly under a vine-covered pergola. Its dead leaves scuffed under his shoes. He came out beside the kitchen. Cantonese voices cut the night. Sharp as their knives. Stoves were hissing, stir-fry was sizzling, woks were clashing. One big door to the rear. A second one the other side of the building. He walked across and tried it. Locked. The trees of an orchard, maybe half a hectare, straggled away into the dark as though in retreat.

He gazed that way, into the night. Uneasiness assailed him. Aged trees. Dark, tortured shapes … but it was more than that. He went back to the front, a shadowy figure moving under the pergola. He'd allowed Dupont enough time to settle into the private room.

The Norwegians had taken the place over. A hostess, a face of flashing teeth, agreed to his jocular suggestion of a particular table. It had a clear view between two large tables of the doors of the private rooms, maybe ten metres distant. It was 7.10p.m.

Matucci ordered a beer. Tonight, there was a bevy of cheongsamed hostesses. For his money the senior, who'd greeted him, was the pick, looked like she knew what was what. He'd never made love to a Chinese woman.

The Norwegians were despatching the delights of southern China with gusto, including Tsingtao beer and the fiery Maotai rice-wine. With both they obviously felt at home: aquavit and a beer chaser were close equivalents. They were as uniformly blond as the Chinese hostesses were black-haired. So ruminated Matucci, not taking his eye off that door.

At 7.20p.m., a plainclothes cop entered and sat down at the bar. His eyes drifted over the scene, over Matucci. A hostess was coming and going from one of the private rooms. Matucci watched beer and a bottle of wine go in. He ordered a meal.

At 8.15p.m., the hostess carried a tray of dishes into the room. Dupont had become impatient. Matucci visualised the bad humour imprinted on the plump features. His own dishes arrived. He was fairly adept with chopsticks, but it wasn't easy to use them with the quick downward glances he was allowing himself. Norwegian conviviality and enjoyment were hitting a peak. At one of the tables a man was on his feet, trying to make a speech while a woman pulled his coat.

At 8.50p.m., the cop at the bar was working on his second bowl of nuts —

Matucci heard it through the din. His chair crashed back, the chopsticks went rolling. He was going through the gap between the Norwegians' tables. He reached the door, flung it open —

124

Upright in a chair, the journalist's eyes were wide-open, directed heavenwards. But his forehead was a write-off from the exit wound. In jellyfish-like pulsations, blood was being expelled. Behind him in the paper-screen wall was a long slit and the wall was wavering slightly as in a breeze.

Metal hard into Matucci's spine. *'Don't move!'* in French.

'Interpol,' Matucci said. 'I'll bring out my ID – slow.'

Sixty seconds later he was in the narrow passage behind the private rooms. So narrow he was moving crab-like, but fast. Another thirty seconds, and he was out the back. He stepped through the now unlocked door. From a different angle, he gazed at the orchard. A corridor of light from the kitchen door jabbed into the trees. The kitchen sounds as before. The breeze was higher, and the branches danced in the dark. No other sounds reached him. No foreign movement among the shadowy apple trees, but it was hard to tell.

The Belgian policeman's partner had appeared. They both watched Matucci with austere eyes while the first talked on his mobile. They'd all screwed up. Outside the death room the Norwegians were singing. The senior hostess had taken one stark look into the private room and closed the door.

Matucci followed Dupont's sightline to the small mirror on the wall. He sighed. How unlucky could a man be? Probably it was a mirror positioned by a feng shui man to ward of evil spirits. Probably, it'd given the journalist a sudden and calamitous view of the face behind him. What had he seen in that last instant? The wide eyes broadcast surprise.

Tonight, even the killer had screwed up.

★

The Reuters' man felt a chilling stab in his gut as he heard the first electronically-distorted phrase from the telephone. Since Kramer's body had been found drowned in its cage this morning he'd been waiting.

'Monsieur Reynard? … Listen carefully … Dupont … cannot call you himself you will hear why soon. Last night Henri Bosson and Herr Klaus Hofmann received a warning. Kramer, the joint architect of the proposed Strasbourg merger is now a statistic. …less an announcement is made by the parties that the merger abandoned … more drastic action will be taken.'

Into the long pause, Reynard said breathily, 'Monsieur, are you the Judgment Day group – or this other group?'

'"Trust not a man in any wise,
The world is false and full of lies;
The raven's black 'neath any skies."'

Unpleasantly the electronic words echoed in the Reuters' man's head. The connection was cut. It had been a sufficient answer.

★

When Anders came out of the chief of police's office, Ferrand was waiting in the corridor, his head wreathed in smoke. 'Monsieur Bosson's secretary's just been on the line. Last night Agribank's mainframe was hacked into. It activated the hacker alarms but they weren't after dough. Went into the corporate centre, then the records of the merger discussions. Like a homing pigeon to the joint board meeting where the decision was taken. Looked at how each director had voted.' He shrugged heavily. 'That's all.'

Anders stood as though transfixed, listening.

'Did they get a fix on the hacker?'

'No. She said the entry point was hidden by jumping between telephone networks. The break-in only lasted five minutes.'

Anders had had a half hour with Commissaire Rolland discussing the Kramer murder and the Paris bombing. 'It's a copy-cat group,' he'd said of the Daughters of Europe. 'One starts up, then they come out of the woodwork.' He'd raised Rolland's eyebrows when he'd told him that the Stuckart-Munich connection was a dead-end. A smoke-screen. He'd explained what Matucci was doing, though was sure the police chief would've heard it from Ferrand, who seemed to go in and out of Rolland's door as if were revolving.

He'd found a few minutes to phone Erhardt, who said that the Chemtex deputy chief of security appeared to have vanished off the face of the planet. Anders told the commissioner of his Stuckart conclusion. A smoke-screen, he'd said for the second time. The ebullient German had been silent and sceptical. Where was the hard evidence?

Now, Anders sat up in his room. The evening breeze sighed over the rooftops. The doves had ceased their talk and gone to sleep. He'd unharnessed, showered, and rubbed ointment into his stump. After the Veronese lunch he wasn't hungry. He'd had a brief conversation with the commissaire divissionaire leading the task force from Paris. The man had been clearly mystified as to why Interpol was on the scene, but he'd been anxious to talk to the forensic people. No doubt they'd meet again tomorrow.

This hacker. According to *The Economist*, the Frankfurt joint board decision on that merger had been unanimous.

Not so with the Strasbourg deal. Anders frowned, and tapped his fingers on the chair's armrest. Sorting out the good guys from the bad guys? Was that what it'd been about? If so, did it mean no repeat strike against the boards, en masse, was planned? He shook his head wearily, and left it.

The cage dropped from Raven Bridge, connected to the past, just as surely as *The Ship of Fools* did.

The phone in his room rang.

It wasn't Matucci. Anders sighed to himself. The familiar, fruity tones of Dottore Guttaso, the Milan publisher who was bringing out his book, engulfed him. How many phone conferences had they had? The dottore exhibited bursts of unbridled enthusiasm, followed by long periods of apparent inactivity. A week ago Anders had called and been told he was in South America.

'Inspector! Concerning the *paper*, I've discovered marvellous stock in Zurich. Acid-free, the pages will live forever – as they should. It'll cost a little more, but my dear friend, worth it. Dottore Romani is well-advanced on his very judicious editing. He's complimentary of your style. Absolutely devoid of *frills*. Incidentally, he loves the book. Knows how much it's a labour of love. Anton Anders, the fine poet, will be brought back into the mainstream. *To life.* My dear Inspector, what an achievement!'

Anders wasn't interested in the paper, or the dottore's opinion of his style. He asked a question – yet again.

'*Aha,* publication date. We're confident of the spring. That's our firm intention. I've sent a progressive account to your address in Lyon. Lira 5,000,000 will keep us moving forward. At your convenience, of course.'

After Anders put down the receiver, the silence flowing over the roof-tops seemed absolute. He took up another book, the Dover edition of *The Ship of Fools*, and began to read it from the first page. He'd the strange impression that Marguerite Dauban, in spirit, had come to sit with him. Just before 10.00p.m. he was startled out of his absorption by the beep of his mobile.

Matucci ... he listened.

'It wasn't intended,' Matucci said rapid and dogmatic. He explained about the mirror. 'My friend had the great misfortune to see a face. You can imagine the moment of pure terror he experienced. Frozen on his dial.'

After a moment, Anders said, 'Perhaps not just terror. Perhaps he knew his assailant. A well-known face?'

'Whoever. He came and went like a damned will-o-the-wisp. He's a risk-taker.'

Anders remained seated, his face severe, considering this fresh drama. Matucci would be tied up with the Brussels police for several hours and would return in the morning.

Almost immediately the phone rang again. 'Eh, Anders! Listen to this,' Matucci said. He told Anders what had come in from Reuters, the text of the message that would break in tomorrow's media. 'The bastards are consistent. Gotta go, these Belgian cops are ace bureaucrats.'

Anders sat for a long time thinking. *The raven's black neath any skies.* Kramer's death was part of the Judgment Day machinations – or was being so presented. This time they'd had to convey their message personally. But the electronic voice again.

A strong gust of autumn air hit his face. He stood up. Abruptly, a certitude came upon him that everything thus far, despite its bloody ferocity, had been a prologue. That this night city, locked in its historical silences, was awaiting the main play.

Fanciful, he thought. Nerves were working away in his

stomach, and the flicker under his left eye had increased its tempo. He felt like a drink, but there was nothing to hand. Instead, he breathed in the flatulent odour of the Ill River.

He found himself listening: to the hotel, the street. The notion came to him that on these dark, bitter nights the city unleashed a legion of medieval ghosts to gambol in the streets. To play out old tragedies, as these ghost-like terrorists enacted the new.

He'd a grim picture of Henri Bosson dancing with them.

XII

THE FOURTEENTH OF OCTOBER

A.M.

'DEATH OCCURRED from drowning,' Inspector Ferrand said in his Gauloise-thickened voice to the assembled detectives. 'The deceased received a blow which broke teeth and cut his lips. Insufficient to render him unconscious. A second blow, to the back of the head, did that. Neither blow caused serious trauma. Clearly, they were to incapacitate him so he could be placed in the cage.' The periods in the French detective's presentation had as much weight as the words.

'The cage,' the man from the central directorate of criminal investigation said. 'What do we know about the cage?'

'Nothing as yet,' Ferrand said, eyeing the Parisian respectfully.

'Except its use, and the drowning off that bridge, has some historical significance in this city.'

'That is correct, sir.'

Matucci came in and sat down behind Anders.

'Time of death is fixed at approximately 1.10a.m.?'

'Yes. The driving licence is a fake. The hirer's name given – Sag – presumably is fictitious.'

Ferrand went on to report that the vehicle had numerous fingerprints, though none on the steering wheel. Not much was expected from this source. He explained how Kramer had given his security men the slip – as he had the previous night.

'An idiot,' the Paris man said gesturing irritably. 'Did he think these terrorists are playing games?'

No-one ventured to guess what the strategist of Deutsche Rural-Credit Bank had been thinking, and after a pause, Ferrand continued, outlining the upgraded status of the security arrangements.

Commissaire Divissionaire Dubost from Paris was a short, energetic man with a thick neck and huge shoulders. He was dark-complexioned and a dense, bristly moustache covered his upper lip. Sardonically, he examined the detectives' faces, his own team, urban and regional detectives, and Interpol. 'Very well, get cracking. Monsieur Anders, could you give me a minute?'

Anders sighed inwardly. Pugnacious in appearance, and in temperament, he thought. In a moment, he and Matucci were alone with the Paris investigator.

'Now, Inspector, *why* is Interpol *here*, and *what* has Interpol found out that I should know? Hopefully there's something.'

Anders' glance brushed over the heavily-fleshed, demanding face. 'We're here because of two factors. Brant's *The Ship of Fools* and the Agribank–Deutsche Rural-Credit merger. It's the biggest on the EC's current horizon. In my view, the prime candidate in terms of the terrorists' manifesto.'

Matucci grinned to himself, and thought: and because

of your special radar.

'What amuses you Inspector?' the French investigator demanded suspiciously.

'I was thinking of a beautiful girl I've just met,' Matucci replied off-handedly.

The Paris man stared at him for a long moment.

Anders glanced warningly at Matucci, and said, 'My colleague should brief you on last night's events in Brussels.'

Matucci gave a concise and selective version of his night's odyssey in that city.

'So, you just walked into it *without* the knowledge of the Belgian police? ... Christ,' the Frenchman said, shaking his head.

'We do have an independent role,' Anders said quietly. 'And we do co-operate to the maximum. The journalist Dupont had twice been used by the terrorists to publicise their demands. We considered a third occasion following Herr Kramer's murder was likely. Unfortunately, we couldn't control the situation as we'd hoped. *Another* connection is the three articles that Monsieur Dupont wrote for *Paris-Match* on EC captains of industry. Two are dead, Henri Bosson remains alive. There's no doubt in my mind that this so-called Judgment Day group's chief ambitions are here.'

Dubost stared, eyes wide-open, at this milky-seeming personality he'd had landed in his lap. The man's reputation was different. At least he had something to say.

'What about Country Fresh's chairman being blown up?'

'Another group's claimed responsibility. Personally I believe that is the case.'

The French investigator thought. 'Why would they go to the trouble of disposing of Kramer like that? So risky it's crazy.' He manipulated, re-set his shoulders, and stared at Anders.

'We're dealing with persons of a weird mind-set, don't you think, Commissaire? When Herr Kramer went on his run the previous night they saw an opportunity. They've a sense of history, and the bizarre. A nose how to maximise *publicity*. To me that's the way it seems.'

But it was only part of the reason, Anders had decided.

Dubost sucked at his teeth. 'And what is Interpol going to do next?' he demanded.

'I'm considering that,' Anders said.

'I expect to be the beneficiary of your maximum co-operation, Inspector.' He stared at them. 'Listen Anders, our police, the Germans, the Belgians, have been running around with their heads stuck up their backsides. The whole case's crying out for a strong co-ordinating hand, and now it's going to get it.'

The Interpol men left. Outside, Anders said, 'I suggest you tread carefully with him. He's a sensitive individual.'

'Bull's bollocks,' the big detective replied.

'As to his ego, I meant.' Dubost was case-hardened and bombastic. Himself? Case-hardened and reticent. It took them all differently.

Behind his flippancy, Matucci was downcast. Anders could sense it, and guessed the reason. They walked the corridors and the blond detective said bitterly, 'It appears Dupont was on the level. Not in with these bastards as I suspected. He might still be alive if I'd played it differently … another mistake on my part.'

Anders glanced at his colleague's grim face. 'Matucci, if I worried about *my* mistakes I'd have been in a straitjacket years ago. Forget it.'

Matucci grunted thanks, or something.

In their room, Ferrand joined them. He was still assigned to the Interpol men. The Strasbourg chief of police had had an argument with Dubost about it. 'This Dubost, he's tough,' Ferrand said. 'He was head of the regional crime service in Bordeaux. Solved a string of big country house robberies. A gang with Land Rovers and Armalites. Big shoot-out. He personally shot two of 'em dead.'

Matucci grinned. 'I'll watch him for pointers.' He turned to Anders. 'I spoke to Frankfurt. That bit of circuit board – they've pinpointed the firm that manufactured it. Zurich. The Swiss police are reporting back, Erhardt says.'

Anders nodded. An identikit picture of the face Renata had described had appeared on his desk. Black and white, no shades of grey, he'd think about it. 'I'm going to take a walk around town, I'll see you back here at 2.00p.m.'

He left Ferrand staring after him, and Matucci lighting up one of his foul smokes.

★

Klaus Hofmann was driving through the city in his Mercedes, a policeman seated beside André, preceded and followed by unmarked police cars. Like a hurricane, the Brussels' murder and the terrorists' new threat had burst upon the air-waves and the front pages. He'd no doubt now that their two boards were in great danger.

With Kramer's death, the voting was unbalanced between the boards, to his detriment. Finding a new director who would satisfy his board colleagues would take time. He gazed blankly at the old city's streets, calm and collected beneath the falling rain.

The crisis looming in his bank's mortgage portfolio would be more manageable from the new entity's top job.

His spin should predominate. Overweight Henri, with his deep-sleep voice, was more complicated than he looked. More street-wise, too. And clearly he'd decided to do a bit of fence-sitting on the merger's go-ahead. While the chairmanship wasn't due to be settled yet, the man who displayed leadership qualities in this terrorist crisis *would* promote himself as the prime candidate. The time had come to take a risk.

The graphic photos were a sordid option which could twist like a knife in your hand. He'd keep them in reserve, and take the *heroic* alternative. He punched his mobile. His PA had moved here from Frankfurt into the Agribank building a few days ago. 'Everything set up?'

'They're waiting in the street. I'll be there. Good luck, chairman.'

The Mercedes and its escorts swept around the corner, André using the klaxon, and approached the Agribank building. The PA had understated the situation: it was carnival time. The police escort were panicking. Hofmann slipped from the back seat into the scrum. In a moment he was standing tall, debonair, athletic, gazing with steely eyes into the lenses of a battery of television cameras, engulfed by bodies, the clamour, with five detectives fighting to position themselves around him.

In clear, authoritative tones, he said, '*We will not bow to threats. Whatever the personal danger, we will defy it. These bloody-handed terrorists seek to turn back the clock in the EC. To defy the fact of the global village. To spit on our democratic rights as citizens. It will not be tolerated. The merger has overwhelming benefits to all stake-holders − to the European Community. Abandon it − says this so-called Judgment Day group. I say to them: abandon your futile efforts to stand against the march of economic history.*'

His PA had appeared at his side. 'That's enough. Don't overdo it.' They moved away in a wedge of bodies, Hofmann giving sober smiles, sober waves. The senior detective, sweaty-faced, said, 'Don't do this to us again, sir.'

From the third floor, Dominique Bosson gazed down on the media-fest. The nature of the event was plain. She whirled around on Henri, her hair flying across her brow. 'He's stolen a march on you, Henri. He's taken a quantum leap forward. Jesus Christ! He'll be on every TV screen in the world tonight – a hero, standing against terrorism – while the chairman of Agribank hides in his bunker. *Jesus, Henri!*'

The fact that her husband showed no disquiet at all at this development was further infuriating her.

He returned to his desk, a hard smile on his face. 'My dear Dominique, calm yourself.'

'Calm myself!'

'Yes, please do. Klaus has suddenly become a gambler. An occupation he's really not suited for. The chairmanship, really, is now going to be a case of *last man standing*, isn't it?'

He gave her a long, steady look. The deep timbre of his voice resonated in the room. They said it was a disguise for his semi-impotence. One of his many disguises. He'd sent her to the Sorbonne to study economics and business. She'd come away with two degrees, and new ideas. From the footlights to top-level banking! A progressive move. But had it been a mistake?

Now she became intensely still. The severity gradually melted, replaced by a measuring look that brought a broader smile to Henri's face.

★

Anders gazed at Raven Bridge. Yesterday's crime scene had been freed of its police tapes and was back to normal. Four white swans, the cruising icons of a million postcards, elegantly rode the current. On the bank of the Grande Ile, a fisherman tended a taut line that had been cast out and carried downstream. The river slid by, dead silent.

'The raven's black 'neath any skies.'

'It's crazy,' the Paris crime chief had said, referring to the cage, and the appropriation of the bridge's sinister history. But there was a weird sense to it.

His hands on the riverside metal rail, it came like the sudden heart-stopping tug on a fishing line after a long, long day of no action. Heart-stopping! In a flash, he stepped into new territory.

The Judgment Day group was a myth. A phantom. They were dealing with one individual. An individual with quite alarming abilities. An individual, who was zealot, mass-murderer, *and* joker. He gazed down at the sliding water ... a devious individual rather than an organisation was much more likely to appropriate a bizarre historical incident to a murdering scenario. To have extracted *The Ship of Fools* from the lode of the past ... to've woven in the personalities and the situation of the *Paris-Match* articles ... to've made the fantastic use of Dupont to get the threats out ... to've set-up this amazing media frenzy – in order to maximise the propaganda, the message.

How cunningly it was all put into place! *If he was right.* Anders, at the railing, was transfixed. It had emerged – partly from his cold-eyed deliberation on the facts; partly from his accumulated experience in dealing with devious minds; partly from the way his subconscious sifted and sifted.

The fisherman, ten metres away, was staring at him.

138

Anders was back in the world. Mutual recognition came simultaneously to each. 'Inspector Anders,' the tall, fair-headed man said, bowing slightly over his rod, 'we meet again.'

'Monsieur Bayard.' Anders was mystified. The competition directorate official he'd met briefly with his two colleagues in the Frankfurt bank, here on the bank of the Ill. Fishing.

Bayard laughed. He was reeling in line. 'You've caught me with my mistress. Fishing's my passion. Fly, live bait. All types. I fish the Ill for two days each October ... even we bureaucrats deserve a change of pace.' The silver hook glinted in the dull light. 'Bait's gone.'

Anders nodded. His thoughts of a moment before had swooped elsewhere. What decision had the Brussels directorate reached on the Strasbourg merger? If it was negative, the whole terrorist threat would dissolve before their eyes. The two banks seemed confident of the green light, but nothing had been announced. He dropped his own hook into the water. 'Can you tell me Monsieur Bayard, when a decision will be reached on the Agribank –Deutsche Rural-Credit merger?'

The EC man was casting out again. The hook and sinker plopped into the stream, were taken by the current and instantly the line became taut. He glanced up at the policeman's face, just as taut. 'Very shortly.'

Anders frowned, and stepped from behind his usual correct formality. 'Is there anything you can tell me – in the strictest confidence?'

The man looked up, smiled sympathetically. 'I wish I could.' He hesitated. 'If I were in your shoes I wouldn't stop your investigations.'

Anders nodded. 'I see.'

'It's fascinating Inspector, we are all fishing for answers in our work. The major corporations I deal with are often fishing for each other.' His tenor laugh rang out across the water. 'I'm enjoying my little holiday.'

He was staring up at Anders, as though he thought the detective could do with one too. Gazing down at him, at the water, Anders felt the river-world flowing into his mind ... momentarily adrift ... again, he snapped out of it, raised his hand in farewell and crossed the bridge.

Anders entered a crowded cafe facing the Place Gutenberg. Nerves writhed in his stomach. An individual! That had swooped back. He ordered an espresso and drank it quickly, nearly burning his mouth, and ordered another.

Marguerite Dauban's copy of *The Ship of Fools* was heavy in his overcoat pocket. Were the release of these verses significant clues – to the identity of the perpetrator? To what was to happen next? Or merely embellishments – a device to enlist maximum public attention? Just like the *Paris-Match* trio. The other layer of complexity rose in his mind: the mysteries of the bomb placement, the access to Servais' apartment. The extraordinary aura surrounding them seemed to be playing continuously in the back of his mind like a persistent guitar solo. He grimaced. And the investigations in Germany and Paris appeared bogged down.

While he sipped the second cup, he took out the book. He found the chapter with the raven quote. He read the two pages. Nothing new occurred to him. He sat back, and finished the coffee. Henri Bosson, and *some* of the members of the two institutions' boards, were in terrific danger. Individually, as Kramer's demise had shown. And that was the difference from Frankfurt. Here, there were good guys.

This terrorist was unusually fastidious.

The statue of Gutenberg gazed with a tortured expression towards the investigator. The great printer of the Bible seemed agonised at his bronze inarticulateness. Anders thought: he would've known of Brant and his *Narrenschiff*. If, in the verses, there were messages to decipher, he would have been the one to do it.

He smiled and went to see Marguerite Dauban, passing chic women's boutiques. The new season's colour was red; all the show-windows were filled with red garments. Quite appropriate.

All morning Marguerite had been thinking about the Italian detective: the handsome, narrow face; the sympathetic aura; the serious blue eyes; the walk. Anders' query about an unusual visitor to the library to examine *The Ship of Fools* had been a dead-end for her and her staff. But the Raven Bridge and its macabre story had opened up another avenue of inquiry. The library was a repository of Strasbourg's history, the open section, mainly modern books, was freely accessible to readers. The rare and old books were a different story. Now she had a register on her desk. Occasionally, she brushed her dark hair back. She'd sprung out of the shower, pulled on a jumper and skirt, her overcoat, and rushed to the library, pausing briefly to eat a croissant, drink a cup of coffee at a corner cafe.

Anders, as he was shown into the room, absorbed her pale-complexioned appearance. As she looked at him the preoccupation dropped from her dark eyes. 'Inspector Anders. Again!' A smile flickered on her lips. 'Should I enrol you as a friend of the library?' He could see that she was a little excited, and wondered.

He'd removed his hat. 'I would very much like to be

141

one, but, perhaps from Lyon it's not a practicality.'

'Please sit down. Excuse me a moment.' She regarded him curiously. Then she was running a slender finger up a column in the register, going back into the past. She turned a page, then another, the finger kept travelling. Zipping up the page. Anders watched her. The moving finger had to do with him. She was a woman of both sharp comments and soft looks. 'Again' she'd said. And again he felt the overwhelming attraction. Her eyes, slanted downward, searched for a title, as the hand brushed back her hair. Was Jewish correct?

'*Ah*, Inspector. Here we are. Perhaps we've something after all.' She shot him a look. 'A rare book entitled *Old Strasbourg Tales* was examined by a man nearly five months ago. A book dealing with bizarre events in the history of our city.'

Anders leaned forward.

'Our talk about Raven Bridge started me thinking last night. Of course, someone could have a perfectly legitimate reason for consulting such a book. And some of the information it holds has been reprinted elsewhere ...'

'I would be discreet.'

'His name was Monsieur Gas.' She read out a Paris address, quoted a French driver's licence. Anders' eyes flickered, his pulse had risen. She pressed a buzzer. A minute later a young woman entered the room.

'Louise, on 6th of April last you showed a Monsieur Gas this book. Do you remember anything about the occasion – about him?'

Hands on her hips the young woman stared at the threadbare carpet. 'I do. It was the morning my aunt died. I'd obtained the book, he'd put on the gloves when Carrie came in to say the hospital was on the line ... I asked

142

her to take over and I rushed off.'

Anders said, 'This man, Mademoiselle?'

She was thoughtful. 'Unusual. He was looking at me as Carrie came in … had said something. Then Carrie was there.' She shrugged. 'A tall man, monsieur, straggling black hair down to his collar. A very pale face. A slump to his shoulders. A black overcoat. That is all.'

Anders stared at the desk-top, then smiled his thanks. The young woman left. Anders looked up into Marguerite Dauban's eyes. A bit of sunlight had shot down through the clouds and the high window and was dancing amber lights in them. She nodded, and rang for Mademoiselle Carrie. The girl flashed a questioning look at Marguerite.

She couldn't remember a single thing about the visit she'd supervised. Nothing beyond the urgent message she brought in to Louise. She frowned in puzzlement, then shrugged, and returned to the stacks.

There it was again.

'What does that mean, Inspector? Does it help you?'

'An extremely interesting piece of information,' Anders said. He was thinking of the man Renata Huber had called him to Munich to tell him about. Of the man who'd hired the vehicle from a clerk who could not recall a single thing about him other than what was transcribed in the leasing record. A man called Sag, and a man called Gas who, quite obviously, shared a certain power. And whose identikit was lying on his desk.

'Carrie seemed to have a mental block,' Marguerite said. Anders agreed.

Marguerite Dauban was frowning. Something was teasing at her own mind. For a micro-second it had flashed out of the shadows, as quickly darted back into them, like a fish in the Ill..She flexed her commonsense lips, and dismissed it, as Carrie had done.

Anders had come to ask her to dinner. He was reflecting that the breaks in an investigation often came out of nowhere. *If* this was one. Then he issued his invitation, and she accepted it.

'Have you a mobile phone?' he inquired. 'Just in case.' He shrugged: personal arrangements were uncertain when one was dealing with the world of crime.

When Anders left the Libraire Kleber it was a few minutes to noon. For a moment he stood, indecisive, then he turned in the direction of police headquarters. Outside the cathedral a crowd was passing through the doors into the south transept. Anders, the guidebook man, remembered this. On an impulse he went with them. Perhaps a hundred tourists had gathered before the famous atronomical clock. They gazed expectantly up at gilded angels and figures. The hour of twelve struck and the figures began their performance: the four stages of life paraded before Death, while an angel turned an hourglass.

Someone directly behind Anders was sniggering. The malevolent sound seemed to bubble up from dark depths. The detective edged to his left through the crowd, and glanced back. A man with smooth-brushed blond hair falling to his shoulders, harnessed with paraphernalia, pockets stuffed with newspapers, was gazing up, mesmeric, at the automated figures in their *danse macabre*. The blue eyes were starkly wondering, and child-like, the sniggering sound from the mouth was not.

XIII

THE FOURTEENTH OF OCTOBER

P.M.

ANDERS FELT the prickling on the back of his neck. The crazy hobo had tautened his nerves, but it wasn't that. He was under surveillance. No evidence of it, only his mind feeling the sudden tension, his stomach the surge of nerves. His experience and instinct could be trusted. Absolutely. He kept his glances casual. It wouldn't fool the trained watcher but he did it anyway. He continued across the Grande Ile, a man awkwardly treading this medieval ground with his high-tech artificial leg, a new alertness in his brain, his eyes.

He reached police headquarters, and cast a look back to the street. Not a thing suspicious. The pressure was gone, as covertly as it'd arrived. But he knew he'd had a warning.

He took the lift. He didn't want anyone but Matucci to know what he'd concluded. He deliberated on whether it was premature to impart it even to him … decided he would. He needed Matucci on-side, and obviously his colleague was becoming frustrated.

He looked into their room, gestured to the big detective to join him in the corridor. Not Inspector Ferrand, though. Not yet. The local detective appeared well-disposed, but the commissaire, and the over-moustached Dubost were expecting daily reports on Interpol's activities.

Matucci lit up as they paced the corridor, then he gazed at Anders.

'Matucci, I'm going to tell you something that you might find unbelievable. This campaign of threats and mayhem's the work of *one person*. Each time, that electronically disguised voice. Each time, the same description – in Munich stealing the suitcase, on the bridge, at the library. No-one else's figured.' He clapped his hands together. 'What we're up against is one person: a zealot with a Machiavellian imagination. A savage and mordant sense of humour. A person who'll take risks just to get a weird commentary into play alongside his objectives. A trained killer. It's been staring me in the face.'

'Hell!' Matucci exclaimed. 'How the ...?' He shook his head. 'An ace publicist.'

Anders halted and stared out the corridor windows at the distant cathedral's spire as though it was another revelation. They *all* had that knack. Terrorists were wasting their time without the media. But he'd never seen it to this extent. 'Disguise and deception, death-dealing skills – and publicity, it's all there, Matucci.'

Matucci gazed along the corridor, thinking. He shook his head again, slowly, turned to face Anders. 'Is it possible? One man, up against the whole EC?'

Anders nodded grimly. 'I think it is. Once you get past the Frankfurt bombing – the big production – the other killings have been straightforward. Within the competency of any trained killer, if we put aside, for the moment, how he got to Servais.'

'Yes, but —' Matucci began, then shook his head again. 'The bastard's everywhere: Brussels, Munich, Paris, here!'

Anders nodded emphatically. 'This tight little world of the EC. The marvels of the modern commute. I've looked at the timings, it's feasible, he could've been at each crime-scene.'

Matucci grunted expressively, still doubtful.

Anders' eyes had remained locked on the steeple. Abruptly, he turned his head. 'There's another dimension. I suspect he's got an extraordinary skill, but as to what,' he shrugged, 'I'm still groping in the dark.'

A French detective passed by, waving papers he held to dispel the tobacco fog.

Then Anders instructed Matucci on the meeting that he wanted set up in Frankfurt tomorrow morning.

'Gas,' Matucci said, 'what kind of a name's that?'

'A name as fictional as Sag, my friend,' Anders replied. He didn't tell his colleague about the surveillance he'd sensed on his walk back to headquarters. He'd watch and wait on that. 'It's going to get nastier and nastier.' He nodded, conveying his pessimism. The flicker beneath his eye was locked in an uncontrollable spasm. After a few moments' silence, he departed down the corridor.

Matucci went back to their room, stunned at the turn of events, and by how energised Anders was. How decisive. He supposed if you were always expecting disaster, you reacted quickly when it came. But *nervous* energy. His senior colleague's nervous system seemed a frail base to sustain the endeavours ahead.

At 3.00p.m., Ferrand called them into a room to see Klaus Hofmann's performance on the TV newscasts. Anders watched in silence. 'An extremely brave man,' Ferrand said. His voice betrayed a hint of sarcasm.

'A damned idiot,' Matucci pronounced. 'What he's saying is here I am, come and get me.' He went to phone Frankfurt.

A zealot's taking risks and a man of ambition is taking risks, Anders thought. The headlines in the French language Strasbourg paper had said:

BELGIAN JOURNALIST SLAUGHTERED
JUDGMENT DAY GROUP'S LAST CHANCE
WARNING TO AGRIBANK–DEUTCHE
RURAL-CREDIT DIRECTORS: KILL YOUR
MERGER OR BE KILLED

At 5.00p.m., he and Matucci left headquarters and walked smackbang into the kind of scrimmage they'd just been watching. 'Shit,' Matucci said lifting his eyes skyward.

A TV reporter had a microphone in Anders' startled face.

'Monsieur Anders … as the leader of the investigation into the Judgment Day group's terrorism against major EC corporate mergers what's your report on progress?'

Anders blinked at the bright lights, at the cameras. 'I'm not the leader of the investigation. The French and the German police forces have that distinction –'

'But Inspector, as Interpol's foremost anti-terrorism expert do you have a comment for the French public?'

He shook his head. Impatiently, another voice cut in from the side: 'Inspector Anders the threat now appears centred in Strasbourg. You were the first crime specialist to arrive here, to pick up on that. How did you do it?'

'I've no useful comment at this stage,' Anders said turning away to push through the bodies. But they surged at him, nearly knocking him off his feet. Matucci thrust his bulk forward. But a sharp-faced French woman reporter with short black hair and bird-like black eyes had gripped Anders' overcoat sleeve. 'Marie Ledru, Channel 4, Inspector – weren't you retired from active duty by the Italian police? With respect, you're a cripple at the forefront of the criminal investigation of the decade.' She was shouting. 'Are you competent for this assignment?'

No respect in her spray of saliva and sarcasm. 'Sweetheart, why don't you go to the ladies' and powder your fanny?' Matucci said forcibly, in Italian.

Someone laughed and translated it for the raven-haired dynamo. 'What d'you mean by that?' she demanded.

Matucci was shoving aside bodies making a passage. 'For our sizzling rendezvous later tonight, of course,' he said over his shoulder in French.

'Smug Italian bastard,' she spat out.

Inspector Ferrand came running out, was hauling bodies aside. A camera crashed on the cobbles.

Then they were out of it.

★

The leader of the police detail was breathing more freely. Chairman Hofmann and his partner were home in the apartment. Hofmann was well satisfied; he'd just watched himself on TV for the second time. He could imagine the conversation Henri and Madame would be sharing over dinner. His thin lips twisted in a smile. He'd heard nothing from them as yet.

In the kitchen, André was whipping up one of his masterpieces, and he'd opened a bottle of a favourite '84 Bordeaux. Celebration!

Two detectives sat outside the apartment's front door.

Two more were outside the big door to the courtyard. Fifty metres up the street, another duo sat in an unmarked car listening to the police radio. 'All quiet tonight,' the control room sergeant reported to bored but captive listeners across the region.

Halfway through its voyage, a glass-topped tourist boat was in the lock. Mindful of the Interpol man's warning a few days ago, Hofmann turned off the lights and stood back from the window, his thoughts on his next move. Henri couldn't afford to be seen wavering on the merger now, and Madame would see that he didn't.

The police inspector in charge, a man named Gerard, left the car and looked up and down the street. 7.15p.m. The nearby restaurants were moderately busy. The breeze was coolish, and ruffled his hair. Lights laid yellow curvy daggers on the choppy surface of the coal-black canal. The old tanners' houses stood in conclave like old-time burghers. He approached the two men outside the gate. 'Keep alert. Watch out for diversions. If they blow up the fucking town hall, don't move from here. Remember Felix Servais.' Then he went upstairs to give the same message to the men outside the front door.

André had produced a dream-like souffle. The fragrances of cheese and wine suffused the apartment. Hofmann's eyes lit up, on two counts, as he saw the slim Moroccan bearing it elegantly to the table where the ruby-red Bordeaux waited, with its own superb presence, in La Lit crystal glasses.

★

'Oh, God, it's driving me to distraction,' Marguerite Dauban said. She peered at the old, poorly lit street. The undefined pressure in her mind would neither declare its mystery, nor decently go away. She could not pinpoint it. Might never be able to. Was it one of those thoughts that fell, irretrievably, into the abyss? *Something* was in her head connected to the library and its visitors which was important — she'd become certain of that much. Should she mention it to Inspector Anders? But it was so vague.

Anders had asked her to choose the restaurant. He took in her thoughtfulness as she entered the place of dark panelling and dozens of antique rocking horses. Standing to shake her hand, he wondered at the strained look in her eyes.

She glanced at the menu immediately proffered by the waiter. 'Are you hungry?' she asked.

He nodded, and she ordered local delicacies.

He'd asked to see *Tales of Old Strasbourg* and had leafed through it carefully without comment.

One other table was occupied. Immediately, Anders had seen Professor Lestang. They exchanged nods. He smiled warmly at Marguerite. The tall, handsome man with his light-coloured hair was gesturing to the five other men at his table, emphasising a conversational point. They laughed. The proprietor was fussing around, saying 'Professor this', and 'Professor that'.

Academic patrons in an old university town: restaurateur's bliss, Anders thought. Abruptly, Lestang rose and came over to them, his eyebrows lifted, as if in surprise.

'Marguerite,' he said from his height, beaming over the hand that she raised to be kissed. 'Beautiful by day, superb by night.' He turned to Anders, who had stood up. 'A night off, Inspector?' The professor of economics smiled as if he found that surprising. 'You certainly have your hands full. Is it a second German Autumn?'

Anders shrugged slightly in response. That was on quite a few minds. They were both gazing down at the dark woman whose lips, tonight touched with a trace of lipstick, had also moved into a faint smile. Again the amber glints in the eyes, Anders noted. This morning sunlight had done it. Tonight, it was the vellum-shaded restaurant lights. Had this spellbound academic noticed too? He was gazing at her as though soaking up every gram of her essence. He and his colleagues had already drunk several bottles of wine. Presently he returned to his table. 'Very much an admirer of yours,' Anders commented.

'We've known each other a long, long time,' she said. She drew a line on the tablecloth with a fingertip. 'He's against neoclassical economics and his comments cause a stir in the press, at the university.' She gave him a quick look. 'I've similar ideas.'

She produced her cigarettes, and Anders reached for his lighter. What was this – sadness – about her? Wariness? After each utterance, each slight animation, she fell back into it.

The pile of choucroute, ham and sausage was formidable, but Anders persevered. Before he'd departed, Lestang had pointed to the large sausage. 'You must try the *maennerstolz*, Inspector,' he'd said with a mischievous grin.

'*Maennerstoltz*?' he'd said to her.

She'd hesitated, then said, 'It translates as "men's pride".'

'Ah.' Instead, he drank Sylvaner poured from a jug, and they talked about the library. She'd found another book which would interest this Inspector Anders. But she wouldn't mention that tonight; she had a decision to make about it.

At 9.20p.m., they left the restaurant and walked through a maze of pedestrian-only streets to the Place Gutenberg. The moment they stepped into the street Anders had become alert. His leg creaked softly. He was surveying the precinct. The sensation he'd had this morning had returned.

'Should we say goodnight, here?' she asked. She glanced at his leg. 'It's about ten minutes more to my flat.'

He shook his head and took her there. Strasbourg, this part of the Grande Ile anyway, wasn't a nightowl's town.

'Does Professor Lestang take many trips?' he asked in a dark street.

She looked at him. 'He's always away, lecturing. Was in Paris a few days ago.'

He awaited an opportunity to ask Lestang about his recommendation of the *Paris-Match* trio. What did it signify? They weren't far from the southern branch of the Ile. He smelt it. She stopped on a corner under a doorway. 'Here we are.'

Anders stood close, absorbed the fragrance of her hair. Was she one in whom he could find a communion of mind and body? He now found himself doubtful, an unusual indecision in him.

'Goodnight, Inspector,' she said.

'Goodnight, Doctor.'

An organ erupted in a blare of sound, vibrating the cold, moist air, making him jump. They seemed to erupt without warning in this city; the sound drummed away against the low clouds. In this case he identified the source: a church where Albert Schweitzer had played. Late at night, did the ghosts of dead players return?

An individual! Based where? In cellar, office block, flat?

153

The German Chancellor and the French President had exhorted citizens to keep a close watch, to report anything suspicious. Thousands had, and it was part of the problem for the police. He turned for home.

A few streets later it struck him, like eyes burning on the back of his head. It was that strong. Stronger than this morning. The recollection of old dangers, past emergencies came in an adrenalin rush. 'Quieten down.' Urgent instruction. He entered an alley heading to the river. He calculated it'd come out near the Raven Bridge. Distant voices only, and the occasional creak of his leg.

The face of a man glowed on a wall poster. Anders approached it … found himself staring hard.

It'd sprung from the wall. Was coming towards him at speed. Spinning like a Catherine wheel. Blur of revolving colour. Anders ducked, and staggered. With the sound of rushing wind the image shot away behind him. He leaned against a wall, gasping from the shock. His heart was pounding, his chest had a steel-band crushing it. He turned his head, squinted in the poor light at the wall. The poster was there; had returned. Like a boomerang. 'My God,' he muttered. He sucked air into his lungs, put his hands flat against the wall, waiting. Never left, he thought grimly. Hallucination. It was early-Lyon, back again, worse than ever.

He pushed himself off the wall, approached the image, trance-like. An elderly man, with a Van Dyke beard.

ON STAGE
THE GREAT FRANKMAN
FAMOUS STRASBOURG HYPNOTIST

The poster was old and tattered, the show it advertised as dead and gone as the summer. Plastered immovably on that wall. Yesterday, he'd thought: it's starting. And tonight, starkly, it had. But how much of it was in his mind, how much reality?

Mademoiselle Nightshift gave him a look. He must appear shaken. Anders showered and sat on the side of his bed. Tonight the breeze was strong and the timbers of the old inn creaked with its secrets – or its boredom.

Sleep was impossible. The lights off, he shifted to the chair facing the open window, surrounded by the forest of pillars, communing with the night. He sensed he was waiting.

The phone rang. 11.30p.m. He picked up the receiver. 'Yes?'

An out-of-the-world synthesised humming sound. But no words.

Again. *'Yes?'*

'Today I've been very close to you Inspector Anders ... I could've touched your sleeve.'

Anders' heartbeats thudded in his ears. 'I know that.'

'Of course you do ... a detective of your experience. I was fascinated to read about your presence here, of your fine record. One policeman among all those agencies, coming like a bird on the wing to the correct location ... not only experience – intelligence. My congratulations. And doubtless you've been making other interesting deductions. By the way, code 7429.'

It wasn't a pretty sound – the brief electronic laugh. Anders was frozen in his chair, but his mind and nerves were absolutely concentrated. Nothing to do but listen; that was what this was about.

'You did make my task slightly harder when you stopped their

board meeting ... but in the event, it's immaterial. Inspector Anders, I'm not in the business of killing the innocent if it can be avoided ... several directors are against the merger. Unlike that gang of Frankfurt criminals, economic fascists to a man. So in Strasbourg a revised strategy is called for ... a selective pruning of the corporate tree. What is the extent of your influence, Inspector Anders? If you could persuade them to abandon the merger it'd all stop. Quite dead. The same if the Competition Directorate declines the merger ...'

The discordant laugh. Anders felt tight in the chest.

'Dupont saw me in Brussels, an accident with fatal consequences ... What did you think of the cage? ... Kramer's past, as well as his present, made him a deserving case to grace it. The opportunist provided an opportunity! Ah yes, but the purpose of my call ... you are wondering that. Klaus Hofmann has been dealt with ... A foolish prisoner of ambition, and duplicity. Henri Bosson was to be next, but Hofmann thrust himself forward didn't he? If Henri had gone next perhaps the German might have seen the light and saved himself. Perhaps this, perhaps that ... By the way, the Daughters of France ∴. someone takes the lead, others spring up. But listen ... just for you "Some trees do burn in hell below/On which good fruit would never grow."

'Blood, Inspector Anders. You will see it.'

Anders had a dead line. He was dazed. Then he was up on his one leg. Balancing like an acrobat on a tightrope. A zealot? Yes. A madman? Maybe. *Klaus Hofmann?*

He got through to Ferrand in a few seconds. He'd be at the hotel in two minutes. The inspector was still on duty, sitting down the street in his car, Anders realised. Whose orders? Not his. Methodically he re-connected his leg, strapped on the Beretta. He walked along the passage, knocked on Matucci's door.

'Matucci. Downstairs. Now.'

'Oh no!' – a plaintive female voice. Going to the lift, Anders decided it belonged to Mademoiselle Dayshift. Or Nightshift? No-one was at the reception desk. Code 7429. What was that?

In the short drive to the Petite France quarter, Anders didn't tell Matucci and Ferrand about the phone call. It was still reverberating in his head. Today this individual could have touched him. Could have put a knife, or a bullet, into him, or poison in his coffee. He believed it.

Instead, the terrorist had done something to Klaus Hofmann. It wouldn't be pretty. He wound down his window. The incoming breeze seemed to enclose his heart in a block of ice.

XIV

THE FIFTEENTH OF OCTOBER

A.M.

THE STREET beside the canal was deserted – except for the police car. Ferrand pulled up beside it, and introduced an Inspector Gerard to the Interpol men. Anders and Matucci alighted, as did the inspector, who was one of Commissaire Dubost's Paris contingent.

What's he up to now? Matucci wondered. Christine had complained with spirit as he'd withdrawn from their embrace. Morosely, he speculated whether it was territory he'd ever regain. No briefing in the five minutes' drive from the hotel. The silent treatment again. What had Anders been up to since they separated earlier in the evening? He shrugged.

Anders looked Gerard in the eye, said, 'I think we should check the security of Herr Hofmann.'

The Paris detective shot a look at this man in the black overcoat and hat. 'My men are in place –'

'I've received some information,' Anders interrupted politely, 'it may be nothing, however ...' Frosty breath hung in the air.

Oh, Christ, Matucci thought.

'*Information*,' the Paris inspector repeated. He looked uncertainly towards his men posted at the building's gate. '*What* information?'

'I'll explain to Commissaire Dubost,' Anders said. He was perspiring. The unearthly voice, the whirling poster seemed to be loose again in his brain.

Gerard turned and approached the gate. At a sign from him, the two men swung it open and the Paris inspector, Anders, Matucci and Ferrand entered the courtyard. The inspector punched his mobile, spoke to the men upstairs. They rode the lift to the third floor.

'All quiet?' Gerard growled at the men in the foyer.

'Yes,' one of the unshaven cops said. 'They've gone to bed I think, maybe about 10.30p.m. No sounds inside since then.'

To bed to sleep? Anders asked himself.

Gerard looked undecided.

'The bell,' Anders suggested.

Gerard whistled air through his teeth, turned and pushed. It shrilled in the interior. A lament, sounding in my cold, cold heart, Anders thought.

They stood there. Perspiration had broken out on the Paris inspector's brow. 'The key?' he asked one of his men.

Anders put his hand on the handle, and tried it. 'It's open.'

'*Merde*,' Gerard muttered. The two men stationed in the foyer looked astonished. They'd heard it noisily double-locked from the inside, hours ago.

The Frenchmen drew their weapons. Anders turned the handle and stepped into darkness. His eyes adjusted. He was gazing down a long corridor to where a vase, on a pedestal, was faintly lit.

Anders walked towards the vase, reached the light. He

looked into a sitting-room, softly lit by side-lights. No Hofmann. No manservant. On Anders' left, a door led to the room which overlooked the canal. He looked that way, then at another door to his right, which was closed.

Inspector Gerard was breathing heavily over the Italian's shoulder. Anders moved to the closed door and swung it open. Another corridor. Shorter, and no vase. And another door.

Anders' deliberate progress through the apartment was mystifying and agitating Gerard.

But there was no great hurry now, Anders knew that.

He opened the door and gazed into the startled eyes of the chairman of Deutsche Rural-Credit Bank. Hofmann was propped up against the headboard of a double bed wearing a sky-blue silk pyjama top. His naked legs were stretched out on the sheets.

In the centre of the birthmark was a red hole. A stripe of blood ran in a straight line down the bridge of his nose, over his lips, his teeth, onto his chin, as if drawn with a ruler.

Gerard gasped.

Anders had frozen in the doorway. A careless move, and his nervous system would fracture beyond repair. He took in the banker's face, centimetre by centimetre. The surprise on it was history. Due to a micro-second of confrontation with imminent death, or to his recognition of the perpetrator?

Matucci, casting quick glances around, recalled Dupont.

'No,' Gerard groaned.

Where was the Moroccan? Anders moved to another closed door, and pushed it open wide. André's head was thrust into the old-fashioned toilet bowl. Gerard pulled the body back. Drowned. Face still contorted, brown, glazed eyes up-turned. No pants. Bloody knees. He'd fought to get a purchase on the ceramic floor to break his assailant's grip. His left arm looked broken.

Except for Gerard, the others were keeping back, grouped in the corridor. The Paris inspector was stunned. His late-night beard seemed smeared like dark paint on his ashen face.

'Not again,' he said in a low, depressed voice.

By 1.10a.m. Commissaire Dubost, visibly pumped-up, had viewed the corpses, and now he was examining Inspector Gerard, who was nearly as inanimate as them. Clearly, he'd zero information to convey. None of the police had heard a gunshot. Silencer?

'The second time, Gerard.' The intonation conveyed total disbelief. The unfortunate inspector had been in overall charge of the protection on Felix Servais the night he'd been killed. 'You're done for, Gerard. Though I hear the Minister of the Interior needs a new kidney. Perhaps if you donate yours, you might survive,' he added sarcastically.

Gerard was speechless. At this moment, retirement and oblivion didn't seem a bad option.

The Paris crime chief turned on Anders. 'Now, Inspector Anders. What brought you to this scene tonight? Obviously with certain expectations. Perhaps Interpol now possesses a connection to the Almighty? Though, going on my ex-colleagues in your service, I strongly doubt that could be so.'

Matucci was leaning against a doorway. He'd dressed in a hurry and his usual sartorial appearance was absent, which didn't please him. He hated sarcasm; had been the butt of it from his last commissioner in Italy, now deceased.

162

He said, 'Why don't you go f—'

Anders' head had turned quickly to cut him off.

'I received an anonymous phone call at approximately 11.30p.m. A disguised voice. Perhaps the same voice heard by Dupont in Brussels. The caller said the situation here should be looked into. He signed off with a verse.' Anders repeated it, then was silent. He'd said all that he intended to say at this point.

The Frenchman was staring at him intently.

'Why you?' Dubost asked.

Anders shrugged slightly.

'Anders, if you're holding anything back on me I'll have Lyon take you back to your desk quicker than you can say "pension".'

Anders nodded slowly, as though that would be a perfectly understandable outcome, which would get no argument from him.

'No-one talks to the media but me. Get it? I saw you on TV, Anders. Don't do that again. I won't have Interpol hogging the limelight.'

Anders wandered out to the front door. The forensic people were at work. A key remained inserted in the lock from the inside. He regarded it thoughtfully.

A few minutes later he had a depressed and introspective Gerard alone. They walked across the street and stood beside the black waters of the canal. It was 1.30a.m. 'How the fuck?' Gerard said almost to himself. His face was stricken.

'Precisely. You were there on the spot when Servais was killed?'

Gerard sighed. 'I was. Up the street, sitting in a car, just like tonight. Although in that case I'd arrived *after* the event.'

'What was your impression of the security men, at the time of their … experience?'

Gerard glanced at Anders, mystified. 'Experience – they didn't have one. They were like zombies. The Paris boys got nothing out of them. Weren't you there? Absolutely no clues as to how access was gained. The poor prick was shot just like Hofmann. Right through the centre of his brain-box.'

At 1.45p.m., Ferrand drove the Interpol duo back to the hotel. Sadly Matucci looked at his empty room. *Coitus interruptus* was clearly not something Mademoiselle Dayshift would take lying down. Anders went on to his own room, a faint smile on his lips despite everything.

★

'Monsieur Bosson, on no account should you make a pronouncement on the merger to the media. Except – I strongly recommend you consider a statement to the effect that the merger's being actively reconsidered. Give us a breathing space to nail these fanatics.'

Dubost stood in the Bossons' super-chic drawing-room, looking like a bear who had emerged from a forest. The Bossons, in dressing-gowns, gazed up at the policeman, hirsute as to face, as to overcoat. Henri seemed in a trance.

He came out of it. 'I've no intention of acting like Herr Hofmann did yesterday with the media, Commissaire. That was ill-advised.'

Dominique, a blonde vision in a peach-coloured robe, was absolutely unshaken. But thoughtful. Different from when Paul Kramer was killed, her husband noted.

Away in another world, Dubost concluded. He didn't know whether he felt admiration or irritation at this. Did she have a shred of fear? Any human being should have. He cleared his throat and said, 'The strictest security is paramount. I emphasise it. Public appearances should be cancelled. Extra resources will arrive from Paris this morning. Monsieur Bosson, you are the terrorists' principal target.'

Dominique Bosson spoke at last. 'It doesn't seem that the strictest security is proof against these maniacs. Your men appear to be total incompetents. Are they trustworthy, Commissaire?' The disdain and suspicion was clear in the stainless steel voice.

'What do you mean?'

She smiled coldly. 'Must I spell it out?'

The Paris chief looked appalled. '*Madame*,' he exclaimed, more in shock than anger.

After the police had gone, Henri regarded his wife for a long moment, and said, 'Klaus was so wrong about his destiny.' She looked away. What is she thinking? he wondered. She seemed to have got over Kramer's death already.

'Last man standing,' she said suddenly. 'My dear perceptive Henri. Shall I come into your bed? All this drama and danger seems to be doing something to me. I always thought Klaus's birthmark was significant to his personality, didn't you? Just as your voice is to yours.'

Bosson smiled cautiously. Life was full of all kinds of surprises. Go with it, but be ready, and never let down your guard.

'I *am* a little tired, darling,' he said.

★

165

Ten thirty-five a.m. Frankfurt. Anders had flown in first thing to talk to the Chemtex security chief, who was back on duty. Standing with Commissioner Erhardt, Anders gazed at the scrubbed clean fish-tank. He could see now that the thick, ultra-toughened glass had fractured into a myriad of small cubes.

Erhardt said, 'It's being dismantled.'

Perfectly understandable, Anders thought. He wondered what progress was being made in finding new directors. It had been announced overnight that the Chemtex–InterDrug merger had been abandoned.

The Strasbourg papers, the TV screens at the airport which yesterday had been showing Hofmann in all his defiant glory, were this morning blazoning his – and his partner's – murders, and what the 'voice' had released through Reuters for Henri Bosson: *'The hourglass is running on your life. Abandon the merger and live.'*

On-screen, the two body-bags being taken from the old tannery building added juice to the chilling words.

Erhardt reported on the search for Chemtex's deputy security chief, Hermann Haug. The trail had gone cold at his abandoned car. The commissioner, a naturally ebullient man, looked tired and glum. There were multiple theories as to why he'd disappeared, but they led nowhere. Nothing in the fellow's past raised an eyebrow. 'Till we find him, or his body, we're running on the spot,' he burst out.

Anders nodded sympathetically. 'How much explosive was used?'

'Six or seven kilos. It was a delicate calculation for those bastards. They didn't want to explode the walls. Wanted to create a bloody icon for the media. And they did it.'

'It could've been carried in a small bag then? A briefcase, for example?'

The German nodded.

The German police had conducted rigorous interviews with all the staff who'd had access to floors thirty-two and thirty-three. Apart from Matucci, Anders had told Erhardt more of his thinking than anyone else. An *individual*? The German had been incredulous. Curiously, they watched the company's chief of security, Kleist, walk painfully from the lift. The man, a grizzled veteran, released from hospital two days ago, with his deputy missing, had insisted on returning to duty.

Anders shook his hand, inquired about his injuries. Concussion. Perforated eardrums. Broken ribs when he'd been thrown to the floor. All were progressing satisfactorily, the pale man replied.

Anders nodded sympathetically, and said, 'I know you've been asked similar questions before, but please bear with me. You were present on the thirty-second floor on the day of the explosion, and the day before? In charge of security?'

'Yes, sir.'

'Access is strictly controlled to thirty-three. Both lift and stairs require a special code to be punched in to gain access?'

'Yes. Myself, my deputy, Haug, and Herr Bosch's PA also had the code to the actual boardroom. Three others to the floor.'

'What were the numerals to the boardroom?'

'Seven four two nine. Of course, it's now redundant.'

Anders nodded, and gazed into the distance, recalling the electronic voice from the other night. *Code 7429.* He came back. 'I've seen the desk on thirty-two where you sit – adjacent to the lifts. You're out of sight of the main reception area. Is your desk always manned? For example, if you're called away?'

'Yes. A senior security person is called to the post if I need to leave it.'

'Did that occur on the day before the bombing?'

'Only during my lunchhour. And about 4.00p.m. A call of nature. The toilets are next to the lifts. My deputy came up on those occasions.'

'No new thoughts on how the survellience system was de-activated?'

'No sir.' He dropped his head.

'Until what time were you present?'

'Nine p.m. when the last director left. Then the whole floor was vacated and made secure for the night.'

Anders' eyes drifted off. 'Who went to the thirty-third floor that day and the day before?'

Two cleaners had cleaned the boardroom the day before. The chief of security had been with them all the time. On the morning of the explosion, the chief executive's PA had taken up board papers, together with the dining-room steward who carried bottled water. Was Herr Kleist with them the whole time? Absolutely.

'No service people?'

'No-one else at all.'

'No unusual event occurred?'

'No, sir.'

Anders gazed at the carpet, looked up. 'What was the boardroom-table constructed of?'

The chief looked surprised. 'An oval table made of black glass. It was supported on a steel frame.'

'If you were sitting at it was the frame visible?'

'No sir.'

'Magnetic material was found –' Erhardt interposed.

'Yes,' Anders said. 'A bomb could've been attached to that frame in seconds.'

Anders turned back to the chief of security. 'Thank you for your time.'

As they walked away Erhardt said, 'That all checks out. Except we've been unable to confirm it with the late Herr Bosch's PA, she's in a catatonic-type coma. But some murdering bastard got in. Maybe aided and abetted by our Herr Haug.'

Anders nodded. The German police had now questioned hundreds of 1970s and 1980s ex-terrorists in and out of prison. Leftists, anarchists, political extremists. They'd up-ended that nether world like a garbage can and raked through the contents. The intensity of that was running down. Karl-Heinrich Stuckart was dead. Anders believed Erhardt, despite the absence of hard evidence, had finally accepted his verdict on that.

'All the visitors to the company the day before have been interviewed – except the Goddamned West Africans. We can't find a crack of light in any of it.'

'Could I see the reports on that?'

'Sure. Come back to my office. A report's in from Zurich on that fragment of circuit board.'

Anders glanced at the German. He'd been holding that in abeyance during the rush of the past two days. He stopped, staring into the distance again. A long shot? He turned and went back to where the security chief stood.

'Excuse me again. I presume the visitors that day entered by the front door, through the security machines?'

The veteran stared. 'No, sir. VIPs are often brought in through the underground garage and go direct to thirty-two. The checks at the main entrance are for ordinary visitors. The West Africans, the union people, the politicians, and the gentlemen from the EC all were VIPs.'

Anders smiled bleakly.

At Frankfurt airport Henri Bosson was on television. 'In view of the recent tragic developments, the boards of our two companies have decided to reconsider the merger. A new announcement will be made within a few days.'

His voice was still sounding in Anders' ears when the jet took off into the pollution-smeared sky. Dubost had swung into action. It'd cause a stir on the heels of the collapse of the Chemtex–InterDrug deal.

A folder containing the report and transcripts relating to the visitors to Chemtex that day was folded in his overcoat pocket. However, he was thinking about the last thing Commissioner Erhardt had told him. The small specialist Zurich engineering company that had made the bomb's detonating device, after backing and filling, had disclosed that a man identifying himself as a member of the French Directorate of Counter Espionage – DST – had ordered it. The company had done business with that bureau in the past, though not for years. The man had known what he wanted: the specifications had been precise. A tall man with hunched shoulders, long black hair, using the name of Sag. The information had thrown the French into a new panic.

Why did *some* people remember their contact with this merchant of death, while others had it wiped out? This man Gas, or Sag, or whatever? This tantalising skein in all the events.

He's in Strasbourg – or coming there after Henri Bosson – Anders thought bleakly. He watched the green German landscape unfold beneath the plane's wings as he flew north. From this height, it all looked as innocent and as harmless as a nursery rhyme. Though, he'd read that psychologists propounded that sugar-coated nursery verses frequently had a dark heart … the jet engines droned on the edge of his consciousness ... whether this zealot would wait for Bosson's announcement, or proceed on his course anyway, was the question.

The thinking he'd revealed to Matucci yesterday in the corridor at police headquarters was nagging in his brain. *At least some of the time, a special power was in play.*

Until now, regardless of the state of his nerves, events such as posters whirling off walls like missiles hadn't featured in his world. But twelve months ago he didn't dream those dreams, either. Grimly, he wondered what his mind was trying to work out. What worm was feeding away in his brain? Once, he'd been horrified to read that, in Mexico, larvae in under-cooked food got into the bloodstream, into the brain, and hatched into a worm with chaotic outcomes, physical and mental. A worm in the brain!

At the airport, he went into a bar and ordered a cognac. Needed it. An old chief of his had told him alcohol was all about nursing the nerves. He sipped the drink and gazed at himself in the mirror. The bar was filled with travelling yuppies. The vision of a woman in Trieste, about three years back, came into his mind's mirror. Brown, oval face. Nerves as brittle as fuse-wire. Trying to grin, and bear her life. She'd a birthmark on her left breast roughly shaped like Australia. 'Anders,' Colonel Arduini, his old friend in Rome had once said, 'your head must be totally filled up with a card-index of women.'

If only it was!

His eye had caught that of a man of about his own age in the mirror. They exchanged slight, companionable, same-generation nods. At that moment they recognised each other.

'Monsieur Fouralt.'

'Inspector Anders.' They shook hands. The competition directorate man appeared harassed. His hand was wet. 'I see you in the papers, on television ... any news?'

Anders shook his head. 'I presume you're here on the bank merger.'

Fouralt's tall frame inclined towards the shorter man. 'We've moved on to other matters.'

'The directorate's taken its decision then?'

The Brussels man hefted his attache case. 'It has. No doubt the parties will release it shortly.' He grimaced. 'Unless they're blown to kingdom come.' He added hastily, 'Heaven forbid!'

The tense man hurried off, and Anders downed the cognac. According to the morning paper, the blood-letting was going to come in the French and German provinces, with the shedding of 21,000 jobs – if the merger went through.

Twenty-one thousand lives disrupted! He tried to recall if this sort of thing had happened in the past, merely to increase profit. It seemed monstrous. What would future generations think?

From his respite, Anders slotted himself back into the EC commuter-world, and the ominous and unrelenting present.

XV

THE FIFTEENTH OF OCTOBER

P.M.

STRASBOURG LOOKED as sedate and chilly as a grey-cassocked monk in a medieval church cloister. So thought Anders, driving in from the airport. Moodily, the overcast sky sagged on the city's spires and towers. The temperature had dropped five degrees on yesterday's; another north European winter was moving closer.

At 3.07p.m. Anders arrived at police headquarters and took the lift up to his room. The Swiss police's report of the man who had bought the detonator had precisely backed-up Renata's description. Each was supported by the young fellow's observation at the Raven Bridge, and by the librarian who'd shown the man calling himself Gas *Tales of Old Strasbourg*.

The building was full of new bodies, and new voices. Dubost's extra resources had arrived. Inspector Ferrand glanced up as Anders entered, and rang for coffee:

'It's just come through on the wire – the Paris merger's been called off. They say strategic obstacles have arisen.'

173

Anders stared. Two down, one to go.

'And the Paris boys have taken over the Bossons' protection,' Ferrand said gloomily. 'In normal circumstances you'd have to think he was pretty well protected.'

'Yes.'

Anders went back to the door, and gazed along the corridor at all the activity. He realised that he hadn't done anything about the identikit, and wondered if he was losing his grip. He turned and smiled at the stolid Strasbourg cop.

'Inspector, we're now in a position to level the playing field. Isn't that how the EC economic gurus talk?'

While he'd been in Frankfurt, the identikit had been revised. He took it from his desk, studied it afresh, and handed it to Ferrand. The detective went out. Within a few hours, every cop in Strasbourg would be primed with this image. The media would go crazy, and not just in France – this was an international story.

He stepped into the corridor and gazed across the city. During the return flight, his thoughts had returned to that whirling poster. And now he made a decision. Abruptly, he went back to the office.

Matucci came in and sat down. Immediately, he'd a cigarette alight flavouring the room. He exhaled luxuriously. Anders had his hat and overcoat on. Not unusual, Matucci thought. He always appeared ready to depart, as if he was at home nowhere. It was a hint that his best work, best thinking, was to be done in solitary perambulations around whatever city was outside. Ferrand returned, and Anders brought them up to date on Frankfurt. He took off his hat, thought for a moment, then looked up at his colleagues. 'This individual has special powers. Is pulling tricks to get the access he needs.'

Ferrand gazed at him in mystification. 'Individual?'

Anders repeated what he'd told Matucci yesterday; what he'd later put to a stunned and incredulous Dubost. He'd left the commissaire staring after him, and shaking his head.

Ferrand blinked. In a reflex, he pulled out his Gauloises, and lit up.

'Special powers,' Anders continued.

'Black magic?' Matucci inquired sardonically.

'Why not? To be effective in our world you need to be able to suspend your disbelief, Matucci. But, no. Hypnotism.'

He gazed at their surprise, then wrote on a piece of paper, and passed it to Ferrand. 'See if you can locate this man.'

Ferrand took it and ambled from the room. Anders turned to Matucci. 'I didn't tell you the full story of that phone call last night.' He gave it to his colleague, practically verbatim.

Matucci realised that Anders hadn't wanted to spell out that communication in full for Dubost. Not a surprise. Anders was adept at holding back enough to maximise his own freedom of mind and movement.

Anders added, 'That electronic voice is in my head like the Eurovision hit-song of the year.'

Matucci stared.

Nightfall had obliterated autumn's dressy, amber shades, and the streets in this quarter were under-lit and populated by shadowy hurrying figures. An imprint of seediness, and over-use. So thought Anders, as Ferrand stopped the car outside a dingy apartment building, which a long while ago had been painted black. Matucci was whistling

175

tunelessly through his teeth, at home in any urban ghetto.

'Wait, please,' Anders said. He didn't know what kind of man he was going to meet. Low-key would probably be best.

He crossed the pavement, opened a gate in a rusted ironwork grille, and stepped into a foyer with two tubs of malnourished plants. A pitbull terrier powered out of an alcove to his left, an insane snarling buried in its throat. Attached to its lead was a skinhead. Two-handed, he was hauling back. He had tattoos across the knuckles of both hands. Rapidly Anders focused on that grip.

Crunch. Anders' shoulders hit the foyer wall. Bone against concrete. The pitbull was mad for his throat, his crotch, whatever anatomical point it had been trained to attack. Inside two coats his hand found the butt of the Beretta. The dog's reddened eyes were less than a metre from his own. The man's were the same hue and temper. He was really heaving back. *'What yuh doing here?'* A grunt of effort more than a challenge.

Anders' hand had frozen; he couldn't get the gun out in time. The fellow looked as crazy as the animal. 'Police,' he said sharply. 'If you want to keep your dog – back off.' He made this calmer and authoritative. An effort. The skinhead fought to hold the muscle-rippling killer with his own whipcord arms. His knuckles were white beneath the crude blue letters. The dog was choking on its collar, in its fury. Ferocity-overload. 'Only way he knows is *forward* ... You want to see Monsieur Charles?' Breathing really hard now.

'Yes.'

'Seeing nobody – especially no cop.'

'Why don't we ask him?'

'Why don't I let Gladiator 'ere sniff your pisser?'

176

The iron gate crashed open.

'Back off,' Matucci snarled, 'or you'll be holding dead meat.'

Anders' eyes deviated a fraction. Matucci was balanced in the gateway, his pistol, held two-handed, lined up on the pitbull whose blood-hazed focus hadn't changed from Anders' throat. The skinhead laughed contemptuously: '*Tough* bastard –'

Matucci fired. A flat *crack*. In the middle of a blood-lust leap the pitbull lurched sideways. *Crack.* The second bullet splattered its brains on the concrete wall and it thudded down on the tiles, a quivering deadweight of flesh. His mouth open, the skinhead stood frozen, his arms sagging. Like an automaton he swung on Matucci, his right boot going into action. *'Bastard!'*

'Wait!' – Ferrand grated in an alarmed voice, springing forward, a truncheon already into a swing that sang down to crack the skinhead on his shaven skull. A second thud, and they were looking at the soles of his huge metal-rimmed boots. 'Wasn't going to shoot him,' Matucci chuckled. 'Nowhere vital anyway.'

Ferrand gave him a look. He didn't believe that. Anders gazed at the scene, turned, and nervously flexing his shoulders, disappeared into the building.

After the violence below, Anders was surprised at what he found in the flat above. And at how easily he'd gained access holding his ID up, conscious of the scrutiny through the spy-hole.

Monastic. The room was as scrubbed and unencumbered by possessions as a cell. Except for the books. They covered the four walls from floor to ceiling and the shelves seemed to be leaning dangerously inwards like a masonry wall whose foundations have settled. It looked like an optical illusion, and Anders felt claustrophobic.

He was sitting opposite a man whose face was both pleasant and curious. A man dressed in a suit, with the serene air of a sympathetic churchman. A man with a Van Dyke beard. The Great Frankman.

'I'm afraid there was trouble downstairs,' Anders said apologetically. 'We had to shoot a dangerous dog.'

Monsieur Charles might've been seventy. He shook his head sadly. 'Ah, Hans our resident neo-Nazi. He's staked out a claim to this building. He protects us ... runs our lives, up to a point. The pity about the dog is that it's replaceable. He'll have another in a week. A badge of office.'

'The police –' Anders said. 'Couldn't they move him on?' 'Better the Hans you know than the one you don't. I no longer receive clients, don't much go out. I pay him 400 francs a month. To me, he's as civil as he's able to be.'

He had blue eyes deep-set under a craggy brow. His arms rested on the desk, bony wrists displayed, long-fingered white hands cupping each elbow. He smiled and looked inquiringly at the detective. 'Interpol? As neo-Nazis go I'd say Hans is the smallest of the small beer.'

'I'm not here for that reason,' Anders said politely, his hat on his lap. 'I'm here because of your profession.'

The man's eyes hadn't moved from Anders'. 'I'm retired, as I said.'

'I saw your poster.'

'Ah, my farewell performance. Over twelve months ago.'

'In the intellectual sense, from some professions a person never retires. I suspect hypnotists and detectives are in that boat.'

178

He laughed softly. 'Inspector ... Anders? You could be right. How can I help?'

Anders outlined the events in Frankfurt, in Páris at Servais' house, and asked his questions. He'd intended to pose them hypothetically, but it was apparent this man had read about him in the papers, perhaps seen the TV. Clearly knew the context.

'Is it possible by *some* means, to approach a trained guard, have him provide information – for example a code – or do as he's bid? Then erase that act from his mind?'

The man considered the Italian as much as his questions.

'Nothing in this world's impossible, Inspector. You *may* be dealing with hypnotism.'

The blue eyes maintained their gaze. 'Of course, there are degrees of skill. The known boundaries are progressively being transcended. I was a hypnotist for forty-five years. What I knew, what I could achieve in my early days, bore little resemblance to what I became capable of.' He paused. 'I was taught by masters, I experimented. If the circumstances I envisage pertained in your cases, I can't really say with exactitude what might have been done. But hypnotism is a possibility.'

At last he lowered his eyes. Anders kept quiet, recognising the sign-language. He looked up. 'I've been aware that an advanced practitioner's been in Strasbourg this past six months. Coming and going. I've perceived a change in the energy field.' He shrugged slightly. 'One acquires a sensitivity to atmospheres within one's realm.' He smiled gently. 'Trade secrets.'

Anders nodded slowly. He understood about that. After a moment, he said, 'You say you were taught. Is there someone in Europe who's the acknowledged master?

Someone whose tutelage would be imperative to a practitioner – even a skilled one – if that person was to
maximise their skills?'

Monsieur Charles took a pen and a piece of note-paper
from a drawer. The fountain pen scratched in the silence.
He passed the note to the detective. 'I was a humble stage
hypnotist, here is a man at the top.'

'It's a long shot,' Anders said. Suddenly he was sweating.
Moisture on his brow, his body. He could feel the fluttering of the skin beneath his eye, like an insect's wings.
Momentarily, the crushing walls of books swam before his
eyes, were closing in. Then his vision jumped back into
focus.

Monsieur Charles was watching him intently, the blue
eyes wide open, clear as a child's, penetrating. An overwhelming compulsion came down on Anders to unload
his mind, to put all the strangeness and trouble in him out
on the table. Before this priest-like man. His eyes were
locked onto that gaze. He did not fight against it, but now
the compulsion was leaving him ... was being rolled into
a small bundle, and put away in a recess. He heard the
words: '*You* must take care, Inspector Anders.' The hypnotist was standing, head inclined. Anders read sympathy in
the eyes.

Down below, the pitbull's corpse and the skinhead were
gone. Matucci and Ferrand were sitting in the car. Anders
lingered outside the iron grille, gazing along the street.
He'd settled down. Even felt a faint sense of release. He
dried his brow with a handkerchief. Staring at the neighbourhood, he might have been putting his tradecraft to the
test – as Monsieur Charles had. But his mind was reaching
out afresh, for an identity as illusive as a phantom.

He turned around to stare at the building. He pitied

anyone living there. But the Great Frankman seemed at home. He turned, crossed the street and got into the car's rear seat. Matucci and Ferrand were smoking, and listening to the radio. He nodded to Matucci, 'Thanks.'

An hour later Anders, alone, tilted back his head to stare up at the cathedral's soaring steeple, and the waterfall of golden light it shed. It gave him a crick in his neck. He brought his gaze back to street-level. An identikit image of Gas would be on the late-night news. This was a small city – 420,000. Someone must have seen him. His appearance was distinctive, and he wasn't holed up. He was coming and going.

The streets were de-populated but the cafes were crowded: the onset of the colder weather had shifted people indoors. He entered the half-timbered Kammerzell house which faced the Place de la Cathedrale. He removed his hat and overcoat and was shown to a table by a waiter. He winced at the noise: the restaurant was crowded with German tourists. The smells of damp clothes and the kitchen co-habited in the smoky interior.

He glanced over the tables, the faces, looking for the face, the figure, the black clothes of Monsieur Gas. Or was he the invisible man? He smiled a tight smile. *Not* listening for the voice; he doubted if he'd hear that – except on the phone. Nothing.

He knew something about this venerable building. Its façade seemed to have a thousand windows. Characters from the Bible and mythology, signs of the zodiac were carved in the wooden window-frames. Anders gazed around. Many things in this city were grist to his mill ... he'd come here because of the fresco. *The Ship of Fools* glowed on the white wall, a copy of a depiction by

181

Rhenish artists of the sixteenth century. He stared at the pot-bellied ship, breasting the waves, pennants flying. Its cargo of faces, headed˝to hell.

He felt a little hungry and ate *baeckoffe*, a hearty meat and potato casserole. It seemed the night for it. He washed it down with a mug of local beer. As he ate he wondered how Monsieur and Madame Bosson were passing tonight. Commissaire Dubost and his Paris task force now had them in a virtual straitjacket. Or should have.

Deep in the boisterous crowd another man sat alone, reading *The Economist*. A man who in his appearance was interchangeable with many of the fair-headed German men present. He didn't look up when the Italian detective left, standing at the door, putting on his overcoat and hat, re-appraising the scene.

Nine-thirty p.m. Sleet in his face, Anders walked back across the place in the direction of the river and his hotel. He turned and stared back at the Kammerzell house's mullioned windows, aglow like bits of amber, faintly heard the human noise contained therein. The intervening cobbled space was black and devoid of humanity. He was waiting … but he felt no pressure of surveillance. Not like the previous occasions. Tonight, maybe it was at a distance. Or, maybe, the perpetrator was in another city.

He froze. Gazed into the night. Abruptly, a new atmosphere was sharp in his brain. He turned off his route into a maze of streets west of the cathedral. His stump was playing up but he ignored it. This was against his better judgment. Could he keep his unstable nerves under control? That is the question, he muttered.

He walked into darkness.

He came out into the Place du Marche Neuf, cobbled and 'overhung by trees. He glanced around. Leaves were sailing down in a soft silence.

He realised he was light-headed. Surprising: he'd eaten, and had only had one beer. He paused at the fountain, which tinkled sedately, his hands resting lightly on its masonry edge. The cafes and the shops fronting this small place had closed down. In an archway, shadowy figures flitted by. *Organ music again.* Abruptly, a sonic wedge had shot up into the heavens; church-organs seemingly lay in ambush everywhere. Their sounds smashed like bludgeons out of the dark.

His eyes swept the environs.

'Special powers.' If he could understand how they'd been used to place the bomb in Frankfurt, kill Servais, maybe Hofmann and his partner, it *might* finger the perpetrator. He turned his head quickly, and swept his eye around the dark scene again.

It was singing in his ears, throbbing in his veins. The pressure was back. He couldn't get his breath. His right hand went to his chest.

It was turning red. The fountain's water. Anders stared uncomprehendingly. Bubbling from the outlet. Blood-red in the dim light. *Blood*, his brain told him. In a few seconds the bowl was frothing.

He turned in a half-stagger, then walked quickly from the place, his leg creaking. Nothing rational was at work here. 'Blood, Inspector Anders, you will see it.' It came from the source of the flying poster that had sent him ducking. The worm, had a worm somehow been placed in his mind?

★

'You're going soft on me, Henri,' Dominique Bosson hissed in the darkened room. 'Keep it up. *Concentrate.*'

Beneath her swirling loins he was gasping raucously. He'd had a few minutes on top. Now, her long white body upright, that morning's hairstyle out of danger, she was astride his flaccid torso. The second time tonight. She'd got into her rhythm, her shapely hips gyrating, the slapping suck of her seemed resolved to drag every drop from his deepest recesses. Chest heaving, heart going like a hammer, he attempted to thrust up into her. He must keep going for a few more seconds. But it was dying on him ... it'll drive her crazy.

She screamed as it fell out. *'Henri you bastard.'*

'Sorry,' he gasped.

'Merde! Henri, you'll have to do better than this or I'll get a toy-boy.'

He didn't think he'd ever regain his breath. As for the pounding of his heart! Through his pain, he was embarrassed. What had got into her? She never talked like this. Elegance and a kind of supreme control were her way. Was it Kramer's death? Had there been something going on there ... these last two nights!

He found he could speak again, though his voice had a quaver. 'My dear Dominique, may I ask – are you finding the danger we're in an aphrodisiac?'

Lying beside him in the dark she laughed briefly. What an interesting mind he had, she mustn't underrate him. She smiled, fecund with ambition, as simpler sisters became with pregnancy. Opportunities kept opening up like the sun streaming through holes in the clouds. Her smile broadened in the dark.

★

184

In a daze, Anders crossed Place Gutenberg. No-one there in the cold breeze. A sprinkling of patrons sitting back in the depths of the cafes. He came past the statue ... stopped, staring up. The great man's hands were bloody. Both of them dripped red. He'd come out of the daze, now had the taste of metal in his mouth. A small red pool had formed on the pedestal. He dipped a finger in it. Holding his hand clear of his coat, he went on.

His stump was chafed. Understandable. After he'd showered, he rubbed in the ointment. He'd settled down, but the blood-spouting fountain, the statue's hands, were stark in his mind. The first: hallucinatory. The second: red paint on his hand. As if they were trying to drive him mad. He was moving into the territory he'd been in during the early months in Lyon. Maybe deeper.

He went to the bathroom, returned the ointment to its shelf in the cabinet. The unopened packet of Ativan seemed to stare at him from the shelf. He slammed the door shut.

Slammed it shut on tonight's blood.

Matucci wasn't in his room. He thought of calling him on his mobile, then left it. He wondered whether to go to Paris to seek out this master. It could be a wild-goose chase. The chance that Gas, in whatever identity, had been to the master seemed remote. But maybe in that closed world, it wasn't ... he'd decide in the morning.

He sat in the chair. *The Ship of Fools* made much of dunces. Dunces in the sense of types of fool. Was he seen as one such? How much did this perpetrator, this Monsieur Gas know of him? Were his mental state, his hallucinations, known? Impossible that he could know. The triggers were in Anders' own brain.

185

Forget it now.

He moved between the ex-tree-trunks to open the windows. Returned to the armchair. The sleet was whispering down again onto the rounded acres of tiled roofs. Cold. He dozed.

He woke up, breathing hard, heart pounding. It was ringing. The phone. His neck was stiff. He reached out:

'Yes?'

'*Good evening, Inspector. I've been close to you again tonight. Where are we all going? Henri Bosson to Hades. But not just yet. He attempts to buy himself a little time. Did you suggest that? No matter. Bosson might see the light. But is it possible, with Madame at his elbow? A simple, but irrevocable decision to abandon the merger and this game ends. We put Brant's book back on the shelf. But who's next? The Economist is writing about the big Dutch petroleum groups. Alas.*

'*You are following a certain line, my congratulations. You're committed to investigate as I am committed to my cause. But think about it. We're not poles apart. I've eliminated the Frankfurt sixteen, criminals against society, you've eliminated forty mafia bosses, criminals against society. We've each selected the bomb as a wake-up call. We've been forced to act because there was no other way. My friend, are you my alter ego, or am I yours? You've been a socialist all your life. But do you really understand what is at stake? We gaze into a black hole and see inequalities growing like cancers, high unemployment, jobs disappearing, becoming dead-end and part-time, depression, rising suicide rates, the implosion of communities, cunning privatisation of essential public utilities. I could go on and on. Its proponents see this, but they ignore it. Or as brain-washed ideologues they can't understand the true outcomes. Therefore, intervention is required.*

'*Dr Dauban is a worry. Will she remember? I wish to avoid*

harm to the innocent but the crusade comes before all.

'I feel you there like a sounding board, a silent sounding-board, listening to a madman?'

A metallic chuckle that sickened Anders.

'A man drowned in a cage. And statues with bloody hands. So confusing. The last – even to me. But be assured, I'm looking into it. I resent plagiarism. However, take heart, you're ahead of the field.

'Tonight I'm going to kill another man – metaphorically speaking – with great regret.

'Inspector, you've been given to me by a special dispensation. My alter ego.

'"Yet many are there left who trip
And prance about the dunces' ship."'

Anders was listening to a fading echo.

Marguerite Dauban!

It was a full minute before he was breathing more or less normally. He'd been holding it in. 'Special dispensation' – by whom? Forget the past, look at the present, he told himself in the dark room as he began hurriedly to harness up. Why warn him about Marguerite? Grimly, he thought: the terrorist's trademark. The way they give warning of their acts. He'd not arranged for calls to be traced. With this perpetrator that would be useless.

And will she remember *what*?

The church on the corner of the hotel's street was black. He crossed the road and went towards the nearest bridge. In the distance, a hint of motor vehicles, but nothing here. He stared into doorways, cast glances down the side-streets he passed. He walked onto the bridge.

Below, a white thing fluttered. A feathery, anguished thing on the far bank. Other white things glowed in a

187

contrasting stillness. He went forward, ten, fifteen metres, stopped, his hands gripped the railing as he peered down in the light cast from the bridge-lamps. It'd ceased to flutter. The swan. It was dead like its three companions. Decapitated. Anders gazed down. In a trance. The second time tonight – uncomprehending. Blood was still ebbing from the severed neck of the last victim alive – as it'd bubbled from the outlet of the fountain. Everything was in sharp focus.

He stared and stared. A frozen solitary witness – to what – madness? To a reality which wasn't reality? He felt nauseous, yet fully alert. There were no heads. The river flowed past on its way to the Rhine; not involved. He left the slaughterhouse scene and went into the streets of the Grand Ile, walking the smooth concrete ribands through the cobbles. Raven Bridge was a few hundred metres away. He was seeing Kramer's pale face when they hauled him up again into the morning light.

Where were the heads?

'You!' Marguerite's utterance came like an exhaled breath out to the landing where Anders stood in the dingy light. Strangely, at the point in her sleep where she'd been woken by the shrilling of the doorbell, she'd been dreaming of the Italian detective with the artificial leg. Now here! This was *unreal*. Even more so than his leap from the front pages that first morning. She gazed at the considering, concerned face, in her doorway at 11.06p.m. on this cold October night, and felt herself falling back into reality.

'I apologise for the hour,' Anders said, 'but I wish to discuss a very urgent matter with you.'

She'd pulled on a pale woollen gown, her hair, which

before had seemed to him to be on the verge of wind-blown, tonight had crossed that line. Straightening it with quick hand movements, she gestured him to enter. He closed the front door. Many women wouldn't welcome being discovered in this state but, in a blink, the surprise and sleep had cleared from her eyes. In the living-room, she faced the pale, strained man.

'What has happened?'

Standing with hat in hand, he hesitated. 'This may seem strange ... are you trying to remember something that might have happened at the library? Possibly in connection with *The Ship of Fools* — possibly connected to a visitor — or other contact? Is there something like that on your mind.'

They were both standing. Almost without thinking she'd turned on the bright central light. He took in every tiny imperfection on her face, her neck. His investigator's mind was trying to enter hers.

He witnessed the dilation of her pupils: surprise at his questions. Her hands were clasped. 'How do you know this?'

'A message — from the unknown person who is, as you've said, debasing *The Ship of Fools* for his criminal purposes.'

'*One* person?'

'I believe so.'

She nodded slowly. 'There is something at the edge of my consciousness ... a tantalising thing.' She shrugged. 'For a person whose profession is retrieving information, it's extremely frustrating.'

Ah! Sickeningly he felt the danger. Extreme danger, he thought. That the brain behind the electronic voice was uncertain about it made it so. He wondered if a psychologist's probing would bring it into the light.

'Do you think that puts me in danger?'

He lowered his head, thinking. He'd have to bring in bodyguards. 'Yes.' Then he advised her about answering her door, about phone calls where no-one spoke. He repeated the description of Monsieur Gas.

'Him,' she breathed, remembering her assistant's description.

Cautiously, because it had the elusiveness between dream and reality, he told her about the swans, the bloody hands. 'God!' she exclaimed. 'What is this about?' She sat down, pulling the gown over her legs. 'The swans ... there was such a case in the fifteenth century.' She gave him a look which said: that's something in my memory which is retrievable.

'May I sit down?' he asked.

She made a gesture of apology, and told him of the medieval legend that tonight had been replicated. He listened intently. The work of a lunatic weaving a different kind of madness. He thought intensely: everything I need to know is out there. The vital question was, would it come quickly enough.

They communed with a silent look. She was an expert on the past, he a practitioner in the present. Put together, it's just a shaky bridge into the future. What he'd done in southern Italy against the mafia had come out of desperation and hopelessness. Could he find something like that in himself again? But his nerves, his energy, seemed to be flickering like a fuel indicator on the edge of empty.

XVI

THE SIXTEENTH OF OCTOBER

A.M.

ON THE corner outside Marguerite's apartment, Anders inspected the street. Each pool of shadow. It was in his head: *'I've been close to you tonight.'* His mobile phone rang: 12.05a.m.

'Matucci here. Something's broken. I'm at headquarters. Where are you?' Five minutes later, Ferrand's car screeched to a stop beside Anders. A moment later a patrol car did the same. Anders spoke briefly, and concisely, to the two uniformed cops in it. Bodyguards for Marguerite. He'd asked Matucci for them. They'd have to do for the moment.

Tonight, behind the wheel of his Renault, Inspector Ferrand's phlegmatic expression was unchanged. He was just driving like a maniac. Over his shoulder, Matucci explained the situation. The identikit broadcast had worked! A woman had seen it. Made a call. The man was there *now*. It looked good. In the back seat, Anders breathed, Thank God – if it wasn't a wild-goose chase.

'Five minutes,' Ferrand growled as he swung the vehicle around the Place de la Republique, missing a street-sweeping vehicle by centimetres. The transplanted architecture of old Leipzig flashed past. This was the quarter where the Bossons lived. Tucked into bed behind their police guard, Anders trusted. Another water-spraying vehicle. Ferrand was coasting now. He turned a corner into a street of plebian apartment buildings. Vehicles stood in the middle of the road.

Commissaire Dubost nodded to Anders. A dozen plain-clothes and uniformed police stood around watching six colleagues, fifty metres away, about to enter a building.

'Gerard's going in now,' the Paris crime chief said tersely.

Another car entered the street and halted. Commissaire Rolland emerged from it. Dubost grunted, said aside to Anders, 'The glory-seeker.' Rolland came over, nodded to them, and surveyed the street. It was plain what was happening. They all concentrated on the steps.

Quietly, the police, bulky in their protective vests, went up them. A tense moment. *THUD!* And the crouching figures were swarming in.

Presently Inspector Gerard, pistol in hand, came down the steps. 'Not here,' he said. 'But it looks like his place all right.'

Dubost swore. Rolland shook his head.

A few minutes later they were in the elderly woman's flat. She eyed the circle of staring faces. 'I don't think he was there very much. I only noticed him a few times, coming and going. And his friend. They never spoke to me. We don't in this building.'

'His friend?' Dubost said.

'He came and went, too. A younger man, monsieur. Fair as the other was dark. Taller, straighter. A gentleman.'

'Madame did you ever see them together?' Anders asked.

'No.'

They stood in the cold street. People were hanging out of lighted windows gazing at the activity. Dawn still seemed an age away. Anders was thinking of the tall man in a light-coloured raincoat carrying a bag, whom he'd glimpsed walking away down a street minutes before they'd arrived at the scene. Him! He was sure. They'd nearly had him. Which meant he was human. The others hadn't noticed him.

'So –' Dubost said. 'Now we're looking for *another* bastard.'

Anders nodded. 'Yes. Obviously, those two men were one. But which is the real identity? Monsieur Gas has been doing the dirty work – so I'd suggest the other. But maybe neither is.'

Dubost grunted.

'I think he'll have planned for this,' Anders continued. 'He's an individual who sees himself set on a long journey. The fact that he used Gas as a cover – at least for a lot of the dirty work – shows he's committed to keeping his real identity under wraps. I think he'll have dropped into another cover.'

Rolland spoke for the first time. 'The disguised voice. I've the feeling that the perpetrator could be reasonably well-known. At least, enough to be worried about having his voice recognised.'

Anders nodded. 'We're hunting him harder. As you know, we must hunt the terrorist. Hunt him all the time. He'll get jumpy, make mistakes. Even this one will.' His breath made small white clouds in the cold night air.

Rolland nodded. He walked away a few paces, and turned back to face the Italian. 'The Frankfurt merger's off, the Paris one, ditto. And here in Strasbourg, my impression is that it's wavering. *His* success ratio is a lot better than ours, Inspector Anders.' He got into his car, and left.

The Paris crime chief's moustache looked frosty. He flexed his heavy shoulders, and grimaced. 'Thanks very much for that wisdom,' he muttered at the chief of police's departing car. 'Who can predict the real intentions of Bosson. As for that dragon-woman of a wife ...' He cast an expressive look to the heavens.

Anders smiled slightly.

Grudgingly, Dubost said, 'You did well to dig up this Gas. It's a pity –' With a shrug, he turned to his car. 'I'm heading back to brief the media.'

The technical group had arrived. Anders looked through the flat, took in the abandoned life. Really the abandoned phase, he thought. He'd been so close.

The technicians looked grumpy, but were working quickly.

'No prints,' Ferrand said. 'The place has been wiped clean.'

'Thoroughly,' the head tech said.

'Toilet seat?' Anders suggested.

'Zero,' the man replied.

Anders wandered away. 'Light-bulbs?' he said over his shoulder.

He had a definite image of Gas moving around the EC, in the streets of Strasbourg. The slump-shouldered, black-clad emissary of terrorism. Now what did he have? A sketchy description of a tall, fairish individual; almost an everyman, in this part of the world.

Day did break, eventually. Mistily and with extreme reluctance, Anders felt. Another morning of news of European politics and economic moves. Ad nauseam. A major train crash in France. Mad Cow Disease. *No Decision*

Yet on Strasbourg Merger – the front page of *Les Dernieres Nouvelles d'Alsace*. It depressed him to see in the article Judgment Day this, Judgment Day that. As a group it'd never existed. But the Ministry of the Interior in Paris had decided to keep that under wraps. They mightn't quite believe it yet, he thought. Perhaps the discovery of the flat would persuade them.

French and German Investigations Enter a New Phase, another headline announced. Anders regarded the dawn-lit street. What were they on about now?

It was ridiculous, but it was troubling him. The words going around and around in his head in their electronic whine. Those concerning Marguerite had shocked him, and he'd acted. The ones equating him with this terrorist had been more slippery. Cunningly planted. The way he'd ushered out the forty top mafioso from their existences *had* been an appropriation of justice. A shattering of the fundamentals of law and order. Granted. In the aftermath, the late Judge De Angelis, rising from the grave, had told him so: *'I understand, of course, why you did it. But it's not the way.'* He'd put that down at the time to his brain being scrambled by the explosion. But it still was, going on the past few days. Was it ridiculous? Dully he considered the proposition: that he and this perpetrator were identical zealots.

It was 7.10a.m. He was drinking coffee with Matucci outside a cafe beside the canal in the Petite France quarter. Overcoats made it tolerable. Matucci was also eating a breakfast of ham and eggs and sausage. A white bread roll, and an out-sized cup of milk coffee, satisfied him.

'Alter ego.' He dropped it out of the blue on Matucci. He told him about the latest phone call – eight hours back in the past. Before this rush and excitement.

The big detective stopped eating and pushed his plate away. Abruptly, the blue eyes gazing at Anders' were shrewd. Anders was a socialist, his father had been an active communist back in the '50s and '60s. So – deep down, were his sympathies engaged? For this ruthless bastard – for his objectives? But to put them on the same plane was ridiculous! The borderline between their respective actions might be smudged – but it existed, and therein lay a world of difference. But could Anders still see it?

He picked his teeth and said, 'The bastard's trying to get into your mind. Jesus, let's catch him, or kill him, and let everything else lie where it falls.' He shrugged emphatically. The shrug said: for much of your career, you've been a terrorist-hunter, what is there to change that?

Anders smiled thinly. 'I value your views,' he said.

Across the street was the late Hofmann's apartment on the top floor of the old tanner's house, one of a row of such houses now converted to apartments. The roofs had large openings which, Anders had read, had aided the airing of the attics and the drying out of the skins. He eyed the roof-line and said, 'Doubtless Madame Bosson is overjoyed at Herr Hofmann's exit from the scene. There's a lot of ambition being played out.'

'Eh, did you see the way that little dog sniffs her?'

Anders smiled slightly. 'You're not a dog-lover.'

The blond detective shrugged, sipped his coffee.

'They're companions, Matucci. Given our relationship, if you and I survive into retirement, having a little dog might make a big difference to us.'

Matucci stared incredulously.

Bang! Behind – a crash like a gunshot – Matucci almost choked on his coffee. They were sitting under horse chestnut trees, and one of the hard fruits had plunged down

196

onto a metal table. *Bang!* Another.

'*Christ*,' Matucci said, 'a man could get brained. Or have a heart attack.'

Anders gravely acknowledged those possibilities. Matucci wasn't one for nature. Brought up in the backstreets of Naples, apprentice and practitioner of his trade in a half-dozen other urban stew-pots, he was deeply suspicious of it.

Anders looked towards the canal. Mist skimmed its surface. They'd found an excellent set of prints on a light bulb over the computer. But whose? Nonetheless, it might be something.

Anders turned to page two of the paper. A slight surge of relief went through him.

STRASBOURG'S BLACK NIGHT
OF CIVIC OUTRAGE
SWANS SLAUGHTERED
STATUES DESECRATED

Early this morning residents were shocked to discover the carcases of the four swans usually to be seen near the Raven Bridge. The birds had been cruelly decapitated. The heads were not found. About the same time city officials discovered that the statues of three of our city's famous sons had been vandalised overnight. The hands of Gutenberg, Goethe and Kleber had been painted red. Police, are unable to say if the outrages are connected. The Central Commissaire, Monsieur Rolland, has taken personal charge of the investigation.

Three statues. Anders scanned further. No report of vandalising to the Place du Marche Neuf fountain.

Matucci glanced down at the page, and scowled, 'Crazies.'

Briefly, Anders reported what Marguerite had told him about the swans. He thought: the heads? The incident had a different smell from the others on their plate. He glanced at Matucci. 'The cage off Raven Bridge ... once you start playing around with things like that, all sorts come out of the woodwork.'

'Copy-cats!'

Anders recalled the terrorist's resentment against his imitators.

Bang! Another missile clanged down. Choosing a table in this season at this cafe was clearly akin to playing Russian Roulette.

'Let's get out of here,' Matucci muttered. 'It's more dangerous than Palermo.'

'Up you go,' Anders, holding the ladder, said. 'Better take your overcoat and scarf off.' The blond detective gave him a look. Yesterday he'd found time to trim his slim moustache; today he had put a sky-blue silk scarf around his neck.

Matucci spent a half-hour climbing through the roof-spaces of the tanners' houses. The stench of tanned skins had long since gone. He grunted when he saw it. In the space above Hofmann's apartment, there was a recent disturbance of the accumulated dust: footprints. Probably the cops. He looked down at Anders through the manhole. 'The killer could've got into the roof space three houses along, come in that way, and left that way. There're small openings between each property. I got through.'

Inspector Gerard's men were claiming the killer had got into and left the apartment via the roof-spaces. Anders had wanted to check that. They might've been trying it on to get off the hook. Matucci came down, ruefully brushing off his suit. 'He *could've* been waiting when they got home. And left the same way.'

Anders gazed thoughtfully across the room. It appeared that the perpetrator had very quietly turned the key in the front door to unlock it. Why? To spread confusion in the mind of the police – and DP Anders?

It seemed that this time no special powers had been employed. No tricks needed. If there was a rational explanation as to how access had been gained here, was there something that had been missed in the Frankfurt and Paris killings? His notion of extraordinary powers a blind alley?

He dismissed that thought. It was more a force than a notion, and he had to follow it through to the bitter end. He had learned to trust his instincts. Although the state he was in now … One thing, the man they'd sprung out of his cover, and probably his identity, this morning, must have counted on eliminating Henri Bosson before his bolt-hole was discovered. But had it been Gas? They'd found nothing in the flat to tie him in. There'd been no clothing at all. But they had the woman neighbour's description. He stared at the floor. They'd gained a march on this Gas – and therefore, the individual behind him.

Throughout breakfast, Anders had been thinking about that shadowy master in Paris. But a pragmatic mind, and a clear-eyed approach, should confront him. He no longer felt he was pragmatic, or clear-eyed.

He turned to Matucci. 'I want you to go to Paris.'

★

At 8.45a.m., the minders who had just come on duty painstakingly examined the Roll Royce's underside with mirrors on sticks. Henri and Dominique waited in the

199

apartment lobby. They were going to a meeting with the new chairman-elect of Deutsche Rural-Credit's managing board, and the delay was making them late. Henri complained to the inspector in charge, who made a show of hastening it along. The policeman would've been far happier if the Bossons hadn't been going anywhere at all. Inspector Gerard had been pulled off minding duty. 'You're too damned unlucky,' Dubost had said.

At 9.15a.m, the Bossons were in the boardroom when the German who had just flown from Frankfurt was shown in. Henri came forward to shake his hand. They'd talked but not met since Hofmann had been killed and for a moment they soberly discussed that 'shocking business'. Dominique, seated at the boardroom table, sat like the Sphinx.

The man's name was Wilhelm Rath. He'd taken a back seat to Klaus Hofmann during the negotiations. However, he'd declared himself fully in support. But where does he stand now? Dominique thought. Now he's to be chief of his bank. Maybe he'll see that as more attractive than playing second fiddle to Henri. With the demise of Hofmann, Dominique saw her husband as a certainty to head the merged institution.

But where did Henri stand? He'd gone strange and mysterious. But things were moving – the competition directorate's approval had come through.

Rath passed his lips above her hand. He was short and pink and fleshy and extremely urbane. Klaus had excelled in downhill skiing, Rath's forte was clearly more in the domain of *après-ski*. He'd been twice divorced. 'Madame,' he smiled, 'always a pleasure.'

Rath wasted no time. 'Monsieur Bosson, we're concerned the delay in an announcment is creating an adverse climate among our stake-holders, and in the market. As a board, we remain absolutely committed to the alliance with your fine institution. If *your* board remains similarly committed we believe that, despite the terrorists, the earliest announcement should be made of our joint resolve to proceed, and that the official approval's been obtained from the EC.'

Henri was nodding continuously. Whether in agreement or because he'd expected the development, wasn't clear. Like Hofmann, this German also seemed in a great hurry to cement the merger. Actually, Henri's nodding was covering his thinking: overnight, he'd reconsidered the fact that neither side had carried out a due diligence study of the financial health of the other. Each was a famous institution, and it had been decided that such matters could be amicably adjusted after the event. 'Sign now, talk later. We'll work anything out.' A handshake deal. But now, the suspect condition of the Frankfurt bank's mortgage portfolio was in the forefront of his mind. For Rath to be so keen, after recent events, was strange.

Rath said, 'As *you* released the news that the decision was being reconsidered, it would be correct for you to announce it's now full steam ahead. Our boards' approvals are really formalities which can be dealt with shortly.'

Dominique's brain, as usual, was moving fast. She smiled brilliantly at the German. 'Herr Rath, we agree entirely. This is the time for strength of purpose, to display our boards' unwavering commitment ...' Henri was sitting stony-faced '... and, quite frankly, with the uncovering of the base of this terrorist who's apparently at the head of the Judgment Day group, and the more precise focusing of the police activity, the threat's diminished.'

Rath was smiling warmly at this blonde, articulate

beauty who he knew, confidentially, from the departed Klaus, had been in Kramer's bed.

'However,' she said, 'we are of the opinion that a joint announcement would be preferable. Showing a unified front. Why not this Friday, in Strasbourg? Our PR departments could set-up a major media event here. Both boards should be present in full. Enough of this hiding in corners. Let's show our mettle to all of Europe. Fire our merger into the EC like a rocket into space.' She tossed her head in an imperial gesture, and glanced at her husband.

Rath gazed in admiration. Was this couple for real? Real enough, he decided.

Henri was also gazing at her, the understanding that he'd been on the brink of grasping for days now dawning. Sooner or later, by this or that means, his wife saw herself in the top job. Amazing!

'Bravo,' Wilhelm Rath exclaimed. 'Monsieur Bosson?'

Henri's voice rumbled, 'Let me think about it.'

The German sat back, a surprised look on his face. What had happened to Bosson's terrific ambition? To be chairman of the merged group. Had he turned coward? He frowned.

Dominique shot her husband a furious look. Similar thoughts were racing through her mind.

'I'll call you,' Henri said with icy calm.

After the German had gone, Henri, his large soft hands placed on the gleaming oak, said: 'Rath should sweat a little. Like Klaus. There's no hurry now in my opinion. Dominique, I don't think the threat from the terrorists has diminished, nor do I think that you think so. And, in future, please note that I'll lead the discussions. Not you.'

★

Matucci arrived at Orly Airport before ten, and took a cab into Montmartre. At 10.50a.m. he was outside a narrow, shuttered house at the top of a vast flight of steps. Its small iron-railed balcony projected above a precipice.

Matucci approached the door, pressed a bell, and turned to inspect the street. On the way from Strasbourg, he'd thought about Anders. Would the guy listen to what he'd said at breakfast? He'd been worried about him in Lyon. No social life, apparently no love-life, and even quieter in himself than usual. He'd spent his days glued to a monitor canvassing the nitty gritty of the terrorist world, going home at night to cook his pasta in that black hole of a flat.

Nothing much worried Matucci, but he knew what worried others. His attempts in Lyon to snap Anders out of his contemplation of his past had been courteously rebuffed. But this morning Anders had allowed him a glimpse of his inner world. A bloody wonder!

No answer. He pressed the bell again. Was it working? He couldn't hear it ringing. He knocked.

Despite everything, his colleague was as sharp as ever. Some persons might see Anders' theories, this mission to Paris, as crazy. And going to Strasbourg had been seat-of-the-pants stuff. But his colleague dealt in craziness. Of one kind or another. It was all the more surprising when you considered his calm politeness – his reluctance to fire his gun, even to draw it. Sometimes men who'd killed went like that. He'd shot more than Anders, and it didn't prey on his mind. Given the type of criminal in his sights, why would it?

Aha. The door was opening. He became alert.

The master was home, but very cautious. A woman examined Matucci's card as though she was learning to read, and went away. The big detective shrugged, and waited. No sign at the entrance indicating the master's profession.

Clash-crash. She was back, opening the grille.

'Interpol?' The huge man with colourless eyes and iron-grey hair rolling back from his brow looked at the detective.

'That's right,' Matucci said, 'attached to the Judgment Day terrorist investigation.'

'Ah ...' Almost a sigh.

They sat in a room beside a wall of caricatures of forgotten politicians in old Paris restaurants.

'You're a famous man in your profession,' Matucci ventured, 'which is why I'm here. Does the name Gas mean anything to you? In appearance a tall, slump-shouldered man with long black hair who, apparently, always dresses in black.'

The master watched the investigator with no sign of curiosity or surprise. 'The whole of Europe knows of Mr Gas. Since the circulation of his description yesterday, since last night's events in Strasbourg appeared on TV screens this morning.'

Matucci nodded. 'Do you know him in any other connection?'

'I do'. Said without hesitation.

Matucci gazed at him, and relaxed slightly. Anders had been right. Another of his long-shots had come in.

The man's eyes were lazy, yet ready to leap forth, Matucci assessed. His voice was lazy too. 'May I inquire what process of thinking brought you to me?'

Matucci's ice-blue eyes were unblinking. 'In connection with these terrorist acts, there're difficulties in establishing how access was gained to perpetrate at least two of the crimes. There may be explanations which have not yet come to light. On the other hand, there's a case for examining whether the perpetrator employed special powers. Maybe the kind of powers in your field.'

He explained the backgrounds of the Frankfurt bombing and the Paris assassination. He gave all the detail they had. He stopped, and spread his hands. The man pushed a box of cigarettes forward.

Thank Christ, Matucci thought. They both lit up. 'At this stage, for us, Gas is interchangeable with the perpetrator,' Matucci said. 'Though it seems that it may be a false identity. That another stands behind him.'

The master nodded very deliberately, the cigarette stuck between his lips. With a smooth hand movement he took it out. 'Since the TV this morning I've been thinking back over my relationship with Monsieur Gas. Normally, confidentiality wouldn't allow me to talk of it but in these circumstances ...' A bowl for ash had appeared midway between them. Matucci frowned, he couldn't see how it had got there.

'My association with him was in three consultations. Each of two hours. In April last. Gas, of course, isn't his real name. That was clear. His skills as a hypnotist are highly developed. He'd studied under other masters. He wasn't specific about that, but I could see the influence of a man in Prague, and perhaps, another in Brussels.

'He impressed me as an individual obsessed with perfecting his powers. Hence his visits to me. Probably, I was his last port of call. There's no-one beyond.'

He smiled faintly. 'I could tell immediately that he wasn't driven by commercial motives, that he was an obsessive in our field, maybe a zealot in other facets of his nature.' The master delicately tapped ash into the bowl.

'What specifically was he boning up on?' Matucci asked.

'He was careful not to put emphasis on any one facet. He asked a great number of questions. I guessed that he knew the answers to many, just sought confirmation. Even such a plebeian topic as auto-suggestion was discussed. He paid me in cash, by the way.'

'What's he capable of? Could you give me an example?'

'If he wished to persuade *certain* people that he was walking on water, he could do so. His hypnotic powers, I'd suspect, could achieve most of his desired ends.'

'About Frankfurt and Paris – what do you think?'

The master puffed on his cigarette, holding it between the last two fingers of his left hand.

'Monsieur Inspector, I cannot know what he did, assuming that he did anything at all. But if he did ...' He leaned back in his chair, gazing beyond Matucci. 'I will tell you what *I* would have done in Frankfurt. This chief of security. My objective would've been to meet him somewhere prior to that incident, perhaps a bar. A park. The place would require a study of his habits. Assuming I could introduce myself into his company in reasonable privacy it would be quickly apparent to me if he were a suggestible subject. That is, readily hypnotisable. Assuming that he was, I would induce a trance – it would take a few minutes only – plant the suggestion in him, that when he next heard a trigger-word, say, 'Codex', he would give me the sets of required numbers, and not be aware of what was happening.'

Matucci listening intently, and frowned. 'Is it necessary to see him on this prior occasion?'

'It's what I would do. Firstly, to establish his suggestibility, as I said. If he weren't, then another method of planting the bomb would be needed. Or, presumably, the project would be abandoned. Secondly, it is easier and quicker to induct subjects if you've hypnotised them previously.'

Matucci nodded.

'On D-Day, so to speak, I'd approach him, induce a trance, trigger the post-hypnotic suggestion with "Codex", and obtain the codes. A waking trance. I would not put him to sleep. The placement and arming of the bomb would take five to seven minutes you say? Before leaving him I'd plant another post-hypnotic suggestion that he would become completely normal in eight minutes, and that he'd remember nothing of what had occurred. The amnesia might not last forever. Spontaneous breakdown can occur. But then few things are totally risk-free. You've said his control desk is not overlooked, but no-one could guarantee the coast would be clear for those eight minutes.' He shrugged.

'This is a trained security guard we're talking about, Monsieur,' Matucci said, his eyes narrowed against the tobacco fug.

The famous man sighed. 'That does not have much to do with it. The most strong-willed and intelligent subjects are frequently the most easily hypnotisable. During the Cold War the Russians used hypnosis to extract secrets from trained agents with good success.'

Despite his natural cynicism, Matucci was impressed by the master's easy confidence. 'Paris?' he prompted.

'Ah, yes. Two guards you say, and presumably no chance of preparation. That is much more difficult. I don't think I would attempt anything. The situation appears to require a Mandrake technique.' His lips were touched with humour. 'But Monsieur Gas apparently brought it off.'

'Mandrake technique?'

'Ah, you're too young. Once, there was a famous comic-strip character – an illusionist-hypnotist – who could do the most remarkable things. I speculate that Monsieur Gas experimented with inductions and found a Mandrake way. Perhaps it was based on the rapid confusion of the subjects, or a domineering technique relying on fear and authority with a chilling coldness of voice … Whatever, it would have to be at very close-quarters. Again, it depends on the suggestibility of the subjects. I suppose, from what you've told me, if he hadn't succeeded with them, he'd have killed them to gain his access.'

The apartment was absolutely silent. The vitality of Paris wasn't even a suggestion in this spellbinder's world.

The man's big head was lowered, the grey hair displayed to the detective. 'The world is largely misinformed about hypnosis. We hear that to be hypnotised a subject must be gullible, that a subject can't be hypnotised against their will … do they speak of the conscious or the unconscious will? That only those of low intelligence can be hypnotised, that subjects can't be made to act against their moral standards. What is their *real* morality, though? And so on.' He laughed quietly. 'Inspector, I assure you that the facts are different from this misinformation.'

Matucci stubbed out his cigarette. Subjects? More like victims, he thought. 'We're grateful for your time, and your information.' He stood up. 'You have my card if anything occurs. We don't know really know where we're going with this one, what might happen next.'

The master smiled. 'Monsieur, I would forget about Mr Gas, it's the man behind him who's of the main account. Each time we met I felt the strength of that man.'

Matucci leaned across the desk to shake the proffered hand, and found himself deep in the colourless eyes. 'Take care, monsieur,' the master said, 'you are about to see *two* doors.'

Matucci turned, and was indeed confronted by two doors. There had been only one when he'd entered. He stared at them. Then he turned back to the seated man.

'Which door is out?' the master said.

The Italian faced away again. There was only one door.

'Do you see what I mean, monsieur?'

In the street, Matucci stood lost in thought at the top of the steps, gazing out over the infinite airspace which was becoming hazier by the moment.

'We would like a word.' A thick Parisian accent broke his reverie.

The Interpol man turned quickly. Two men had materialised while he'd been in his daze. Both were short, wide, muscular and were scrutinising him with care.

What's this? the Italian wondered. Carefully he reached for his ID.

'Don't worry about that,' the balding one said. 'We know who you are. Matucci from Interpol.'

'And you?'

'Police. Let's go to the bar over there and talk.'

Matucci stared at him, at his colleague, who was darker and more phlegmatic, prolific of eyebrows and nose-hair, and smelt of garlic.

'No thanks. I'm off –'

The first man smiled affably. 'Commissaire Divissionaire Dubost, presently in Strasbourg, has detailed us to find out where you're going. We've found out that. But we haven't found out why. Give us a break, Matucci. That man's a career-killer. Come and have a drink. Ten minutes.'

He laid a hand on the Italian's forearm. His colleague

stood there, appraising Matucci's suit. Matucci shrugged. Half the time in this EC you never knew who was up who. 'ID?' The policeman showed it. 'Inspector Roque,' the Italian read aloud.

They entered the bar. The Frenchmen ordered red wine, Matucci nothing.

'A visit to France's greatest hypnotist, what's it mean?' Roque asked.

'Dubost'll have to ask my boss,' Matucci replied evenly. 'Which should be fair enough for you.' He looked at the silent one. He could almost feel the man's brain moving. You couldn't lay too much on Dubost. Anders had been only forthcoming with the French cops on what he was certain of. Not beyond that. It was the way he worked. It was the situation. It was his present mood.

'Okay,' he said. He stood up, and turned for the door. They watched him go.

In the street, Matucci was both angry and amused. Had their helpful shadow, Inspector Ferrand, tipped off Dubost on this mission? God Almighty, if this mad terrorist found out that the police were now running around after each other, he'd be laughing all the way to his next act of mayhem.

XVII

THE SIXTEENTH OF OCTOBER

P.M.

'INSPECTOR ANDERS, Commissaire Roland wishes to see you.' In the phone's receiver Ferrand's voice sounded terse. Lack of sleep. Anders consulted his watch: 12.05p.m.

'I'll come straight in,' he said.

After leaving Hofmann's apartment, and parting from Matucci, Anders had returned to the hotel. He'd been almost out on his feet and he'd slept for three hours. Then he'd showered and shaved, and settled down with Erhardt's report of the events at Chemtex's headquarters. He'd studied the transcripts of interviews. Apart from the gap relating to the West Africans, they all appeared bona fide. He'd laid it down as the phone rang.

Now he put on his hat and coat and went to police headquarters.

Commissaire Rolland had a restless air, and an autumn cough and sniffle. He kept dabbing his nose with the handkerchief taken from his sleeve. When Anders was safely seated, he got up to pace the room. 'Good work on

211

flushing out this Monsieur Gas, Inspector. Bad luck to miss him. You're a step ahead of Dubost – all the time. What's your next move?'

Anders noted the derisory emphasis on Dubost's name. The Strasbourg police chief and Dubost were at loggerheads. He'd heard each was complaining to Paris about the other. Rolland had given Anders' conclusion, that the Judgment Day group was a front for one individual, a better hearing than Dubost.

Anders said, 'I believe the perpetrator's slipped into another counterfeit identity – or returned to his own.' Rolland ruminated on this, stifled his cough. Then Anders explained Matucci's mission to Paris, and the thinking it was based on.

The police chief returned to his seat and stared at the Italian. He'd been briefed on Anders' visit to the Strasbourg hypnotist. That had given him pause for thought. He'd been about to bring it up.

Anders said, 'I'm trying to find a route to this individual's real identity. If I'm wrong about the Judgment Day group and it does exist, then I'm hopelessly out of my depth.'

'What about a phone tap on these calls?'

'He's too clever for that to tell us anything important. And I don't want them to stop.'

The intercom buzzed. Rolland picked up the receiver. 'Tell him to wait,' he said tersely.

Anders continued: 'This mental block of Marguerite Dauban's. Could you arrange for a police psychologist-hypnotist to see her?'

'I'll set it up. Check with me later.'

'I may have to persuade her –'

The door was flung open and Commissaire Dubost

strode in. He was surprised to see Anders, and glared at the Interpol man. He addressed Rolland. 'You wanted to talk?'

Anders stood up politely, ready to withdraw. This looked sticky.

'Stay,' Rolland said. 'This affects us all. Dubost you've had another media conference – without me present. Don't do that again. From this point on, I must be there.'

'Is that *all?*'

The Strasbourg police chief nodded. His face was taut with anger. The moles on his face were stark against his pallor.

'I'll bear it in mind,' Dubost said curtly, and strode out.

Anders resumed his seat. The phone ringing broke the uncomfortable silence. Rolland listened, and put his hand over the receiver. 'Professor Lestang's on the line to my secretary. He wants to see you urgently. Can you go out – now?'

Anders nodded. What was this about?

Rolland replaced the receiver and glanced sharply at Anders. From his expression, clearly he was having the same thought. He took up a newspaper. 'Did you see his article this morning?' He held it up. 'No? He's written about the case. Dispensed another dose of his oppositional economics to the French public. Listen to this, "While the terrorism and those behind it must stand condemned in the strongest terms … the sinister hand of the prevailing economic theory in the business life of the EC, its anti-social and flawed self-serving capitalist fallout, is engendering a ground swell of grave discontent – from which history shows us organisations like the Judgment Day group emerge, as surely as night follows day."

'Here, take it. The EC establishment regards our crusading professor as dangerous; he considers them economic lunatics. But I've got decapitated swans and vandalised statues on my turf. You don't know anything about those, do you?'

Ferrand drove Anders to the university. The streets were shiny wet and leaf-splattered. They passed Raven Bridge. No signs of the overnight outrage. Outside the university, workmen were washing Goethe's hands.

'First place to look for all of that,' Ferrand growled, 'is the university's medical school. Ratbags.'

'The Professor will be here in a few minutes,' his secretary said, ushering Anders in, and hurrying out.

The academic had personal memorabilia spread around. Hat in hand, Anders surveyed it. In one corner, there were half a dozen framed photographs obviously from his military career. Anders wandered over. The helmeted, camouflage-uniformed youth at the instant of parachuting from a military aircraft, his face tight against the slipstream. Lestang, again in helmet and camouflage, electronically detonating an explosion. Beyond him in the photograph, a house was imploding in a cloud of dust. Now in dress uniform, captain's rank, with red beret. Anders' eyes swept over it.

'Ah, Inspector Anders, you've discovered my past.' He'd entered silently by a side door, had been watching for a moment, Anders thought. Even at rest his vigour and athleticism were evident. His tall, fair, brown-eyed presence, his words, were tinged with amusement – as though commenting on a misspent youth.

They shook hands. 'What's it like to jump?' Anders asked.

'You're loaded up like a packhorse, forty seconds from

exit till you hit the ground. Over very quick.' He smiled, and shrugged. He indicated a chair to Anders, and they sat down. 'Inspector, I'm conscious that I rather rudely ended our previous interview. I had no choice. A lecturer whom I'd dismissed for grave misconduct had turned up on the campus and was making trouble.' His hands spread in a gesture. 'I left one or two things unsaid.'

His expression neutral, Anders nodded politely.

'It's not generally known, but I'm the one who recommended Bosch, Servais, and Henri Bosson to *Paris-Match* as the subjects for that series of interviews. It's something that weighs on my mind. My intention was to show them as black knights against my white knight – in the economic war.' He shrugged. 'Naturally, I had no idea that these terrorists would convert this to their own ends. The others, alas, are gone. But poor Henri Bosson – I fear he is in a terrible situation, for which I'm partly to blame.'

The academic stared at the Interpol investigator.

Surely Lestang would've assumed the police had unearthed this information? After a moment, Anders said, 'Yes, it's to thicken the campaign for publicity, we surmise. Obviously, it's the merger activity involving these institutions which is the key determinant of the terrorist campaign.'

Lestang nodded slowly, and sat back as though something had been got out of the way. His face became more acute. 'As a psychologist with an interest in terrorism, I've been carefully studying the events, the content of this group's press releases, and the possible personalities of the perpetrators.'

'Oh?'

'I wish to place my thoughts – and a theory – at your disposal.'

Anders blinked. 'Please go ahead.'

'Have the police considered that within the EC's multiplicity of governments, agencies, and bureaucracies, there is terrific corruption, deep covert influences, conflicts of interest, corporate and personal agendas, which transcend the so-called interests of state? That the perpetrators of this terrorism, may not be the run-of-the-mill activists and anarchists of the past? In our midst, we see government ministers on trial. Great government frauds being covered up – all of it the tip of the iceberg. And does anyone ever quite know what the proliferation of state intelligence services are up to, behind their overt strategies? It is all a great mystery, which no-one can unravel.'

His brown eyes held Anders'. 'Does this terrorism lie within the black heart of all of that? Is it a game being played out on a grand scale by those with interests hidden beyond the objectives in view?'

Anders was silent. The man was clearly serious. What was he up to? For a long moment, Anders stared at the face in front of him. 'The police agencies try to collect evidence pertinent to a case, to unravel the mysteries, unmask the criminal. What you theorise makes the police task almost insurmountable.'

The academic nodded. 'I feel I'm in sympathy with you Inspector Anders; with your record. Otherwise I would not have put this before you.'

'I will certainly think about it.'

Anders thought: Sciascia's worm in the Sicilian apple. There's something in what he says, but it's not the real world for me. He decided to move back into familiar territory; he told Lestang about the phone calls. About his theory: the Judgment Day group being a front for a single perpetrator.

Listening, the academic had rested his jaw thoughtfully

in a hand. He looked up quickly. 'He might've been quoting from my anti-neoclassical articles and speeches. The political terrorist's compelled to rhetorically justify his deeds. He gives warnings of acts to come, claims responsibility for acts done. *I am omnipotent*, he's saying. His acts of violence are done solely for heroic purposes. He's the total egotist.'

He paused, his gaze locked to Anders'. 'You've no doubt heard of Walter Laqueur's adage: "One man's terrorist is another man's freedom fighter." That's how he sees things.

'Ostensibly, you're heading the investigation against his crusade. Hardly surprising you've become a focal point for him. Your celebrated case involved a quantum leap beyond the normal parameters of law enforcement. Forgive me, a matching of brutal ruthlessness with the same dark commodity. Does he see you as ... an alter ego?'

Lestang spread his hands. His eyes assessed Anders.

We're back to that, Anders thought.

'None of that takes anything away from the theory I've outlined. Some cabal in government, some cell in the bureaucracies, could be running a dark agenda. The spectrum is wide – nothing can be counted out.'

Anders thought: paranoia? He didn't comment again, but decided to play another card. 'I await confirmation, but the terrorist's diverse abilities may include a highly unusual skill ... Hypnotism.'

Lestang's face changed. Anders thought: he's fascinated by this. Almost as much as by his grand theory. The rain had begun again, whispering insistently against the lead-framed windows. Abruptly, Lestang relaxed. 'I know something about that.'

Anders said, 'The Frankfurt bombing, the Servais killing have extremely puzzling features as to how access was gained.' Lestang had large white hands with prominent knuckles, and abruptly he cracked them. Anders blinked.

'What are you looking for, Inspector? Hypnosis is induced by verbal suggestion. It can be induced without sleep – "waking hypnosis". The person focuses on the hypnotist, accepts suggestions, experiences amnesia for a suggested time period.'

He went on, *his* voice seeming almost hypnotic in the quiet room.

There was one other thing.

Anders said, 'I fear Dr Dauban is at risk.'

Lestang became extremely still. A muscle flickered in his face. Anders felt a surge of uneasiness. He related what the perpetrator had said, what she'd said. Lestang was shaking his head now. He'd become silent. Anders said, 'Could hypnosis unlock what's frozen in her memory?'

Lestang stared. 'It's possible. With her co-operation.'

Anders found himself standing. About to leave. Lestang said, in a strained voice, 'I hope I have not muddied the waters for you, Inspector.'

Ferrand was reading a newspaper in the car. 'Matucci's back,' he said. 'Dubost wants to see you.'

Getting into the car, Anders looked back to see Lestang still watching him from the steps.

Dubost sat astride a reversed wooden chair glowering at Matucci. The Parisian had dark circles under his eyes, and one hairy paw grasped a coffee cup. It wasn't clear whether he was going to drink from it or throw it. Inspector Gerard, very uneasy, sat nearby.

Something had popped into the commissaire's mind, unrelated to the business at hand, but nasty. His seventeen-year-old daughter had had an image tattooed on her bum.

Left cheek. During a recent shout-fest she'd whipped down her jeans and flashed it at him: a snake about to strike. He'd almost choked. 'Your face, my bum,' she'd chanted.

He shook his head, and came back to this room. 'I'm going to ask you about Paris, don't worry, but in the meantime where in God's name is Anders?'

Matucci shrugged, and lit a cigarette. 'Don't know. Want me to inquire?'

The Paris crime chief put the cup down on his desk. He glared at the big Italian. 'Let me guess. Would he be loafing around town gazing at architecture, waiting on messages from God – or this maniac he has his heart-to-hearts with?'

Matucci was silent, blew out smoke, and watched the hairy, angry face.

'You're an arrogant bastard, Matucci. If you were on my team, I'd have the blow-torch on you.'

'It's been tried. However, I'm not, never will be.'

Gerard cleared his throat nervously. Dubost's huge shoulders and torso seemed to have expanded. The chair was looking fragile.

Anders was standing in the doorway. Dubost's thick neck twisted. 'Oh thank Christ! *There* you are. We're saved.' The words emerged coarsely from his throat.

Anders stepped into the room, removed his hat, sat down. Ferrand followed him in, leaned against the map of France.

Dubost was battling with himself. Suddenly the shoulders slumped. He growled, 'Anders, do they tell you anything about teamwork in Lyon?'

Anders said mildly, 'Of course, Interpol's objective is maximum co-operation with national police authorities.

That's also my personal aim. However, we've a quite legitimate independence when circumstances –'

Dubost sprang up. The chair crashed on the floor. 'Crap! Crap! Crap! Your colleague's been in Paris this morning. Calling on this country's leading hypnotist. *What is going on?*'

The commissaire's shoulders were shaking with passion. An hour ago Gerard had made inquiries. Monsieur Cage, thirty years before, had been the famous stage-hypnotist The Fabulous Bruno. After a successful stage career, he'd gone legit. He'd been admitted as a member of the French Hypnotherapists' Association. In due course, had become its President. What in the hell did it all mean? Ferrand hadn't told him of Anders' earlier visit to Strasbourg's The Great Frankman, though he'd informed Commissaire Rolland.

Calmly, Anders gave the Frenchman the bare bones of his theory as to how, possibly, hypnotic powers might have been used to gain access to the Frankfurt boardroom, to Felix Servais. How in all probability they'd *not* been used in the murders of Kramer, Hofmann and his Moroccan partner, or of Dupont in Brussels.

'Inspector Matucci's report may throw some more light,' he finished.

Dubost's dark eyes gazed at Anders. The Italian had stopped speaking thirty seconds ago. Ferrand struck a match to light up a cigarette. Gerard winced at the abrasive sound.

'Have you gone off your rocker, Anders?' Dubost seemed to have recovered himself, as though he'd flicked a switch. He grinned, picked up the chair, and sat down again, shaking his head in wonderment. The only sane man in the picture. 'Is this the kind of crap our government pays Interpol for?' He turned to Matucci. '*Now*. What did you find out? And I hope you're not going to tell me the security guards in Frankfurt and Paris were mumbo-jumboed.'

Matucci spoke his piece, addressing it to Anders as though he were the only other person in the room, and saying that this was exactly what might have happened.

★

The Libraire Kleber became busier in the colder months, and Marguerite had been fully occupied. Quite naturally, there had been increased interest in Brant's volume, and also in the bizarre incidents connected to the Raven Bridge, which had been followed closely by the local press. Reporters had called about them, and while she'd been circumspect in her comments, their reports hadn't been.

She'd put out of mind what had been hovering beyond her consciousness. Worrying about it, trying to tease her memory to release it, wasn't working. Perhaps its dismissal might.

Inspector Anders was attracted to her; she felt that, quietly and confidently. It was a surprise, and perhaps it was also one reason for his knocking on her door at 11.00 last night. She was curious and interested in him, and she wondered at herself.

The phone on her desk rang.

'My dear Marguerite, could I come to see you tonight? About nine? I've something important I wish to discuss.'

Marc Lestang's voice seemed its usual breezily confident self, but clearly he wasn't going to say any more on the phone. It was only when she'd put down the receiver that she absorbed the note of tension. Had his article that morning stirred up more trouble for him already? With the terrorist threat, the EC's establishment were feeling vulnerable. The Judgment Day group appeared out of reach, but Professor Lestang could be plucked off his academic tree easily enough. His tenure would be no obstacle to the enemies he had made.

★

A brown paper-wrapped box stood on the bench behind Mademoiselle Dayshift. 'For you,' she said to Anders. Matucci eyed it. Then he winked at the slim brunette, who was blushing. She had a lovely slope to her chest.

'Do you really want to open this?' Matucci said. They were in Anders' room. 'Should I call Ferrand to get an expert?'

'Don't worry. I've no bad feelings about it.' He was already stripping off the paper. It was a hat-box. He peeled off adhesive tape. A strange odour was coming from it. The rank smell of the river. He lifted the lid.

They'd been coiled into it like snakes. White snakes. Anders gazed, fascinated. Matucci stepped back in disgust. The swans' combative eyes were glazed like too-old fish's at the market. Blood streaked the feathered necks. Anders peered in the box, and lifted out a blood-stained scrap of paper. Hand-printed in French was:

'On gamblers God has never smiled,
The gambler is the devil's child.'

He passed it to Matucci. 'Have it delivered to Commissaire Rolland. I think it's a major break in his case.'

Matucci read the note. 'You're not taking this seriously?'

'It's nasty and I am, but there're degrees of seriousness, my friend. And types of craziness.' Anders shrugged and re-sealed the lid. 'Matucci, why don't you phone up that woman TV reporter. The offensive lady. Wasn't she with Channel 4? And give her this little morsel for the late news.' *He* should hear about this development quickly. It might assist the inquiries he was making into his plagiarist.

In a city where old German and French dishes were to be found everywhere, Matucci had to go for Chinese! But not tonight. Anders had his colleague safely within the walls of the Veronese restaurant.

Matucci had given him more on the Paris visit. 'Dubost had me followed. The bastard's feeling left out.'

Matucci lit a cigarette. Decisively, Anders took up the menu and Signor Cantini materialised at his side. He ordered: *pasta in brodo con fegatini e piselli.* They discussed the qualities of the chicken livers, the parmesan, and the method of cooking. The proprietor's enthusiasm lit up his face. When Anders ordered a bottle of the red Valpolicella from north-west of Verona, he gave an emphatic gesture with circled thumb and forefinger.

Professor Lestang's astonishing theory! Matucci was pouring the wine. 'A wine of considerable charm,' Anders commented out of his thoughts.

The food arrived, but Matucci seemed unable to face it. 'Those damned swans' heads,' he commented.

Nature equals nausea, Anders thought.

Matucci was thinking of Philippe Dupont. That mistake continued to trouble him. 'Why wasn't Dupont hypnotised?'

'It's part of the pattern. It seems some have been, some haven't. It might've been too tricky, in terms of what he was required to do.'

Anders shrugged, dismissing it.

Lestang's voice was famous nationwide – as radio broadcaster, television personality. The thought leapt out of his subconscious. Without disguise, it would be recognised immediately by any number of people. But in a monologue the choice of language, the phrasing was harder to conceal. Suddenly the language, the phrasing, he'd heard that afternoon was merging in his head with those of the late-night telephone calls. But it was one phrase which stuck in his head: *alter ego.*

Anders stared across the room, nursing his excitement. The interlude this afternoon *had* been a muddying of the waters. The academic had said it himself! Yet another smoke-screen!

Abruptly, Anders' thinking re-focused and a chill entered him. *Special forces man: trained killer and explosives expert; proponent of anti-neoclassical economics; hypnotist.* The tide in him turned: his brow was hot, his heart was beating quicker. He drained his wine-glass, without knowing it.

And he'd been on the point of asking him to unlock Marguerite's memory!

Matucci was staring at him through his smoke. His colleague's face clicked into focus. 'Lestang,' Anders said with quiet triumph. Then he told Matucci.

'Christ!' the big detective said, but also quiet. He gave Anders an amazed look. 'We should be able to check his movements at the operative times –'

'He was certainly in Paris the night Servais was killed … It's him,' Anders said. 'I've been blind. It fits like a glove.'

Matucci said, 'Maybe too well –'

Anders wasn't listening. 'I'll call Rolland, and we'll pay him a visit crack of dawn, put the heat on.' He was speaking urgently, keeping his voice down.

'Wait a minute, Inspector.' Matucci lifted his hands.

'Why don't we run the checks first on his movements since October 8? I can start tonight –'

'Why don't we ask *him* about that? The clock's running, Matucci. I don't want Henri Bosson or someone else in the morgue while we're tying up loose ends.'

Anders was staring into the distance. He'd become paler. The tremor under the left eye was flickering crazily. Lestang's voice, the phrasings of that distorted voice, were in his head. Stark. 'I'm dead certain. Every moment more –'

Matucci shook his head. 'Eh-eh! Don't do it, not head-on like this. Give it one more day. We'll work fast.'

But Anders still wasn't listening. Marguerite's face was sharp in his mind. What had he done – in revealing to Lestang that she was struggling to remember something? He must go there!

His mobile was ringing. He fumbled it out.

'Anders! Erhardt. We've got him! Holed up with an old flame in the Black Forest! I'm off there now. I'll call you.'

Anders stared out to the darkness. How would the Chemtex deputy security chief fit in? An accomplice? He told Matucci, told him where he was going, and walked out, past Signor Cantini's outstretched hand without seeing it.

Matucci stared after him. Had he cracked? Was this it? Normally Anders was as cautious as hell, and he was the loaded gun. Anders wasn't the only one with a professional nose. His own was really twitching on this. He paid the bill, made an excuse for his colleague to the crestfallen proprietor, and started back for headquarters.

★

Marguerite had washed and dried her hair. She'd put on a skirt and sweater. She'd absorbed Anders' advice and was keeping the chain on the door. The telephone rang.

'My dear Marguerite, my apologies, I can't come tonight. I'll phone again to make a time tomorrow. Early. Are you all right?'

'Of course,' she said, 'why wouldn't I be? Where are you phoning from, Marc?'

'The university. I must go.'

'Goodnight,' she said.

She stood there thinking. There had been a definite urgency in his voice. A strain. What did he wish to communicate to her that couldn't be done on the phone?

★

En route to her flat, Anders passed the madman from the cathedral's astronomical clock. He was eating alone at a solitary table outside a restaurant, segregated from the patrons. Coolish dining. He was surrounded by small bundles of possessions, and talking to himself between mouthfuls. Again the long blond hair was carefully brushed. As Anders hurried past, a waitress came out with additional food. Madman or tramp? Anders never turned his eyes away from weirdos or deviants. He passed close, but smelt nothing but the pleasant aroma of meat stew. The man didn't look up from his plate. It had begun to sprinkle with rain.

Ten minutes later, he reached Marguerite's building. He glanced at the police car, and stepped into the foyer, brushing raindrops off his shoulders.

In the spy-hole, Anders' serious face was revealed to Marguerite. She removed the chain and opened the door.

Coffee in hand, his overcoat neatly folded on a chair, his hat placed on it, Anders studied this woman. He wondered what kind of love-life she'd had in the past; had in the present. What kind of life she'd had in general … her restraint and introspection hinted at something.

He thought of what she'd told him last night about the swans. In the mid-1400s a lecturer dismissed by the university had a long-running dispute with it, seeking re-instatement. He'd lost all his money gaming. One night he cut the heads off four swans and placed them in a box and sent them to a visiting dignitary. It was seen by some as an act of bitter despair, but they'd locked him up as insane.

'The swans' heads have turned up,' he said. He explained the delivery and the message.

She stared, frozen, eyes dilated. 'Mother of Mary! What does it mean?'

'That there's a copy-cat trying to get on the Judgment Day band wagon,' Anders said. 'Possibly a deranged mind. A distraction we don't need.'

He sipped coffee. He was a man who tried to avoid frightening people, but a time came. 'This whole affair is coming to a climax,' he said, carefully setting his coffee cup aside. Lestang was filling his mind. But he talked about the late-night phone calls, and how her name had figured.

Her eyes never left his face.

Finally, he talked of the aura of hypnotism; the gist of the conversations with the two masters. He paused, framing words. 'I believe that what happened a while ago brought you face to face with the perpetrator. He's virtually told me so. I think he may have come to you when he was formulating his plan, to seek information about *The Ship of Fools*. Not Monsieur Gas, but the man behind him. I believe you know his identity, but it's masked by the amnesia planted in your mind.' Anders had watched her brown eyes with the amber flecks as he described the extraordinary aspects of the case.

Softly, she exhaled breath. 'The pressure.'

Anders said, 'The amnesia created by a hypnotist can be finite in time. Can break down spontaneously. He's not been able to check it and satisfy himself. I surmise that's the problem this individual may face. Tomorrow, I expect to confirm his identity.'

She was staring at him seriously.

It was remarkable to Anders how these things happened. At a particular moment, an exchange via eye-contact, or a touch of hands, an unfinished utterance – suddenly accelerated what had been a casual relationship. Such a moment had come now. He gazed at her ample hips, at the profusion of dark hair which spread up her stomach to her navel. He proceeded gently. There had been nothing spoken, just a mutual reaching out. The desire of each to penetrate mysteries; a heightened consciousness – at a crisis point. Her murmurs turned to a gasping. She withdrew her mouth from their kiss. *'Oh God,'* she breathed in a long exclamation.

Afterwards, usually he drew on his sense of humour. 'Close your eyes,' he said. 'I've got to hop off to the bathroom and it's quite a ridiculous sight.'

'No,' she said. 'I'll watch.'

At the bathroom door, he turned, holding onto the jamb. 'Marguerite, what is your relationship with Marc Lestang?'

228

She stared at him. 'Five years ago, we were close.'
'Close?'
'Lovers.'

He was back in southern Italy. That world. Unerringly. A con-crete bunker. The lavatory. Seated on the bowl, his arms raised, hands gripping each elbow. The door was floating … he was air-borne. Red, the colour again. Liquid-red swishing back and forth under his feet. Bloody scraps. A pyramid of swarthy heads, bald-ing, moustached, with and without spectacles, ascended against a wall like a mural. In relief. Against another: a tangled heap of gold watches, chains; another of shoes, shredded expensive leather, some in which an ankle and foot were mounted. The bunker was rotating. Heads were progressively flying off that pyramid going into orbit around him.

He awoke in a terror of pounding heart and hot per-spiration. In his mind, he could still hear them swishing past. But the sound died away with his nightmare. Wide awake, he was listening to the silence of the old city.

XVIII

THE SEVENTEENTH OF OCTOBER

A.M.

AT 1.10A.M. Anders came down the stairs from Marguerite's flat and stood in the lobby. He was still recovering from the nightmare. He couldn't lie quiet, even in that bed. He had to wake up Commissaire Rolland to seek his co-operation. From the lobby door, the street was as empty as if a medieval curfew had been declared.

A police car was parked there. He walked across and spoke to a sergeant. There were no other entrances to the building. Even so, *he* had got past alert policemen before. Anders went on his way, foreboding in his heart for Marguerite's safety.

Checking doorways, the entrances to side-streets, he crossed the Grande Ile, heading for Raven Bridge and his hotel beyond. There was no one around, as if the heritage city had been stripped of living people. He skirted the cathedral, lit-up, with no-one but him to look. His footsteps detonated echoes.

Matucci thought he'd gone off the rails. He'd read that in his colleague's eyes, in his concern. And had he? Was his judgment blown to smithereens? Quickly, he went over it, point by point. It had been building up in him for days, he realised. Piece by piece dropping into place in his subconscious. Then today's meeting! He was walking fast. Circumstantial? Yes. But its weight was overwhelming. He shifted his shoulders. He was committed. The next act was coming, and he had to be fast. Trust his instincts.

As he walked, he thought about how delightful it would have been to have had breakfast with her. But at times like this, approaching a crisis in a case, he needed to be alone.

He came down to the river beside the Palais Rohan. The flotilla of glass-roofed tourist boats were moored in rows. The river's current nodded them this way and that. Beside them was an unlit pontoon. Pitch-black. No lights along the bank here. Something white flashed in the water near the closest boat. Anders paused, then stepped over a low stone wall onto the pontoon, and moved across it. He stared into the water, and was surprised to see a child's stuffed toy bobbing there.

Behind him, the pontoon dipped. Quickly Anders straightened and turned. A dark figure was four paces away. Light from somewhere gleamed on steel. He moved to his left. The figure stepped to block his escape. Anders came back right. The figure backed away, covering him. It was hissing through its teeth as though sorting out a puzzle. Anders had gained a little room. He went for his Beretta. Too late. The figure attacked.

The steel was an extension of the dark arm. Frantically, trailing his left leg for speed, Anders darted across the pontoon. He almost slipped on the damp wood. Then a gunshot cracked open the night. The figure staggered back, reeled away towards the river-bank, fell over the low wall, was up almost immediately and half-running into a narrow street.

'Stay where you are.' A shout. Matucci. He was running across a bridge ten metres away. Pistol in hand, he came down to the river-bank and dived into the narrow street. Breathless, Anders crossed the pontoon and followed. Weirdly, the running sounds abruptly stopped. A single streetlight played on the façades of old houses. From the darkness further up, Matucci called: 'Inspector! Come and take a look at this.'

His colleague stood at the side of the street peering into an ancient stone structure which resembled a bus shelter, but wasn't one. His gold lighter had flared. Now it flared again. Anders had it in a glance. The smooth blond hair. The throat cut from ear to ear still copiously draining gore. The wide-open, surprised eyes. It was the madman.

'Quick piece of work,' Matucci said grimly. His eyes swept the darkness. He holstered his pistol.

'I think it's our copy-cat artist,' Anders said.

'The info about the swans' heads and the verse was on the nine o'clock news,' Matucci growled.

Viewed by a man who hadn't seen the imitation as a compliment, Anders thought. He moved away and put his hand on a house-front. He was still breathing hard. Exertion and shock. Matucci had his mobile out. He spoke tersely for a few moments. Then he came back to his senior colleague.

'Are you all right?'

'Quite – thanks.'

'Why didn't you shoot?'

'Drawing the gun, getting off the safety was a problem, survival was hopping about.'

Matucci shook his head. The safety on his pistol was always off.

'Good shooting in that light,' Anders said.

Matucci shrugged. Suddenly he chuckled in the dark street. 'Eh, Anders you were really stepping it out on that pontoon. It was hard to get a clear shot while you were sambaing away.' He couldn't stop chuckling. 'Looked like you were competing in a Latin-American ballroom championship.'

'For one-legged contestants?' Anders inquired wearily, and turned away for the hotel. 'I'll leave you to take care of the formalities.' He felt drained of strength and emotion. *He* was running rings around them.

Matucci called after him, 'We're doing those checks on the professor's movements. I was on my way back to the hotel.'

Anders raised his hand. That had been lucky for him. He was going to wake up Commissaire Rolland and it wouldn't be an easy conversation.

*

Half a kilometre away, Dominique Bosson shouted angrily in the dark, 'Henri! Don't leave me up in the air!' His heaving, over-fleshed body had collapsed on her. Years ago he'd heard her yell like that on the stage. She extricated herself and shrugged on a silk gown, automatically pushing and teasing her hair into place. Muttering to herself she padded across the room.

Behind her, he'd begun to snore.

In the salon, she paced up and down, her hands stroking her temples, her blonde head lowered. Her lips were compressed, reflecting her thoughts. At the behest of their minders, the curtains had been drawn. She touched a button. They swished back. Delineated by a bracelet of light, the circular Place de la Republique appeared: the handful of trees, the broad paths, the patches of grass. Geometric, yet airy as a French pastry.

It was after midnight, and a few cars crawled around the circuit. She could see the police vehicles parked at the kerb. Police officers were stationed in the building's lobby, and in their private lobby. A woman who was accustomed to slipping away to her various assignations, she found this intensely irritating. The University Library, the National Theatre, and the Palais du Rhin were framed in the cinematic-screen window. Henri was fond of this Germanic quarter; of the giant, neo-Renaissance buildings. 'A junction of Franco–German aspirations and culture – just as we'll achieve with our merger,' he was announcing at select moments.

It made her shudder. To her critical eyes, only the central space found favour.

Her husband's great high-backed chair, eagles in flight in its tapestry, with its padded headrest, was placed where he could sit and savour this view. He sat in it to conduct the stereo system with his antique baton. Beethoven: a favourite. *Mad*. It was the chair that the journalist Dupont had photographed him in. *'Resplendent in his vast chair the chief of Agribank France SA surveys the EC's banking horizons for* Paris-Match. Dupont! Now something less than yesterday's man. Abruptly, she turned from this stage-set and crossed the room to the study. She closed the door behind her and took up the phone. She knew where he was staying, and the hotel receptionist put her through to his room. 'Herr Rath? *Wilhelm*. Dominique. I think we should meet – later this morning. I've a matter I wish to discuss.'

His voice was sleepy, then alert. They made their arrangement, and she replaced the receiver. Had he been alone?
She'd a feeling that he wasn't. Her lovely face was severe
with her thoughts. Suddenly, that expression was wiped
out. Her head swung to the door, listening. What? ...
Only the sighing of the heating system.

Was Henri's snoring and exhaustion as counterfeit as
her own cries of frustrated passion? She opened the door
to the salon. It was empty.

No, she needn't worry. The thought of Henri tiptoeing
around, in any circumstances, defied the imagination.

★

Anders sat in the armchair looking over the roof-tops.
He'd undressed, and unharnessed Mark III; gently mas-
saged the stump. Its reddened surface seemed to stand as a
condemnation. A cold breeze played on his face.

He was in his gown and too keyed-up to sleep. Quite
surprised to still be alive. Tonight had sorted out one
strand of craziness. He supposed the dead hobo would
have a history. He was staring ahead into the future – like
a steeplechase jockey having narrowly surmounted one
fence, focused on the next. *Lestang*. He'd had a fifteen-
minute conversation with Commissaire Rolland. The
police chief had been shocked, then deeply troubled.

Now, instinctively, Anders was expecting a call.

But he did sleep: dropping into a restless doze.

The telephone brought him up like a diver shooting to
the surface. 'Yes?'

'Inspector Anders! What time is it there? It's Guttaso.
I'm calling from Mexico.'

Anders was dazed. The rich tones seemed to have

saturated his brain. 'Dottore … *Mexico*?'

'I haven't received your cheque.'

Anders sneezed abruptly in the cold breeze. Painfully, he was back in the present. 'I haven't sent it.' In the silence, Anders wondered what paper-chase his ebullient Milan publisher was on now.

'No matter. At your convenience. Our editor Dottore Romani has a suggestion. I refer to the chapter where your illustrious ancestor dies in the duel with his land-owning neighbour. The dottore feels it'd have additional drama if the poet made a declaration on the field of honour for posterity. For instance, and this is merely a suggestion: "I stand here, in the name of all women debased by men." The appeal to modern-day feminists, eh! Stoicism won't endear him to readers. What do you think?'

Anders cleared his throat. 'Dottore there's no record of what he said, what he thought, at that fatal moment. It may not have occurred to Dottore Romani, but my objective is to be scrupulously true to what's documented.'

'Of course, of course. And much can be read into a meaningful silence −'

'Dottore, I'm expecting another call. I must conclude this conversation.'

'Understood! My dear Inspector, I'll talk to you soon.'

Anders hung up on his publisher. On Mexico.

Immediately the phone rang again. Here we go, Anders thought tensely. But it was Matucci.

'Our corpse is a sacked university lecturer turned eccentric. He's been on the streets for months, though he didn't have to be. His possessions turned up in a doorway off Place Kleber. There's a wad of newspaper tear-outs on the Judgment Day group, on those swans − on you. A real fan. And a paint-brush with traces of red paint! No sign of the murder weapon. Or the throat-slitter. One thing, a prelim from the autopsy. The knife had a very sharp point. It was thrust in the left side of his neck, exited the right – then the blade sliced out his throat. Filleted. They say it's a trademark of the French army special forces. My slug was in his left shoulder.' He hung up.

Thoughtfully, Anders moved to close the two small windows. Lestang. In the chair again, he reached out for the report that Erhardt had given to him. He read it for the third time. Maybe, tomorrow, the Chemtex security man, Haug, would fit into the puzzle. He was getting sleepy.

'Have you been waiting for my call, Inspector?'

Whirr-whirr-hummm: the electronics were in Anders' brain. He wasn't aware of having picked up the receiver.

'A near thing for you tonight. But as you know the madman's been eliminated, no longer will he muddy the waters. As I've told you I'm close. Very close.

'Congratulations on your elimination of Monsieur Gas. I admit, an inconvenience. The only thing that survives of him is this voice. You're creeping closer. I've never underrated you, but the master in Paris was inspired. And now I surmise you're on the verge of unravelling other matters that are the key to my identity. Matters not obvious, but which are there in the public domain. And so might some others, should their minds and memories begin to work again.'

The faint humming silence lingered in Anders' ear. 'You are going to be caught,' he said. 'The odds against you are too great.'

'That is probable. If I don't move to eradicate those threats. I wish you to know that it will be a grievous regret to me. But your own success is forcing my hand. It's only the arch-enemies who I really want. If they won't recant.'

The brief, ear-jarring laugh came.

'We are cut from the same cloth, Inspector.' Professor Lestang's article yesterday was brilliant as usual. Sums it all up. Are you getting the message? Henri Bosson's game is almost over. Listen:
    '"To earth no power has e'er been sent,
    But in good time its way it went
    When once its usefulness was spent."
'This is goodbye, Inspector Anders.'

Was it Lestang? Sickeningly doubt niggled. Matucci was hardly ever cautious. Bad signs. But without warning, the hatred swelled up in his guts, slopping over like the full shit-cans remembered from his youth. Disgusting and malignant. The muscles of his body seemed locked. His neck was stiff. His hands gripped the arms of the chair as though it might buck him out. He had to follow his instincts.

His coffee was hot and bitter. He sipped it and made a face: 7.30a.m. They've got me in a vice, he thought, eyeing the papers. Reuters was insatiable. For ten days they'd saturated the wires with stories on every conceivable angle. A half-dozen times Anders had seen his own photograph. No longer the eleven-year-old one that the Ministry in Rome had on hand, but one snapped in that media scrum outside Strasbourg police headquarters.

And this Thursday morning here it was again, front-page, with the threat to Bosson, and the verse which had come with its electronic cadences into his ears at 3.20a.m. A headline blared:

D-DAY FOR BANK MERGER.
Strasbourg. Tomorrow evening at 5.00p.m. in the ballroom of this city's Grand Hotel, Monsieur Henri Bosson, spokesman for the joint boards, is to announce the fate of the

Franco—German merger which reportedly would throw 30,000 jobs into doubt. All directors will be present — a defiance to the Judgment Day group's ultimatum, and against the advice of the Ministry of the Interior. Police security is blanketing the hotel. Last night a former Strasbourg University lecturer was killed near the Raven Bridge. Police haven't released more details, but it's understood that Interpol's Inspector Anders, a central figure in the terrorist hunt, was at the scene.

At 8.00a.m. Anders entered headquarters. Matucci hadn't surfaced yet. Still in his hat and overcoat, Anders paced backwards and forwards in the corridor. He was waiting for Rolland and the others. Rolland had insisted on doing this by the book – at a civilised hour.

★

The fear of sudden death was evident in the faces and body language of the half-dozen detectives who were posted in and outside the hotel coffee shop, where Dominique Bosson and Wilhelm Rath were meeting. The policemen were ultra-wary and tense. This hadn't been in their dawn briefing.

Dominique's aura was platinum smooth and shiny. Her blonde hair in its French roll looked salon-perfect. The large emerald ring she wore danced and darted green gleams across the table's white napery, even upstaging her blood-red fingernails.

Rath's face was close-shaven, his expression confident. His thoughts equated to his appearance. But he was also curious. What was this fascinating woman, the surviving creator of their proposed merger, up to now?

They had a secluded table, and could not be overheard. But she leaned close. 'It's been kept quiet. Henri's heart is not in good shape. I think it's important that you know.'

Rath studied her. So this was it! 'I'm sorry to hear that,' he said. Between them, suddenly as potent as the aroma of crispy fried bacon in the room, wafted ambition.

Henri's heart wasn't good, but neither was it so bad – as long as he kept his physical exertion within bounds. Dominique had been thinking about its precise condition a good deal. She said succinctly, 'This has great significance.'

He was having a tremendous view of her breasts, knew he was being granted this privilege. It was mildly sunny but chilly outside. Her mink coat had been borne away by the coffee-shop manager.

She smiled, a delicious, half-meditative smile. 'Henri and I have a very open marriage. That's *one* thing the scandal sheets are correct about.'

What had that to do with the price of fish? However, Rath knew that everything this woman said had its weight. Her fragrance was an overwhelming aroma in his head.

She said in her low, enthralling voice, 'He's wavering, but don't worry I'll persuade him. Succession planning should be high on *our* agenda, don't you agree?'

Neither of them had drunk or eaten a thing. The German reached out with his plump, manicured hand to cover her own. The emerald was cut off from the light. A flurry at the door: three detectives had entered the room, were nodding to their surprised colleagues.

Henri Bosson strode in, his overcoat draped casually over his shoulders. He looked around, spotted his wife, and came over, smiling broadly. 'Fancy seeing you here, Dominique. And you, too, Rath.' He didn't look surprised.

241

Astonishment and consternation were melding on his wife's face.

Rath stood up quickly. 'Will you join us?'

'No, I won't.' His smile had abated, and his eyes were assessing his wife. 'Tell me, Herr Rath, has my dear wife been advising you of my dicky heart? Expressing her worries?' They stared at him. Her superb complexion had become as pale as the crisp white napkin she held, frozen en route to her lips.

He shrugged, looked around and waved two waiters out of earshot. 'I've some news. But perhaps you've seen it. We'll hold a media conference at 5.00p.m. tomorrow to announce the merger, and the regulatory approvals –'

'Bravo Henri!' Dominique came alive and clapped her hands. Rath grinned, and offered his hand.

Henri smiled, and took it. 'My dear, your resignation as a director of Agribank has been accepted by the board in a telephone conference meeting at 7.30a.m. The board's most grateful for your past services and hopes that you'll remain as our chief strategic planner. For the moment.'

Shock. Dominique's classic face had collapsed. On appointment, as a matter of corporate housekeeping all the directors were required to sign an undated letter of resignation, to be exercised at the board's discretion.

Still on his feet, Rath's eyes had narrowed, otherwise his expression was unchanged.

'I must go. We've a busy two days ahead. Dominique, I hope you don't mind me advising you of this with Herr Rath present. We're virtually a family now aren't we?'

They were left with the heavy, sincere tones, not a shred of irony, and Rath felt his admiration rising as he watched Henri and his cavalcade depart.

242

Commissaire Rolland had asked Anders to join him in his car. Gravely, he'd congratulated him on his narrow escape. They followed Ferrand's Renault with Matucci sitting bolt upright in its passenger seat. Responses to Matucci's urgent inquiries were still awaited. With immigration and customs formalities now obsolete for EC citizens, they were reliant on the airlines, based in various cities. He'd been fuming over the delays. Rolland was agitated, and as they drove to the university, made Anders go through it all again. Then the grey-haired Frenchman shook his head, and gave the Interpol man a look of resignation.

Mist loitered along the Ill – the old seducer was slipping its amorous arms around the Grande Ile's generous curves. A chilly tryst. But Anton Anders could've made a poem of it. So thought Anders, seeking relief as the car purred towards this unmasking. He touched the Beretta. They'd have to be fully alert. He'd warned his colleagues.

Professor Lestang was too urbane to show his surprise for more than a few moments. Expansively, he ushered them in, shaking hands, greeting Rolland effusively. 'Gentlemen?'

Anders took his time getting settled. Rolland was staring at him. 'Professor Lestang, I'm obliged to ask you some very direct questions. I trust you'll co-operate.'

'Of course.' He was frowning.

'It would help our inquiries if you'd provide full details of your whereabouts on certain days in October.'

Lestang looked astonished. The commissaire stirred uneasily.

'Perhaps your diary, your secretary,' Anders suggested. He was watching this man as though he might vanish before his eyes. Matucci and Ferrand sat like watchful statues in the background.

The handsome academic's face had flushed. 'Inspector ...?' He turned his head, 'Commissaire, what is this?'

'We've received information which we are obliged to follow up,' Anders said.

'Information!' Lestang locked his hands together and gazed at them. 'What dates do you require?' He was angry now.

Anders, reading from a note-book, told him.

Matucci couldn't remember seeing a case fall to pieces so swiftly, so comprehensively. Lestang's secretary, his appointment book in her hand, went through his movements in October, chapter and verse, and verified them. Only the night of Servais' murder in Paris matched up with anything. That evening, at the critical time, he'd been giving a speech to 500 economists at the Ritz. It had been televised.

Anders listened, pale and serious, as each rebuttal fell like lead into the room. Rolland sat forward progressively in his chair, his face showing pain.

Matucci groaned inwardly. *Why wouldn't he wait?*

The room was silent. A telephone was ringing somewhere.

'Does that assist your inquiries,' Lestang said icily.

'Are you prepared to provide us with a set of your fingerprints?' Anders said into the silence.

Rolland exhaled breath.

Back off, for God's sake, Matucci almost whispered.

Lestang said in a hard and level voice, 'Why not? ... I take it there's an explanation for all this – for these ... accusations?'

'Not accusations, sir, inquiries.' Anders voice and face were devoid of expression.

To Matucci, it seemed that Lestang was about to launch into a major performance when he stopped himself. He'd suddenly become deeply preoccupied, as though this vexatious and traumatic occasion no longer figured.

There were no handshakes as they filed out. Rolland said, 'Professor you'll receive a full explanation.' But the academic merely nodded, hardly taking that in.

Outside, Matucci and Ferrand immediately lit up, avoiding Anders' eyes.

Commissaire Rolland said, more in sorrow than anger, 'Anders! I thought better of you.' Slowly he got into his car and left.

Back at headquarters Anders sat in their room, his hands folded on the desk, gazing into space. He hadn't spoken a word to his two colleagues. They'd busied themselves with various tasks.

At 11.10a.m. a call came through from Frankfurt. Commissioner Erhardt. The German's excitement and ebullience of last night had evaporated. He sounded weary and depressed. 'He's a nut-case, Inspector. The medicos report a complete nervous breakdown. Apparently, after the bombing he just fell apart. He was one of the first on the scene. He took off, heading for this friend's place in the Black Forest. His car skidded on black-ice. He just got out, walked to a station and continued his journey. She just put him to bed and shut the door on the world.'

Anders made some sympathetic sounds.

'Nine days of turning Germany upside down, and what've we got? I'm nowhere. Tell me there's a bit of blue sky your end.'

'Commissioner, I wish I could. But frankly, I've made something of a blunder here this morning. I'll tell you about it some time. But we've got to plough on.'

They hung up amid mutual commiserations. Anders had not, however, been merely staring into space. His mind had been raking back over everything. He felt sick. But the pale set of his face signified nothing but a steely determination to keep going. Harder. Until he, and his nerves, fell apart. When they brought the news that Lestang's fingerprints weren't a match with those in Gas's flat, he merely nodded.

Commissaire Dubost stood in the door, smiling. Matucci and Ferrand had come back with coffee, and put one in front of Anders. Here we go, Matucci thought angrily. The bastard's absolutely cock-a-hoop that Interpol's stuck its head up its backside.

But he was wrong. Dubost came around the desk and clapped Anders on the shoulders. 'Hard luck, Inspector. It happens. If *I* had a cigar for every time I've sucked the wrong titty I'd be set up in a flash tobacconists' salon on the rue de Victor Hugo.'

He strode out, and later, Anders was to think that, in an obscure way, the gesture might have signalled an imminent turning point in the investigation.

XIX

THE SEVENTEENTH OF OCTOBER

P.M.

'EVERYTHING'S TIGHTER than a fish's arse-hole,' Commissaire Dubost announced to the room packed with detectives from the urban police, the regional crime service, and his own central directorate. 'The bomb squad's gone over everything. They'll be crawling through the airconditioning conduits, over the whole building all day and right throughout the event. The hotel's cancelled all other functions, is closing its restaurants for the night. They'll be checking no new guests in, and those there've been vetted to the nth degree as have the staff. There'll be a tighter cordon around the hotel than they gave De Gaulle.'

Central Commissaire Rolland sat silent and sceptical, shocked and angry with Anders. Last night the swans' heads had put him off the roast chicken his wife had prepared for dinner. An academic madman! He'd known him. Now this debacle with Lestang! The Strasbourg chief of police wondered what kind of welcome he'd get at the university in future.

The management of the Grand Hotel had resisted

staging this event. Henri Bosson was adamant that they would. Dominique's dismissal hadn't stopped her phoning its general manager advising him that the whole of France was going to learn from her, personally, that he, personally, 'had a deficiency of balls', unless …

Dubost's dark eyes belligerently swept the assembled police. 'But this bastard can crawl through key-holes, disappear in a puff of smoke, according to Interpol's Inspector Anders, who the shit sees as his window to the world. *So.* If anything goes wrong at the Grand Hotel, a lot of careers will *also* go up in a puff of smoke. Savvy?' They did.

Anders returned to his desk, and continued to gaze into space. More coffee. The sick feeling in his stomach hadn't abated. He'd gone back and forth over Erhardt's transcripts. The Chemtex world the day before the Frankfurt bombing was vivid in his mind. He could almost hear the voices of the various parties at their meetings. And it was a puzzle. But *what* was the puzzle? Again, he rifled through the reams of paper on the follow-up inquiries and interviews. The competition directorate's merger task force … *those* people. The faces of Bayard, looking up from his fishing rod, of Fouralt, tense with nerves at the airport bar, were suddenly in his mind's eye.

Abruptly, out of his unconscious: focus. It sometimes happened like this. A rising excitement. He reached for the phone. Erhardt was surprised to hear from him again so soon. The commissioner listened attentively. 'I'll ring you back,' he said thoughtfully. 'Shouldn't take too long.'

Anders sat with fresh hot coffee brought by a young police woman. He sipped it, and put all thinking on hold. Ferrand smoked and kept silent. After half an hour, Anders went out to the corridor and paced up and down.

Ferrand poked his head out of the room. 'Commissioner Erhardt on the line.'

'Commissioner,' Anders said, and then listened to the apologetic voice. 'I don't know how we missed it. One of them did leave the conference room for a short period, about 4.30p.m.'

Anders felt the pressure mounting. '*Who* was he?'

'The receptionist doesn't know. A tall man. She only took in that. Carrying an attache case, as if to leave. She didn't have occasion to know their names. They'd been met downstairs in the garage by Herr Bosch's PA and the security personnel.'

'Dark or fair?'

'Doesn't have that detail.'

'Must have been either Bayard or Fouralt. Both are tall. But he returned ten minutes or so later ... with the case?'

'Yes.'

'The chief of security was at his post in the lift foyer adjacent to the toilets at 4.30p.m. So?'

'He says he was. That is the peculiar thing, Inspector. We've just re-checked. He did *not* sight the man.'

Anders sighed. 'And we know the surveillance camera was switched off in that short period. Thank you my friend, I'll be in touch.' He sat motionless. The cream of European bureaucracy. *Above suspicion.* In theory. His new suspicion wasn't one that should hold water. And yet he remembered once in Rome, working on a foreign exchange scam in a large bank, he'd seen a giant US bank fall into bankruptcy. It'd been getting away with all kinds of recklessness. The US regulators had considered it 'too big to fail'. Did they have that kind of situation here?

Anders walked down the corridor to Dubost's room with a heavy though excited heart.

'We've slipped up badly …'

The commissaire settled back in his chair, ran a hand over his moustache, preparing himself. Rapidly Anders reverted to the Frankfurt scene, Chemtex's headquarters the day before the bombing, described the visitors. 'The German police went back and forth over the employees – exhaustively. They put the trade union people through the grinder … even those two politicians. They couldn't get hold of the West Africans. But this trio from the competition directorate in Brussels? No.'

'For Christ's sake!' Dubost snarled, and half-rose from his chair in anger. 'Next you'll be accusing the President.'

But Anders went on, remorselessly. 'It shows up in the police transcripts: almost as if they were considered above suspicion. They've been here in Strasbourg, at Agribank.'

Anders related his conversation with Erhardt, said, 'A feasible scenario as to how the bomb was placed is beginning to appear. The terrorist dragnets have turned up nothing. Stuckart's dead. Haug, the Chemtex security man, seems clean.' He shrugged. He hadn't mentioned hypnotism. Yet. Dubost was thinking hard. His face, a few moments ago suffused with anger, turned pale.

Anders said, 'Their names are Arminjon, Fouralt, and Bayard. Their antecedents and recent movements should be checked out thoroughly. Their respected official positions have allowed them a dream-run.' He shook his head slowly. 'I blame myself, but the perpetrator's been stirring a lot of ingredients into the pot.' He stared at the map of France. Was he diving into this gap? Setting himself up for a final fatal fall? He'd been dead certain about Lestang.

Dubost stared at the Italian. The Frenchman audibly drew in breath, like a man about to plunge into icy water. He was a 'facts' man, but he'd seen enough of this Italian's way of operating to modify his pragmatism. Scratch this morning. If he'd had the information Anders'd had he might've gone down that road himself. He picked up the phone. 'We'll have to go through the Ministry. And to get it done fast I'll have to put the fear of death into them. I mean, re their damned careers.'

Anders stayed close to headquarters. A top-level call had already gone through from Paris to the EC's competition directorate in Brussels. Now they could only wait. He still had the sick feeling.

At 2.10p.m. the ministry phoned. There were problems. The competition commissioner was refusing to sanction release of confidential files on the three named officials. The minister of the interior was presently being briefed, and would himself phone the commissioner within the hour. But don't expect anything till evening.

'*Merde,*' Dubost said, turning his eyes to the ceiling. He lit a cigarette, the first time Anders had observed him do that. Brussels wouldn't even tell them where the trio were at present.

Anders got up and stared out the window. He said, 'I trust the Ministry's asked the competition commissioner to keep the inquiry confidential from those three.'

Dubost grunted. That had been his request. 'I'm going to start checking airline movements.'

Anders nodded his agreement and wondered if he should help. However, he'd had another idea. He looked at his watch, excused himself and went to his room. Matucci and Ferrand were back there, silently smoking. Anders gave them a look and went to the phone.

The switchboard put him through to the Frankfurt number.

'Eh, Inspector Anders,' Dottore Zanotti said. 'I've been reading plenty about you. May I ask how it's going? The market is betting that Henri Bosson will chicken out.'

'I don't know anything about that,' Anders said diplomatically. 'We should all have the answer tomorrow at 5.00p.m. Could I ask you something, Dottore?'

'Go ahead.'

'The three officials – Arminjon, Fouralt, and Bayard – of the Competition Directorates' Merger Task Force. I met them briefly at your office –'

'The Takeover Trinity.'

'Excuse me?'

'That's what they're known as. They work as a team. One of several Merger Task forces.'

Anders thought for a moment. 'Do you know much about their background? Each man's?'

It was the banker's turn to hesitate. 'A bit. In this business we study the opposition, and the regulators. Let me see.' For several minutes Zanotti's potted history, and assessment of each individual, crackled in the room. The trio had certain common denominators: each was a lawyer and an accountant, each was in his early-forties. He described their universities, past employment, marital status … the deals they'd signed off on, the deals they'd declined.' Anders was impressed. Zanotti continued: 'Arminjon is the team leader. More pragmatic than the others.' He ceased abruptly. 'That's it.'

Anders had put the call on the speaker phone and Matucci and Ferrand were paying attention. Though Ferrand didn't know Italian.

'You don't have as much on Bayard as the others. Any reason?'

'Well,' Zanotti said, 'there isn't as much accessible on him. For example, past employment. Strangely enough, no-one I know ever heard of him in the years prior to the competition directorate. There's a gap between university-army, and turning up there. I never asked him personally about it. Not *that* important to me. He's a bachelor with no known female or male companions – at the time we looked into it, anyway. He's perfectly open to deal with. Doesn't come across as the mystery man.'

'Dottore, this has been of great assistance.'

'Really?'

Anders hung up. The three detectives regarded each other in silence. Anders explained briefly to Matucci and Ferrand, whose Gauloise seemed forgotten in the corner of his mouth.

'I'll start checking his back movements,' Matucci said.

'Where is he now?' Anders said. 'That's what I want to know.' He showed a spurt of excitement. 'With luck, he won't know his cover's blown.'

The corridor to Dubost's office was becoming home-ground. Anders stood in the doorway. 'Bayard,' he said to the Paris crime man's worried face. 'Especially him.' Then he told the commissaire why. 'We need their fingerprints, and especially his. And we need to know *where* he is.'

Anders returned to his office. Matucci and Ferrand were busy on the phones. He went out again to the corridor, and paced up and down, his head dropped in thought. Could the Takeover Trinity in Brussels be kept ignorant of the French requests for their personal files? Would 'a friend' tip them off? Was the *terrorist* still fighting his battle on two fronts: one, to protect his real identity – so vital to him in the future; two, to inflict a major catastrophe on the Strasbourg merger?

Hands deep in his pockets, Anders continued to pace the corridor, leg creaking, floorboards creaking. Number one might not matter now. He might've discarded his real identity and assumed another false face – Gas's successor. After a while, he stopped the pacing and gazed through the window for a long time at the greying afternoon.

Anders jerked out of the reverie, glanced at his watch: 2.55p.m. This waiting could go on for hours yet. Grimly, he went to Dubost's room.

The commissaire was abusing two detectives. Anders waited in the corridor. The pair came out, glanced at the Interpol man, their faces sour.

The Paris crime chief's head was wreathed in cigarette smoke. He waved his hand to disburse it. 'Until two days ago I'd given up, and it was a success story. *Twelve months.* Now – in ruins.'

Anders looked sympathetic. For him it was five years. He took a chair in the room's corner. Dubost raised his big, hairy hands. 'I've rung the Ministry twice. Just put the phone down. Still no word from Brussels. The competition commissioner's gone into his fucking bunker. I tried direct for their whereabouts. But that organisation's like a clam.'

He gazed at the Interpol man, weighing his next piece of information. 'At 4.00p.m., the Prime Minister will phone him. He's being briefed at this moment. The Minister of the Interior's entered hospital for a kidney transplant.'

The Italian raised his eyebrows, conveying more sympathy.

Dubost shoved his bulk back in the revolving chair, causing it to emit a savage squeal. 'Madame Bosson's been sacked as a director of Agribank. She's taken off in her red

254

Porsche to their country estate. In the words of a jazz-playing black man, Now ain't that something?'

Anders nodded slowly. 'We're all feeling the strain.'

'Not that woman,' Dubost sneered.

Anders said, 'I'm going out to check the men at Libraire Kleber. I'll be back within the hour. You've got my mobile number.' A compulsion had come down on him to make sure the four detectives there were super-alert.

★

Mid-afternoon, Bayard arrived at Strasbourg airport. He'd been accredited to the observer's role for the directorate at tomorrow evening's meeting at the Grand Hotel. He'd come a day early. There were a few matters to take care of at the directorate's office in the European Parliament building.

The tall, blond man strode through the airport building headed for the taxi rank. Lean and loose-limbed, he looked extremely fit. He carried his briefcase, a small bag, and a fawn coat. For the past few days, he'd been flying back and forth on duty to European capitals including Strasbourg. Airports were like bus stops to him.

When he left the building to the taxi-rank he stopped to put on his weather-coat. He glanced at the sky: rain was forecast for this afternoon.

★

When Professor Lestang came to see Marguerite, he was relieved to find detectives on guard at the library. It was nearly three. He'd been shocked by this morning's inter-view but that had been overrun by his mounting concern for his friend. Yesterday afternoon, after his interview with Anders, he'd paced his room for an hour, the Interpol man's remarks about Marguerite running through his head. Precipitately, the notion had come. Certain things had clicked into place, and fear had fallen on him. He'd phoned her to arrange a meeting. Yet it was all too hard to believe. Doubtful and irresolute, he'd cancelled their appointment, decided first to phone several old contacts in Paris and Brussels – people he hadn't been in touch with for years. By the time he'd tracked down phone numbers, it was too late to phone their work addresses, and he had no personal numbers. The police had arrived first thing this morning, and after that nasty session, he'd begun the calls.

Marguerite thought: he looks subdued, quite tense in fact. She was accustomed to his confident urbanity. She was curious as to why he'd sought the late-night appointment at her flat last night, then broken it. Instead, Inspector Anders had called. She blushed at the memory. She could hardly believe it. But it'd seemed so natural. As if the time, the place, the man had been ordained by all the events and forces moving past them – this crisis. Nonetheless, was it an experience she wished to repeat? She shook herself alert. Marc was only chatting about university gossip, mutual friends.

However, Lestang had already twice introduced a certain name into the conversation and clearly it had gone over Marguerite's head. He paused and mentioned the name again. He was holding his breath.

She stopped in mid-sentence. 'There's that name again, Marc, do I know him?'

He stroked his lips thoughtfully. Then he described the individual in considerable detail, the occasion when he'd introduced her to him. Nearly twelve months ago. The topic of conversation that had followed was focused in his mind. He was watching her with scrupulous care for the faintest sign of remembrance.

'God,' she said. 'It must've been a bad day. I've absolutely no recollection –'

She'd stopped abruptly. Here it was! This related to that frustrating pressure she'd felt herself under. She brushed back her hair. 'It's important,' she said tensely.

He was silent, thinking what to do next.

She looked at him directly. 'What's this about, Marc?'

He spread his hands. He'd decided. 'Nothing to worry about.' He smiled tightly. 'What I really came for was to ask you out to dinner. That Italian policeman shouldn't be allowed to monopolise your company.'

Behind a cafe window opposite the library, over the top of a newspaper, eyes watched the professor's hurried departure, and came to a decision. 'What a pity,' the owner of the eyes sighed with resignation.

Five minutes later, standing in the Place Kleber, Lestang felt a deep chill. But for Inspector Anders, he'd still be in his fool's paradise. Anders had made an idiot of himself over one thing, but not over this. He'd observed the police at the library. Alert men. Thank God the Italian had responded to the warning. But they wouldn't stand a chance if *he* was determined. Yet – was he over-reacting? Yet again, he had a sudden doubt as to whether the connections he was making in his mind weren't merely crazy coincidences. Jumping to conclusions on circumstantial evidence like Inspector Anders had.

He gazed at the street. He'd spent three hours on the

phone making those calls to old friends, old army comrades, people he knew in Brussels, seeking confirmation. It hadn't produced a thing. The fellow didn't seem in touch with anyone in their mutual past.

He squared his shoulders, and dismissed the doubts. He must act. Abruptly, he got out his mobile, took Anders' card from his wallet, and punched in the numbers ... no answer. He swore softly. Without warning rain began to teem down. He stepped under an awning, and punched in the police headquarters' number and when it answered, asked for Anders.

A long wait. 'He's out,' the switchboard operator said. 'His mobile number is –'

'Never mind, when'll he be back?'

'Within the hour they say.'

Lestang thought quickly. What about the other police? No. 'This is important,' he said. 'My name is L-e-s-t-a-n-g. Tell Inspector Anders to ring this number urgently.'

The tall man stood in the pedestrian-only heart of the old city, watching passing faces, thinking what to do. He phoned Anders' mobile again. Still no answer and this time he left a message.

Abruptly, he decided to walk to his flat. He'd try to contact him from there.

★

Having checked the arrangements at the library, and spoken to the detectives, Anders returned to the street. He hadn't seen Marguerite. He started back for headquarters. He was passing the Palais Rohan when he was caught in the downpour. He hesitated as the chilly rain swept into his face, then ducked into the palace. From the doorway he looked at the sky. Maybe fifteen minutes. The sign in the foyer said: switch off all mobile phones. He did, bought a ticket and went upstairs to the galleries. He walked through the richly endowed world of the old episcopal palace, the royal apartments, the King's Chamber, where the decorative motifs were of sleep. Feeling that he'd dropped out, briefly, he read of poppies, flowers of slumber, of dragonflies symbolising dreams. He gazed at persons in night-caps, surrounded by bats.

Parallel to the large apartments were smaller ones, facing out to the courtyard. Anders stood and gazed down a long, narrow corridor to a doorway. Twenty metres he guessed. Windows overlooked the courtyard. He thought of a bowling alley. Or, an indoor shooting gallery. He glanced out. The rain had almost stopped.

He went down the curving staircase and out into a dripping twilight. The grotesque figure of the madman, a sculpture on the façade, watched him depart. Well *that* incident was behind him. Maybe his next nightmare would feature not bombs, but the bats of the King's Chamber. This morning Ferrand had told him that months ago the ex-university professor had tried to strangle a senior colleague, that it'd been hushed up and he'd been retired – to the streets. Another ticking bomb.

Outside the palace, he fumbled for his mobile to check for messages.

★

Lestang's flat was on the Rue Finkwiller at the edge of the Petite France quarter – fifteen minutes away. The rain had become sleet, and he turned up his raincoat collar and set off. It was after four, and already almost dark. A gusty wind had got up and pedestrians, heads down, were hurrying to their warm and dry homes.

Following Marc Lestang from the library, the man walked easily and confidently. At home in wind, rain and darkness. Lestang wasn't acting professionally. For a man with his training. But that was the way it went. Unless you kept your skills sharp and shining and in play they became devalued: merely certificates on a wall, cups in a cabinet, photographs in a study, a beret in a drawer. This was a sad business. The tall man sighed, and dropped back a bit as they turned into a deserted street.

Lestang had almost reached a small humped bridge which crossed a canal when his mobile rang. He whipped it out, and heard: 'This is Inspector Anders.'

'Thank God!' he said. 'One moment.' He glanced aside, spotted shelter in a doorway, and moved into it. 'Can you hear me clearly, Inspector?'

'Yes, go ahead.'

Lestang drew in his breath. 'Please listen closely. Marguerite's in danger. I saw the police at the library. Obviously you've reached the same conclusion. It's *extreme* danger. Are you hearing me?'

'Yes.'

'Listen, in case we lose the connection – Pierre Bayard. B-a-y-a-r-d – of the EC's Competition Directorate, Brussels. *He is the man you're looking for.* The danger man for Marguerite. Have you got that?

'Yes.'

'Listen – I was shocked – when you said the terrorist'd told you Marguerite might threaten his identity. Then the hypnotism. In a flash, I had a frightening memory. Though

260

I couldn't believe it. But I do now … this past half hour. Twelve months ago, I casually introduced him to her at a party. I hadn't seen him in five years, he just turned up. I left them, later heard them discussing *The Ship of Fools*. They went on for an hour or more. Till our meeting yesterday, I forgot this.'

He paused for breath, and to wipe moisture out of his eyes. 'Are you there, Inspector? Right. My army unit was a crack group. The best in the French forces. This man, possibly the best of the best. I heard he disappeared into one of our secret services. He would've gathered more skills there. Black arts. I trained, as you know, in hypnotherapy. Years ago, he showed a great interest in that. In the army, he teased me with extreme-leftist doctrine. Today his job takes him all over the EC. Jetting somewhere every other day … I've just seen Marguerite. It's obvious she can't recall meeting him, or their talk that night. What I think is that soon after that talk, he called on her. Eliminated her memory of him, and their Brant conversation. I can only surmise he was exploring ways and means for this mad terrorism. He regretted not taking sufficient care in disguising it. Now, he's come to doubt the reliability of that amnesia. God knows why he hinted this to you. Inspector, it's the mind of the terrorist. The cover he now has is unique and unrepeatable. He must protect it.'

He was excited, nearly breathless. *'Inspector, have you got all that?'*

'Yes,' Anders shouted. 'We know – and we've a dragnet out for him.'

A stunned silence. 'Thank God.'

Anders suddenly had a sickening feeling. One of his instinctive premonitions. He felt an obligation to the crusading academic: for his blundering accusation – and to a sincere man who cared about the under-class – who saw a huge and desperately dark picture. Never mind its credibility.

He said urgently, 'Professor where are you?'

'In the Petite Paris quarter. Ten minutes from home.'

'Don't go there,' Anders said curtly. 'Is there a well-lit cafe or bar close to you now?'

'Yes. Fifty metres away.' He gave its name. 'Do you think –'

'Yes. He's here. Anything's possible. Go immediately to this cafe, we'll be there in ten minutes. Go now.'

Lestang gazed at the dark street as he slipped his phone into a pocket. Quickly he turned and descended stone steps to the river-side promenade, and headed north-east. The lights of the cafe were just ahead. The canal's surface was corrugated with wind. A couple hurried past, laughing, the man's arm around the woman pulling her beneath an umbrella. Fittings on the façades of old buildings high above the promenade emitted bangs and rattles. A baby was wailing. He checked behind. Streetlamps spaced well apart laid pools of light. Nothing.

Ahead: the shuddering of a boat's engines. The cruise-boat was forging along the canal away from him. Lit-up, showing a paucity of passengers.

A sound, he swung around.

A man with red hair, and glinting silver-framed glasses, stood there. Lestang's heart dived. He didn't move, but peered at the stationary figure. Unfamiliar, yet familiar.

'Is it you?' he asked.

'You know that it is,' came the reply.

★

The quarter was hemmed in with darkness. 'Not this place again,' Matucci growled. Ferrand was parking his car across the street.

'Yes,' Anders said tensely, scanning the precincts.

The cafe was brightly lit. Outside was shadowy, the metal tables unoccupied, the foliage of the trees swaying, the last leaves sailing down speedily as though hellbent on disintegration.

Anders stood in the doorway. His eyes swept over the few patrons. No Lestang. Ferrand joined them. 'Not here,' Anders said. 'Split up and search the area. Back here in five minutes.' The three detectives hurried off in different directions. Anders took the canal side. He walked fifty metres along the river-side promenade towards a humped bridge. The neighbourhood was deserted; the population had disappeared. He turned and walked back. They reassembled. The others shook their heads.

Anders' face and hands were cold, but his heart felt icy. Had the professor gone home after all? His nerves were stuck in his throat.

They walked beyond the trees and tables to an iron-railed terrace which looked down on the canal. They gazed at the lock, ten metres away. A cruise-boat was enclosed, riding turbulent water. A crewman with a boat-hook was at its bow, leaning over. Deftly, he hooked something out of the black water. Matucci became tense. 'A wallet,' he said squinting down at the well-lit area.

The man was busy again, and suddenly excited. He called urgently over his shoulder and his colleague in the stern came hurrying forward. Anders peered hard at the water under the boat's bow. He saw the floating human figure flopping this way and that in the foamy water, the boat-hook holding it clear.

The wallet in hand, Anders stared at the sodden pasteboard card with the printed words. *Inspector DP Anders, Interpol.* He thought he was going to vomit, but he controlled it.

It took ten minutes to heave the overcoated, water-logged corpse onto the quay. The two uniformed police who'd arrived turned it over. The three detectives gazed at Professor Lestang's watery, vacant face and the small colourless hole in the centre of his forehead.

Anders just stood there staring, his arms rigid at his sides. Matucci had never seen him quite like this.

Anders was silent for what seemed like an age to the others. Finally, he turned to them and assigned them a task which made Matucci grimace. No bed tonight. Probably this would send his relationship with Christine into a final death-dive.

Anders was dropped off at headquarters. Obdurately he made his way upstairs. His thoughts seemed to be discon-nected. Fractured. But he had to put this tragedy aside. Wearily, he went looking for Dubost. The Paris crime chief's room was empty, the corridors likewise. One of the Paris detectives came in. 'He's at the Grand Hotel. There's been a bit of a scare. They grabbed a plumber doing emer-gency repairs. The guy's bona fide.'

'Has he been informed of Professor's Lestang's murder?'

'Yeah, by me. What happened, Inspector?'

Anders gazed at Dubost's ash-tray, overflowing with butts and ash, as though it were an artistic focal point. He breathed in deeply. 'Bullet in the head. Dumped in the lock.' He thought: he's relentless, ruthless and fast. And cruel. *You're outclassed.* He looked up at the man. 'Anything yet from Brussels, or Paris?'

'They confirmed the Prime Minister made his call.

Otherwise, silent as the grave.' He looked away from the fluttering under Anders' eye.

At 8.00p.m. the same detective hurried into Anders' room. 'Something's coming through from Brussels.'

They went down in the lift. The photographic images were being down-loaded. The three confidential personnel files were already done. Anders seized them and glanced quickly through Arminjon's and Fouralt's. Then he sat 'down and concentratéd on Bayard's. Unlike the others, it was chronologically incomplete. He'd graduated from law school in 1985, and gone into the army. Between 1990 when he'd left the army, and 1997 when he'd appeared at the competition directorate, nothing was recorded. The gap was as sharp as a razor-cut. Anders gazed at it as though he was seeing an unexplained hole in the ground.

The detective passed him the three photographs, he glanced at two, and then studied the third. A head and shoulders shot. The handsome face looked up at him. A face devoid of distinguishing marks. Really, of character. A great face to create other faces on, Anders thought. The face he'd seen at *Banca Internazionali Di Roma*, on the bank of the Ill. The eyes alone had something: faint irony?

Dubost came in, treading heavily, smelling of body odour and tobacco, resonating bad mood.

'They've arrived,' his man said.

'Thank Christ.'

Anders said, 'I suggest we forget about the others and concentrate on *him*.' Quickly he briefed Dubost on his phone conversation with Lestang; on what had transpired. He passed the report and photo. 'The report's been censored – or the Competition Directorate knowingly took

265

on someone with a hidden past.'

A detective entered. 'Bayard. Yesterday morning he flew from here to Brussels at 8.00a.m. Today he came back – arrived 2.35p.m.'

'Bounces around the EC like a ping-pong ball,' Dubost growled.

'He's here now, all right,' Anders said quietly.

Dubost's gimlet brown eyes studied the Italian, then he scanned the report in his hands, grunted and strode to a phone. He'd sniffed as though he'd smelt himself. He gave the switchboard operator precise instructions and put down the receiver. He didn't look at Anders, just gazed at the photograph. After sixty seconds the phone rang.

Dubost jerked alive and answered it. An animated conversation, certainly from Dubost's side, began. The Frenchman knew the person on the other end well. Anders guessed he was speaking to a representative of one of those special agencies tucked away in government which, in the interests of national security, never slept. Dubost lapsed into silence; the other party had obviously put down the phone. Two minutes extended to three. Dubost stared at the wall. Then the other was back on the line.

'Yes, Claude, I guarantee an official request will follow from the Ministry. Claude, this is *me* you're talking to. And doubtless you're taping our conversation.'

Then the other was talking, and the commissaire was nodding and grunting. At last, deliberately, he put down the phone.

'It's a DST wipe-out,' he spat out. His tone made it clear what he thought of the Directorate of Counter Espionage. 'An embargo on the fellow's past. My contact wouldn't be specific on his current status, but Bayard's been an agent with the DST. May still be.'

The room went silent as the implications sunk in. Suddenly Anders was hearing Lestang's voice as he'd spoken earnestly of dark and secret agendas, super-powerful forces overshadowing the state. Then Dubost began talking again. 'I'll get the Ministry probing deeper on it ... but to us, standing here in this damned city, at this moment, what are we looking at? A counter-espionage agent who's run off the rails, or some kind of convoluted business of a government hierarchy which beggars any interpretation you or I might put on it.'

Anders nodded, and stared at the desk-top. The Swiss manufacturers of the Frankfurt bomb's detonating device had suspected they'd been dealing with a DST agent.

He looked up. 'Bayard's fingerprints?'

'No word. The Belgian police are on it. I'm going to put out the bastard's details, all points. Right now. Get a task force onto hotels.'

Yes, he's here, Anders thought, but Gas is 'dead', that flat is blown, so in what skin and with what face – and where?

Anders arrived back at the hotel at 10.45p.m. Dubost had wearily said he was going back to his own to clean up and get a few hours sleep. Tomorrow would be a big day. His eyes looked like they'd shrunk back into his skull.

Showering and shaving, Anders tried to analyse the reason for the wipe-out of Bayard's DST past. No legitimate French agency would seek to undermine the government's policies on the EC. Maybe it was just routine procedure with ex-agents.

Bayard *must* be a man alone, he told himself. The sole human face of the Judgment Day group. What a man! Endlessly resourceful. But Lestang's voice was still in his brain, sombrely stating his overarching conspiracy theories.

Anders tilted his head, listened – a resonance of evil seemed to vibrate in the air. Not fanciful.

He dressed again and sat in the armchair gazing at the dark outside the windows. He'd put on his linen coat. Now he thought specifically about Marguerite, though he'd been thinking about her in gaps all evening. Matucci and Ferrand were guarding her. The experts said a good proportion of human beings couldn't be hypnotised. Whether the tough duo fitted into that category was an open question. And did previous norms apply to a master practitioner, who might've broken through old frontiers? He'd looked Matucci in the eye and said, 'Be prepared for tricks.'

Anders called Matucci's mobile.

'All quiet,' his colleague reported. 'I'm inside her flat, Ferrand's in the downstairs' lobby.'

Anders described Bayard. As he did so, the face in his mind's eye seemed to be assessing his moves. 'Going on his form to date, he might look nothing like that now,' he said, and rang off.

Tomorrow morning he'd take over the task himself.

Bayard wouldn't – shouldn't – know his cover was blown, if the competition directorate had kept the police inquiries under wraps. Until Bayard could be told, or found out for himself that his identity was discovered, she was a target. At this juncture, there was no way the French police would jeopardise the hunt by permitting a leak, so probably Anders was going to have to tell him.

He suddenly realised this. *I must tell him.*

But tell him how? They'd gone past the phase of the late-night phone contacts. Past the joking. Bayard was no longer in control. And doubly dangerous, Anders thought.

He got up and paced between the pillars. Was he a human being!?

He recalled him, fishing on the banks of the Ill. God!

It came at him from nowhere. The room had been invaded by the overpowering stench of the river. The air was deafening with the threatening cries of the birds … a terrible physical disorientation had gripped him. The room was heaving. Then spinning. Nausea rose in his throat. His face was instantly covered with perspiration. The ceiling was sliding up and down. He staggered to the bed, fell down. Oh God! *Worse. Hellish.* The bed was rotating, going to toss him off. He seized its sides with his hands. Faster, faster. The tree-trunks were telegraph poles beside a fast train. He was going to vomit. He lurched up from the bed, reeled away, crashed into a pillar, rebounded and staggered to the bathroom. He fell down before the toilet bowl. Violently ill. Again. Heaving it up. Both his arms were around the bowl anchoring him. He was holding it as tightly as he could. *What in God's name?* Consciousness was going.

He was awake, lying on the ceramic floor. Cold. The horrendous vertigo had gone. He got up stiffly, creakingly, taste of vomit in his mouth, and staggered into the bedroom, crashing into furniture. He wouldn't trust that bed. He fell into the armchair, seized its arms in case, and plunged down again into a black pit.

XX

THE EIGHTEENTH OF OCTOBER

A.M.

FROM THE black mouth of the alley across the street, the terrorist stared into the building's underlit lobby. The detective had moved out of sight, but was still there. Doubtless, others upstairs ... watching the body follow the boat into the lock, from the windy darkness, he had suddenly felt absolutely alone with his responsibility.

One-sixteen a.m. This was no good. Anders had been fast. Tomorrow, he'd choose his own ground. Turning, he moved deeper into the alley.

★

Through sleety rain, drifting leaves, and opaque grey light Anders walked to the Libraire Kleber. He was dead-pale and a trifle unsteady on his feet. His vision was slightly blurred. What had it been? A toxic reaction? A weird virus striking from nowhere? He wished. Grimly, he surmised that it was the next stage; beyond the hallucinations. He was shaken, but for the moment it had run its course. He trusted.

And Lestang was dead. Should he have handled that better? He knew it was a factor in his nightmarish attack.

His mobile rang. It was Dubost. 'Inspector, it's just come through. The fingerprints are Bayard's. Perfect match! The Brussels cops got into his apartment, lifted prints aplenty. Congratulations!' Excitedly, he went on with other information. The dragnet overnight had been negative. 'But thank Christ we know who he is, and we've got the bastard on the run now!' He rang off.

Anders had frozen in the centre of Place Kleber as he'd listened. Relief had thumped him in the belly.

There it was!

He stared ahead, unseeing. He didn't care about the professional vindication. What he cared about was that at last they *knew*. The man could never step back into his own skin again. At last, they were running him close, making him sweat. His face would be on every TV screen in Europe today. It wasn't over yet. But he, Anders, was spitting the contempt, the mockery, back in this criminal's face.

His phone rang again. Commissaire Rolland. 'Congratulations my dear colleague! When you unearthed *Monsieur Gas* from that flat, I was convinced it was a major breakthrough. Keep up the good work!'

All a bit premature, Anders, sardonic now, thought. But they were desperate for a bit of blue sky. He walked on to the library. The whole of the European establishment had been starved for good news. But they'd have to stay calm and clear-headed. It was a major step but Bayard wasn't finished. That convoluted mind, that killing machine, was perfectly capable of turning the heat and flames back on his pursuers.

And they were no longer looking for the man who had stared up at him from the photograph last night.

Anders straightened his shoulders, and went on, sweeping the precinct with his eyes.

He'd thought of keeping her in her flat today. Then he'd had this other idea. He picked up newspapers, and stopped at a cafe. Coffee, hot and black coffee, was vital. Amid commuters eating their breakfasts, he scanned the front-page report of Professor Lestang's murder. It had equal billing with the projected 5.00p.m. event. Lestang had been a celebrity in this city. *Les Dernieres Nouvelles d'Alsace* ran an editorial re-stating much that'd been written about the sinister campaign of the Judgment Day group, sketching a link with this latest atrocity. Beside a photograph of the murder scene and the main report a box said:

MARC LESTANG MURDER

Strasbourg University authorities last night were in shock at the outrage. Tributes are flowing in from the European Community, but what are the police doing? A top-level crime team from Paris and Interpol's anti-terrorist expert have been on the scene for a week – Inspector DP Anders, again, was at last night's murder scene. Are the police agencies anywhere near a breakthrough against the bloody madness which is moving in our midst with increasing virulence? The public has a right to be informed.

Understandable. Dourly, Anders reflected that they mightn't have seen the worst. However, the sensation of the terrorist's identity would today throw them a meaty bone. Dubost and Rolland were putting together a press conference in an hour's time. He paid the bill, and went out to avenue General-de-Gaulle. Pre-1945 it'd been Adolf-Hitler-Strasse, and before that ... the city's shuttlecock nationality was a wonder. Overnight he'd caught a cold, and he mopped his nose.

At 9.00a.m. Matucci and Ferrand brought her to the library. Shocked and ashen-faced, not a smear of cosmetics, and a black ribbon tying her hair back. The unshaven detectives were tense. She gave Anders a searching look, but didn't speak as they climbed the steps and rode the lift up. Anders studied her. Those big eyes ... that lovely, humane mouth. They saw her into her office, and Anders turned back and told them the news. His colleagues broke into grins. They were buoyed up by it. Anders talked to Ferrand for a moment and the Frenchman nodded, and hastened off.

Anders said to Matucci, who'd listened in, 'Go get cleaned up and eat. Then come back. Sleep'll have to wait.'

The big detective padded away, skirting the high aisles, giving them a searching look. A jungle ...

'Marc Lestang,' she whispered to Anders. A catch in her voice. 'Why?'

He regarded her with sympathetic concern. The death of an ex-lover could be one of life's saddest experiences. He told her what had happened last night. What Lestang had told him. All of it. He told her that there was a good chance that this man didn't yet know that his cover was blown. She listened, biting her lip, gazing down at her desk. The amber glints in her eyes had vanished. She looked up, shook her head. 'What a tragic waste.' He could only nod his agreement. Then he told her the man's name, and his high-flying job.

She stared at him in astonishment. 'God,' she said softly, 'I still remember nothing. I've never heard of this man. It's amazing,' she murmured. A nightmare ... what happens now?'

'I think he'll come here.' He watched the black pupils dilate. 'It'll be the opportunity to convey to him that the whole world will know today who he is. He's a zealot whose targets really are as the Judgment Day manifesto set out. People have been killed only because they threatened his 'crusade'. He values his cover. It's been marvellous for him. But once he knows it's blown you're no longer a threat.'

And it's the chance to grab him, he thought. If he doesn't bamboozle us with tricks.

'So we just sit and wait?' she said. With deep regret, he saw the wondering look in her eye. She studied him, an expression on her face he hadn't seen before. She understood that she was bait.

He said earnestly, 'Detectives are moving into position out of sight in the surrounding streets.'

There was a knock on the door and Ferrand came in. He handed Anders the mini-radio transmitter, with its red button. Anders turned to her. 'I can bring them in with a touch of this.' He indicated the button. 'Thanks,' he said to the detective, who went on his way. The library opened at ten — in twenty minutes.

'Please stay in your office. I'll be outside the door.'

He got up, and the leg creaked. 'Let me know if any unusual phone calls come through —'

'Wait,' she said decisively. She opened a drawer, removed a chunky pocket-sized volume and placed it before him. He glanced at her in surprise. It was old, and the title on the thick-boarded front cover was indecipherable. He opened it to the frontispiece —

The Night Serpent & Other Poems
by Anton Anders, Rome, 1872

His heart jolted. Quickly he turned to a page at random and read familiar lines. His research hadn't found this edition of the poet's master-work. He looked up. Her face was serious, yet in the midst of this danger a pleased smile flickered on her lips. He felt the weirdness of it – at *this* juncture.

She said quietly, 'We aren't computerised, but our systems are good. It was acquired in 1880 from an Italian resident of Strasbourg. Take it. Return it when you're ready.'

He nodded slowly, and put it in his pocket. He took his sense of weirdness, of unfathomable connections, out into the library, and watched a young woman open the main doors. The visitors who'd been waiting began to drift in. Swathed in coats and scarves they entered and disappeared into the book-stacked aisles. He'd shaken off the spell cast by the book and was concentrating.

An anonymous medley of faces, mostly male. All ages, but mainly older. No-one set his pulse racing. But that'd be the way of it. He was looking along a clear area to the entrance. To his left was the quarter hectare (he guessed) of dense and narrow aisles. Out of sight, in an area akin to a forest clearing, were reading tables. He sat down on a chair. Determined. Alert.

Ten-thirty. He checked that his communications were open. Ferrand's throaty voice confirmed they were. Eleven a.m. A girl brought him coffee. This was an institution of women. That floated through his mind. His research on the poet had brought familiarity with places like this – where time seemed dead and buried and, in a sense, had been.

The realisation had come to him that their single night of love had been put back like a tiny, intricately embossed volume on a remote shelf in this library. Exchanged for the one against which his heart was beating.

Forget that now. Forget the last ten days, studded with carnage. Sip coffee. The mayhem and madness of last night were still on him like the overnight odour of garlic on hands. *Concentrate.* Stay calm. He'd taken the safety off the Beretta. Had his right hand on the butt in his pocket, the left on the tiny radio transmitter. Matucci would have grunted his approval. Where was his colleague? Should've been back by this.

★

'Short and sweet,' Henri Bosson said with a smile. The PR flacks of both banks had worked late on the statement he was to make. At 9.00a.m Wilhelm Rath came to the boardroom, heard it read out loud by Henri, and signified his approval.

'Very short and sweet,' Henri said again, but the phrases were carefully crafted to present him in a courageous and decisive light – a champion of the new EC. The appropriate man to head the merged banking giant.

Rath cleared his throat, but his face was unreadable.

Dominique's vision was intense, but short-term; Henri considered that his was aligned to the far future and his ultimate personal place in the EC's corporate power-base.

She was fuming away in seclusion at their country estate. He didn't expect her at tonight's event. Her pride wouldn't permit such an appearance. The architect of the merger sacked! 'Dominique is out!' the staff were saying. He smiled. Let her consider *her* future. He'd no doubt that she'd be back before long.

He watched Rath leave. He'd stand throughout tonight's proceedings. Maximise tension. He'd heard back from his highly-placed contacts. His friend at the Bundes-bank had said, I can't talk to you about this, but had then said enough. Deutsche Credit-bank's mortgage portfolio was a problem, but it could be worked out. He was just the man to do it, and he'd force through any adjustments favouring Agribank.

Now he rehearsed the announcement again. His voice reverberated impressively in the empty boardroom. It sparked with verbal flashes. Like thunder and lightning in action above a broad landscape. He turned his head decisively, practised his look, into an imaginary camera lens. Steely.

XXI

THE EIGHTEENTH OF OCTOBER

P.M.

ONE P.M. STILL no Mattucci. The library was closing for lunch. The crowd was going out again. A young woman was locking up. How could they know that everyone had left? It was all so casual and sleepy. Marguerite had been closeted with an assistant all morning. Working on some facet of the library's administration, but thinking about what?

The assistant came out and closed Marguerite's door. She gave Anders a curious look. He stood up, listening. The woman's fading footfalls were devoured by the crouching silence. Despite his intentions, his thoughts were springing away in tangents. But out in that dusty mass of murdered trees, something was at work. *He was here.* Instantly Anders was sweating, but the library was coolish. He slipped the Beretta from its holster. Held the transmitter in his left hand. *Now,* he thought. He stood up.

'Monsieur Bayard! This is Inspector Anders. Your identity is known to the police. Your cover is blown.'

His voice reverberated over the stacks, going away and away. For a mini-second Anders thought he was hearing an echo – then it sliced into his brain:

'Inspector Anders! I have a hostage. Do not call your back-up or I will kill her. Do not move from where you are.'

It was the voice from the Frankfurt bank. From the side of the Ill.

From the heart of the stacks came a woman's terrified scream. On the back of his neck Anders' hair became electric. He flung open Marguerite's door. The room was empty. He turned and slipped into the nearest aisle, moved down it going fast for him. Damn this creaking leg! At a junction he turned right. The scream had been cut off.

A sound. *Behind.*

'Sorry, Inspector, I need to get out –'

Anders whirled, whipping up the Beretta. A sledge-hammer smashed him in the chest. He was flying in space. WHAM! His shoulders cannoned into bare boards. His brain was brilliant with white light. Deafened. His right heel was drumming a tattoo on the floor. No breath. Dust-choking.

Then he was sitting up, arms clasped across his chest, coughing, but breathing a bit, the pain in his heart now absolutely the dominant thing in his universe. Vision blurred. Thank God! Marguerite and another woman: floating towards him along the corridor. Her black hair drifting above her head as though underwater. His left hand had a vice-like grip on the transmitter. He brought his right hand over, and jabbed the red button. He gasped, as a fresh spasm of pain sliced the dream-world clean in two.

Matucci's pistol was out. In his hand before the sound of the gunshot had faded. He bounded up the staircase into under-powered lighting, a landing dim and icy as a chapel.

Library's main door ajar. He pulled up, eyes scanning fast right −

Out of the alcove to his left a karate chop caught his rotating neck below the ear. He pitched forward, was down on hands and knees, his pistol slithering away over marble. Dazed. *Dead* next? But footsteps: retreating fast. He shook his head. Agony! Spat out blood. He'd bitten his tongue. He struggled up onto his haunches, gazed at the floor. His head felt disconnected from his spine.

More running. Ferrand and two detectives came up the stairs breathing hard. Matucci waved them into the library ...

Unsupported, Anders was standing between the two women, but his shoulders were pressed against book-spines. Both of his hands were holding his heart. With the right one, slowly he fumbled inside his suit coat and found the volume. He held it up. The hole in the board cover was precision-tooled. He turned the volume side-on. The bullet was affixed within the pages. Mounted there like a trophy.

He stared at it.

Marguerite began to laugh. An edge of hysteria. It stopped as abruptly as the scream had.

He let his right hand with the book drop to his side, kept his left where it was. 'Who screamed?' She hadn't heard it, had been in her private lavatory, which was behind panelling and was news to him. The answer to that question was never found out. But later, Anders thought of that counter-tenor-like voice. A voice which had surely needed the disguise of the synthesiser.

'He can handle himself, which we always knew,' Matucci said. He was talking about seeing a chiropractor, but

Anders knew it was just talk. The big detective had been on the end of a lot of violence. For his part, Anders expected to have a bruise over his heart the size of a dessert plate. But the morning was history.

Marguerite had been escorted home, and detectives were on guard. But Bayard knew the score now. She's no longer in hazard, Anders thought. If logic prevails.

The Grand Hotel was lit up like a power station, the security as conspicuous as that surrounding the President of the Republic. Commissaire Dubost growled, 'What identity is he going to be in for this junket, Inspector? Houdini?'

Anders was unsmiling. His chest was aching with a dull persistence.

'By God, you nearly had him – or he nearly had you,' Dubost muttered. He glowered at the Italian, 'Bosson's been a total pain in the arse. Turned down the Minister flat when he tried to embargo this little show. The other night, the dragon woman implied I didn't have the balls to work with the situation.'

'Unbelievable,' Anders murmured.

Dubost nodded. 'Everything's under control.' He shrugged. 'But he's got more lives than a cat.' Police with bomb-detection apparatus had been busy all day, as had others with sniffer dogs. The assembling media, queuing up to enter, were complaining volubly about the rigorous checks. The hotel staff's nerves were at breaking point. Matucci lit a cigarette, moved his neck experimentally. A hotel manager stepped forward. 'Please put that out.' He fell back from the detective's look.

One newspaper Anders had seen had said: *'The ballroom will be the stage for the most dramatic corporate theatre seen in a decade.'* Now the TV crews were setting up cameras, snaking cables across the polished dance-floor.

Bayard ... Anders' eyes roamed over the assembled faces. He must've got the message at the library. He'll be as dead as Gas; another 'identity' executed. In that mini-second before he went down, Anders had not even glimpsed him. He won't take a suicidal risk. This was only one battle in a long crusade.

His eyes continued to sweep the ballroom. The chairs on the stage awaited the arrival of the directors. In the auditorium, the rows of seats, flanked by the banks of cameras, were now taken up by a phalanx of journalists. They were screwing necks around, sizing up the occasion. Hotel staff were in position with hand-held microphones.

If by another feat of sleight-of-hand he'd got a bomb in, many bystanders would be killed. That didn't square with what he'd said, what he'd demonstrated thus far. The unfortunate bystanders who'd been eliminated had, by past association, or quirks of fate, become threats. In the end, anyone was discardable: classic reasoning of the terrorist.

Dubost and Gerard and other senior police had ceased hurrying around. The camera crews had become tense. Nerves crackled in the air like radio static. This was going out live and the clock was ticking down. The ballroom's gilt-outlined doors sprang open. Commissaire Rolland appeared, his silver head looking incongruous to Anders beneath a peaked cap. The directors, two by two, followed, Henri Bosson in the lead with Wilhelm Rath, who appeared as calm and urbane as though he were entering his favourite nightclub. Bosson was serious and controlled: a major corporate citizen of the EC, about to achieve star status.

If he lived through tonight.

'What do you think?' Matucci muttered.

'Something's going to happen,' Anders replied, 'but it won't be here. We'll stick close to Bosson.' His colleague looked at him, and Anders wondered if his confidence was another mistake. Where should he be? The trinity of executions set up by Dupont with his *Paris-Match* articles was one shy. The man, Bayard, being what he was, would be compelled to complete it. But how and where? There'd be a plan snaking through all this as twisted as those TV cables.

★

Bayard alighted briskly from the small dark-green van. The two police cars which had earlier been stationed outside the apartment building had gone. He smiled to himself. A tall man with reddish hair, wearing steel-rimmed glasses, dressed in maintenance overalls, a company logo sewed on the left breast. He took a carry-tray of tools and repair materials from the rear of the vehicle. He slammed the door shut, turned his back on the Place de la Republique, and entered the apartments.

The detective in the lobby on the third floor heard the lift coming. It stopped at his floor. He rose from his seat, and put his hand on the pistol in his belt. His companion had been pulled into the Grand Hotel, had left making a sarcastic remark about the inadequacy of his life insurance, adding: 'Have a good snooze you lucky prick.'

Who was this? He drew his pistol.

★

Henri stood at the microphone. The directors of the two corporations clustered behind him. In an uneasy, breath-

284

holding silence a barrage of camera-flashes went off in his face. A man wearing ear-phones was gesturing warningly, suddenly gave a thumbs up. Henri spoke to Europe: 'This will be a very brief statement. It is my pleasure to announce that the boards of Agribank France SA and Deutsche Rural-Credit Bank DG have voted to merge our institutions, subject to approval of our shareholders, and all official approvals have been granted.' He blinked at another frenzy of flashes. The timbre of his voice was at its deepest. 'The merged entity will become a giant institution serving the regional and agricultural sectors in Germany and France. Our shareholders, our customers, our staff will each derive great benefits from the rationalisation and the technological developments that will follow. Indeed, it will be of immense economic benefit to our two nations, to the European Community, and shows the way to other great Franco–German partnerships.'

He dropped his hand with the note he'd been reading and gazed with that steely look into the nearest camera. His voice was lower, even more rumbling. 'We have been under a bitter and fanatical attack from left-wing extremists. It has not swayed us from our duty. Progress will never, never, be stopped by the craven assassin. That is the lesson of history. That is our message.'

He held his gaze into the glinting lens. Then he turned, and Rath and he were shaking hands, then embracing.

Dubost's mobile phone rang. 'Who?' The competition commissioner's secretary in Brussels. He stepped into an alcove to hear, the journalists were now shouting their questions. 'Yes, this is Commissaire Dubost,' he said loudly.

The voice, a male one, was breaking up 'Monsieur Bayard has an apartment in Strasbourg. Also, the Directorate has a small office in the European Parliament building which he is in the habit of using.' Dubost was jotting down particulars. 'Monsieur Bayard travelled to Strasbourg yesterday, the Commissioner's instructed me to offer our full co-operation.' Dubost hurried to Anders, spoke urgently into his ear. *'Monsieur Bosson how many jobs will be lost in the merger?'* an amplified voice was demanding.

Anders went to Matucci. 'We're leaving,' he said.

The Interpol men hurried out through the lobby. Matucci had beckoned Ferrand. Outside the hotel, rows of limousines and escorting police cars were waiting to convey the assembled directors away. Expectant drivers, police, were standing everywhere. Hurriedly they climbed into Ferrand's car and a moment later the dour Frenchman took them out into the traffic and headed for the parliament. Behind them Gerard and several of his men ran to cars. They were going to the apartment.

The competition commissioner, belatedly, was seeing the ramifications of the directorate's unbelievable connection to the terrorism. To the terrorist! He's woken up, Anders thought.

This sortie was a hunch on the run. Bayard should be keeping clear of his old haunts now, but you never knew. They were running him close and maybe there'd be a slip-up. He had an up-market apartment here! He brooded on this man, moving in the city from it to the semi-squalid flat where Gas had done his business. Now both were cut off to him. He'll have another bolt-hole, be a new man on the prowl, he thought grimly.

The tyres slithered on wet tarmac. The old streetscapes jerked past, at this hour as dark and grainy as a 1940's newsreel. 'Be there in ten,' Ferrand growled.

★

286

In the rear of the green van, now abandoned in a back street near the Place de la Republique, he'd changed from his maintenance man's outfit to a smart, pinstripe grey suit. The reddish hair and the steel-rimmed glasses were gone. The fair-headed man, carrying an expensive brown raincoat, walked easily but swiftly to a taxi-rank a few streets away. The area was as quiet in an evening reverie. Under his arm was folded this morning's newspaper. Its headline said: *Bosson Expected To Give Merger Green Light.* Quite right. Wretched Henri Bosson had been playing his little games of postponement, politics, and deception. Now they'd play his dead march.

He would've liked to've stayed and watched, but it was impossible. Every minute he delayed now added danger. It might already be too dangerous; he'd have to size up the situation when he got there. It'd been a mistake to leave the new identity papers in the safe, but Anders had amazingly broken his cover. He smiled. Who'd have thought the inspector wore a bullet-proof vest. He'd have sworn he wasn't the type. He entered a taxi and gave directions. Five-twenty p.m. They'd be embroiled in that fiasco at The Grand, and he'd be at the office in seven minutes.

★

No bomb, no disturbance, nothing! Henri Bosson in the back seat of the Rolls Royce felt euphoric. And of course, no Dominique! He should phone her tonight, commence rebuilding bridges. It shouldn't be too hard. She was the most pragmatic woman in the world. And this had been a monumental lesson for her. He'd call her after he'd watched himself on the 7.00p.m. news.

The drama of the ballroom, the cut and thrust of the

brief question and answer session he'd allowed the crowd of media, were relegated to another world as he rode home to a quiet, solitary dinner. The police had been adamant: no public celebration. All the directors should immediately slip back within their security blankets.

'It isn't over yet,' the tough policeman from Paris had said. But didn't they have the bastards on the run? Too off-balance to mount any further threats – falling apart like the Red Army Faction had?

The two black unmarked police cars moved ahead and behind. Like ravens in flight, he thought. Ravens – those madmen had used that image in one of their insane messages. A regular patrol car led the convoy. The detective-sergeant sat beside Henri's driver, stolid and unspeaking. All Henri had gleaned about him was that a dry-clean was indicated for his suit. The odour.

He grinned. A bottle of champagne. Then he'd put on Beethoven and have a memorable concert.

The usual rush and bustle – as they saw him out of the car, into the building, into the lift, into his apartment. The lone detective in the lobby was on his feet. The returning colleague said, 'Have a good snooze?' It looked like it.

The inspector in charge opened the door and stepped aside for Henri. His overcoat draped over his shoulders, he strode into the hall. Dominique was standing at its far end, her arms held wide. 'Darling! Congratulations! You were wonderful!' The phrases shot at him in her warm and playful voice. The voice he'd first heard on the stage of Bordeaux's Grand Theatre. The red lips were curved enticingly.

He halted, beaming. 'Darling! You're here. This is *so* marvellous.'

'Room 1713,' Anders said tersely. What might he be confronted with there?

The flags of the member countries of the Council of Europe snapped in the breeze as Ferrand squealed to a halt before the vast circular steel and glass construct which housed the European Parliament. He stopped in a no-parking zone and they scrambled out. They hastened across the forecourt and entered the building. Anders was sweating at this momentum and his stump was burning. Concerned, Matucci glanced at him. Through glass, he could see into the great circular heart of the building. They flashed their accreditation to the security guards, and were on the way to the lifts.

'Floor six,' Ferrand muttered.

The floor was quiet. A curving corridor of shut doors, each numbered. An occasional voice, once the tapping on a keyboard – but overpoweringly, silence.

Anders assumed the lead now, and waved the others back as they reached number 1713. He drew the Beretta and gently tried the door. Open. Quietly he turned the handle. His insides seemed to've frozen. The anteroom was lit but no-one was present. A doorway opened to the left and quietly Anders moved to it. He stared, as if mesmerised, at a small safe with a wide-open door … an empty room with an essence of movement, of disturbed air – like a breeze had just passed through. An interior door slammed.

In his awakened shock, he cried: *'The corridor!'*

Matucci and Ferrand ran back into the corridor, Anders followed. It was empty. *'Downstairs!'* They ran to the stairs. Anders making his best speed, took the lift.

Lovely in the lighting, the expanse of pink paving stone outside rolled away before Anders' eyes. The only people on it were Matucci and Ferrand standing there, gazing at Anders. They had an air of mystification, and embarrassment.

Unconsciously, Anders was rubbing the pain over his heart. Matucci was shrugging, Ferrand looking down at his square-toed shoes. They'd heard the door slam, seen nothing else.

'Yes, Monsieur Bayard came in a few minutes ago,' the security guard told Anders. Was he still in the building? No. He'd have his special exits. Anders looked up at his colleagues, as though he'd made a decision. 'This sounds melodramatic, but the only way he'll ever be taken is to shoot first and ask questions later. Are you ready for that, Matucci?'

'Ready!' the big detective responded.

If we ever get a chance, Anders thought. And it'll take a trick shot. The man had been in that room seconds before Anders had appeared in the doorway. Had he vanished in a flicker of an eyelid? God knows, enough flickering was going on. The detective shook his head.

Matucci was staring at him intensely. The flesh seemed to have evaporated from Anders' face, leaving white skin stretched over bone. A trick of light ... had Anders stepped over some sort of line? Then Matucci remembered the two doors in Monsieur Cage's room in Paris. And the dazed mystification of the security guards the night Felix Servais was murdered. And the rest of it.

Even so, 'shoot first' was absolutely opposed to the credo Anders lived by. Until he was backed into a corner from which he saw no way out, apparently, then everything was up for grabs, and a ruthless man stepped from the depths. On the whole, Matucci took it as a good sign.

★

Henri and Dominique had eaten a splendid dinner prepared by their cook, who'd padded back from the food
markets at 5.30p.m., accompanied by the small dog. A
bottle of Verve Clicquot 1984 had been delicious. They'd
watched Henri's performance on the 7.00p.m. news.
During the dinner, she'd reached across the table and said:
'Darling, I'm going to fuck *you* tonight. You won't have to
move a muscle.'

Now she said, as they left the table, 'You *are* going to
put me on the new board aren't you?'

His eyes swept her face. 'Naturally,' he said with a grin.
It'd been a salutary lesson to her. He went into his study
and began a series of phone calls. Ten minutes later he
reappeared. 'It's done.'

She opened her arms. 'Darling!'

Henri reflected that it was a game they were playing –
not dissimilar to the convoluted manoeuvring which the
two big institutions had been engaged in. That game had
been put to bed, where would this one take them? Where
it'd been taking them for the past several years he suspected. At any point in time, Dominique could be trusted
only so far as her ambition was being satisfied. She was like
a leading competitor in the Tour de France. One day winning a stage and wearing the yellow jersey, the next losing,
and surrendering it … the next … As for her sex life, he
was pretty sure that she obtained her satisfaction elsewhere; her performances in their marriage bed had to do
with the manipulation of their relationship.

He smiled happily to himself. For the moment, he had
her exactly where he wanted her. 'Why don't you,' he said,

fondly, 'fix us liqueurs. I think I'll turn on Beethoven.'

He inserted the CD in the sound system, took his baton and went to his chair. He sat forward, gazing down into the Place de la Republique – that bracelet of light – the baton poised. The music exploded in the room. Simultaneously, still leaning forward, his arms swept into action.

'Bravo!' she called from the cocktail cabinet twenty paces down the salon. The orchestra boomed, his exhilaration soared. What a day! He flung his head back against the headrest.

BOOMMM!

The liqueur glasses Dominique held shot ceilingwards, her body seemed airborne, buffeted by a great blast. Her brain was jelly; her eardrums, crazy … She found herself prostrate on the floor, but staring along the salon to the chair. From the headless torso, a stream of red was gushing upwards. The front door crashed open, the two detectives burst in and pulled up, mouths slack. Dominique shrieked, echoing the car tyres below which a micro-second before had done the same, as Henri's head went in spirited bounds across the circular road like a football that'd been mis-kicked over a fence. Frantic horn blowing had erupted.

Commissaire Dubost was speechless. He's not with it, Anders thought. Understandable … he barely was himself. The Paris crime chief was standing well away from the chair and its decapitated occupant, gazing in incomprehension at the roughly circular exit hole in the glass through which the late banker's head had been propelled, and from which a maze of severe cracks radiated.

Forensics had arrived: amid carnage, a touch of what passed for normality. Anders own brain was inert, his nerves paralysed. He hadn't recovered from the overload at the parliament. It was fruitless, and of no consequence now, how Bayard had got in to plant the explosive in the chair's ex-headrest (the chair had been decapitated, too). All that mattered was the *Paris-Match* trinity had been closed out. Having failed to stop the merger, Bayard had exacted the threatened retribution. Now he would disappear. *Finis* – till the next time.

Dubost wandered aimlessly through the debris to where Anders stood with Matucci and Ferrand. The whites of his eyes were a misty red. He was ultra-shaggy. But to Anders, his bear-like image now resembled an air-filled figure which had become semi-deflated. 'He's beaten us. We're powerless,' Dubost was muttering, in a weird way, to himself. 'I'm finished.'

Anders nodded sympathetically. It wasn't the moment to tell how he'd slipped through their fingers at the parliament, though at present he doubted Dubost would take in anything but his own trauma. Apparently, Dominique Bosson was closeted in the study with her maid-servant for company. The two detectives in the hall told Matucci this. 'Eh, boys! Keep up the good work,' he said going back in, followed by their glares.

'He'll be well away by now,' Gerard ventured. 'Tucked into his bolt-hole.' He couldn't bring himself to consider how he'd got into the apartment to plant it.

Anders could. But the solitary detective on duty in the foyer had been adamant: he'd seen no-one. Wearily, Anders hadn't pushed it. He thought: assuming it was done during the Grand Hotel session, he'll have an hour or more start. Could be in Germany ... many places. The police at the airport, the station, would be looking for Bayard. But Bayard had gone the way of Gas.

'She's making calls,' Ferrand said tersely. He'd seen this

when the maid-servant had hurried out. He'd glimpsed the taut-faced woman, hair hanging over her face, being very business-like on the phone.

Soon Henri's PR manager, looking shaken, turned up, and was shown into the study.

Held by the traffic policeman who'd retrieved it, Henri's head was in a plastic shopping bag, imprinted with the name of a women's boutique, and his body was now being packaged up for its trip to its autopsy.

Everyone jumped as the shattered window collapsed abruptly into the room. Anders stared at it, then wandered around the salon. His mind had recommenced functioning. He gazed at a picture of wild horses. The movements of the technicians behind him were reflected in its glass. An idea came. How to devise a situation where it could be enacted? Now his thinking was concentrated on the future.

Below, a commotion had broken out. The media had arrived: the Grand Hotel had been left a ghost town, and Inspector Gerard and a local detective were remonstrating with a crowd of men and women who were paying out cables from vans, setting up cameras, jostling around the building's entrance, shouting questions. Gerard came upstairs to speak to Dubost, but the commissaire remained incommunicado. At that moment, her face pale and severe, Dominique made her entrance. Her white frock was stained. Somehow streaks of red had appeared on it. A blood-like streak traced down her left cheek. The blonde hair was in a semi-controlled, alluring display. Her eyes were wide: horror-struck. 'I am going to give a media conference – in that room. Please allow the press to come up.'

Gerard looked at Dubost, who remained in a private

world. 'Madame, I'm afraid you're not. This is a crime scene.'

Bastard, she thought concisely. 'Then I will give it on the steps outside.'

Anders had put aside his thinking when she'd appeared, and was studying her. How amazing! He'd frequently observed ambition in play throughout his long investigator's career, but he'd never seen it as rampant as this.

She, her PR man, Anders, Matucci, Ferrand, and Gerard descended in the lift. The TV cameras were set-up to take it out live to Europe. Tonight was to've been Henri's really big moment, Anders marvelled. In a way, he supposed it still was. She stationed herself in the place indicated.

He'll be watching. It came to Anders. Wherever he is he'll be studying the impact. Suddenly, he felt excitement building in him.

The ear-phoned men became tense. Dominique had requested the Channel 4 reporter, Marie Ledru, who was keyed-up, moistening her lips, glancing at her board. Suddenly she was doing her business, engaging the world out there with a breathless intensity. 'Henri Bosson, chairman-elect of the managing board of the Franco–German Agribank has been assassinated at his house overlooking Strasbourg's Place de la Republique. At approximately 7.15p.m. Monsieur Bosson's life was ended when he was decapitated by a bomb which had been placed in the headrest of his chair. The Judgment Day terrorist group has carried out its obscene threat.'

The reporter turned. 'Madame Dominique Bosson, who was present when the bomb exploded, will speak to you live from outside the bombed residence in Strasbourg.'

The actress in Dominique had risen to the surface.

Anders was reminded of the pictures of Jackie Kennedy after *the* assassination. She brushed back her hair. Her red nail-polish had been removed. She was ethereal.

'Tonight I stand here a widow. My beloved husband has been foully murdered. Shareholders, staff, and customers of Agribank France and Deutsche Rural–Credit Bank, citizens of the European Community, look at me, see the horror. Look at me, see a grieving woman. The merger we've fought for will go through. Nothing can stop it. You, the assassins! You cowards! You have stopped at nothing and you have stopped nothing. It is true many jobs will be lost in the merger. This is in the price of progress. In the name of efficiency. For the ultimate benefit of all. That is the world we live in. The globalised world.'

She threw back her head and her hair, projected her jaw at watching millions. 'I'm a woman but I'm not afraid. You cowards. Do your worst.'

She stared into the live cameras, her pale lips parted.

Some of the watching journalists were applauding. Matucci spoke into Anders' ear, 'The bastard won't be able to resist a challenge like that.'

Yes! Anders was nodding, it was exactly his own thought. Perhaps it gave him a plan, at last. A double-header. Madame Bosson and himself. Two in one. *His* ego, *his* ambitions would bring him back – like a typhoon circling back to wreak havoc a second time. Perhaps. But what to do?

★

Twenty-two kilometres north-west of Strasbourg on the A4 autoroute driving a big silver Mercedes, he heard the broadcast on the radio. He pulled off into a lay-by and listened intently to the announcer – then to Madame Bosson. His gloved hands rested quietly on the steering wheel. He was dressed in a blue suit, a camel overcoat folded by his side. An elegant moustache had appeared on his upper lip and would be replaced by the real thing as soon as he could manage it. Contact lenses showed brown eyes to the casual observer. A touch of make-up in a couple of places had added ten years. This was aided by the slower and more deliberate body and head movements he'd adopted. In his breast pocket was the documentation of his new identity – recovered just in time from the safe. Timing! In Paris awaited his new apartment.

Madame Bosson was running true to form. She was a type of woman for which he felt the deepest antipathy. He'd got Henri Bosson, but the merger was to proceed. As he heard this, his brain grew cold and he felt a churning in his belly. What would it take to save those jobs? To stop this obscenity?

He started up the engine and carefully infiltrated the Mercedes back into the fast-running traffic. He began to think with even greater concentration.

The green van, which he hadn't planned to see again, remained parked in the back street. They wouldn't be expecting another strike at the same scene. They'd be putting a big effort into watching airports, stations, here, across Europe. It would have to be tonight. Within the next few hours, it was imperative to be in his new identity, to keep it safe and untainted. Possible? Confusion reigned in their ranks. Bosson, the target, was dead. There might be a crack to slip in, and slip out. For a practitioner of his unsurpassed skills, and his unbounded luck. What a challenge! On a second departure, he wouldn't be able to take this exit from Strasbourg. By then there'd be checkpoints in place.

But he'd plotted an alternative exit over secondary roads, and if, unfortunately, he was challenged by a patrol car it'd be tragic for them.

Angrily, he steered off the autoroute and took an over-pass. A few minutes later he was heading back to Strasbourg.

★

Outside in the chill air, Anders was pacing the river-side walk beside the cafe. Matucci and Ferrand were inside drinking coffee, watching him through the window. He was oblivious to this, to his surroundings, to the cold. Into his mind had come a vision of that scene: the duel in which his poet ancestor had been killed in 1875. Anton Anders had taken the field against an evil man; a profes-sional duellist; had taken a stand, made a move in a forlorn hope.

It was the identical vision to the one eighteen months ago, when he'd contrived the monumental strike against the mafia that had mesmerised the nation. He was walking with a measured tread, his eyes on the path. *Was it possible? Madame Bosson, unconsciously, had hurled down the gauntlet – baited the hook. But had he seen her TV broadcast? Would it bring him back?*

Anders paused, and gazed at the river. He was trying to get inside *that* mind. The stakes would be high enough for him, a terrific boost to his crusade if he could bring it off. His rampant egocentricity, his sense of omnipotence might sway him. He was into his pacing again, trying to keep the nerves and excitement down. *Against the run of play, as he had that other time, could he create this opportunity?*

Dubost had said 'We're powerless.' It was close to the

mark. Thus far. Unless, he, Anders, could put himself on the same level as that dark mind.

He took off his hat, and felt the cold air on his brow. It would be necessary to offer him a duelling ground which he calculated he could kill on, and escape from. The place came slipping into his mind as smoothly as if it'd been biding its time, awaiting the trigger to be pulled in his brain.

Inspector Ferrand was shocked by Anders' proposal. But he'd seen enough of the Interpol man, learned enough of his past actions against terrorists, the mafia. If it failed, the Frenchman knew his career would be ruined. But he didn't see how he could stand in the way of it. Not after what had been going on.

He looked at Matucci. What did he think? But the big detective kept his eyes down, fixed on the cafe table. It was a terrific risk. And would this madman be enticed back? He lit a Gauloise with a deliberation which befitted the gravity of the decision.

Anders sat quietly, now that he'd explained most of it. Watching the performance through the cafe's window, Matucci had been deeply uneasy. He said tensely, 'Am I right? You're going to use her as a goat staked out in the jungle at night. To bring the tiger.' He watched Anders narrowly. That was it, all right. How could he think of putting even that woman's life in such terrific hazard, in a solo confrontation with that merchant of death, that mad spell-binder? He took an oblique look at Anders' face. The fluttering under the left eye had ceased. For the moment.

'A colourful way of putting it.'

But right on the nail, Ferrand thought. The excitement had begun in him.

Matucci glanced at his watch: 10.50p.m. 'But where is

he? If his brain's going at its usual rate, he'll be having a drink in a bar on the other side of Europe by now, won't he?'

Anders, his hands lying either side of his coffee cup, pondered the predestination in him. 'Perhaps not. He's still on a winning streak. We've been peeling back his identities, and doubtless he's assumed another. His mind's an enigma. Up to a point. And Madame Bosson couldn't help playing the actor, couldn't help laying down that contemptuous challenge. With his personality, a terrific temptation.'

'She has a way with contempt,' Matucci agreed.

Anders nodded. 'The police won't be expecting him to come back for another strike. He'll see it that way,' he said quietly.

'What if *she* won't play ball?' Ferrand said. 'And what about the cops guarding her?'

Anders gave him a level look. 'That woman isn't afraid of anything. And the police won't have the option.'

Presently they left the cafe and drove out into another Strasbourg night whispering with rain. Anders wondered whether the fates were going to bring it all together for him.

When the trio got out of the lift the inspector and the sergeant now on duty in the foyer looked surprised. 'Is she still up?' Ferrand asked.

'I believe so,' the inspector said. 'She's been on the phone ever since the media mayhem finished.' He looked curiously at Anders, who'd been so prominent in the investigation. He'd not seen him face to face.

'We've got orders to take her to a safe-house,' Ferrand said, ringing the doorbell.

'What?' the inspector said. 'Nobody's told us.'

Anders jerked his head, clicked his tongue, with feigned impatience at this slip-up.

'I report to Dubost, I'll have to have his authority.'

'Call him,' Anders said shortly. Swiftly he'd taken a gaze into Dubost's current mental situation. Hoped he wouldn't have to use extreme measures here. The inspector took out his mobile and punched in numbers.

'He's not responding ... I'll try Gerard ...' He punched in more numbers ... 'No response, either.'

'They're in slumberland,' Matucci said. 'For Chrissakes.'

The door opened and the maid-servant stood there regarding them with reddened, accusing eyes. 'One moment, please,' Anders said to her. Inwardly, he'd sighed with relief at the unanswered phones.

Ferrand said, 'Philippe, you've known me for twenty years. Would I do anything crazy?'

They gazed at each other. Never trust someone that talks to you like that, Anders was thinking. The inspector nodded them in.

Dominique stood in the middle of the study.

'Madame Bosson, I'm Inspector Anders.'

'My memory's not defective.'

He nodded. 'Following your broadcast, we've reason to believe your life is in immediate danger.'

The traumatised but courageous face on the TV screen earlier now wore a hard enamelled expression. 'So?'

'I require you to come with us. We have a safe-house arranged for tonight.'

With an assessing look at the Italian policeman, she took a bag from a side-table and began placing items in it. Then she shrugged into her fur coat as the maid held it.

They brought her out and installed her in the rear-seat of Ferrand's car. Matucci got in beside her. His hand on the door-handle, Anders casually scanned the place. The black-trunked, near-skeletal trees in the centre struck a funereal note. Life was absent except in their own activity. The two uniformed police stood like statues, seeing them off.

Was he close by? Watching? Equipped to follow? If he wasn't, Anders' plan was already in shreds, and he wasn't seeing a thing that looked out of place or gave him any hope.

Despite his confident utterances in the cafe, grimly he faced the fact that Matucci might be correct: Bayard could be sitting in a bar in, say, Amsterdam, slotted into his new identity, planning the next march of his crusade. Anders wondered if his hatred for the terrorist breed, now graphically for this individual, was compromising his thought processes, sabotaging his judgment. Certainly, he was running with the old emotions; back to the worst of the Italian Red Brigade days.

He got in, slamming the door to send the sound across the place like a gunshot. 'Don't be in too much of a hurry,' he said to Ferrand as they started off.

The caretaker-cum-security man of the Palais Rohan, in the small side door, blinked at Ferrand's and Anders' IDs. The former episcopal residence dated back to 1730, standing between the cathedral and the quietly flowing Ill, seemed steeped in its accumulated history, in the autumn night. Frozen. Silent.

Ferrand had explained their requirements. The man, mystified and nervous, stood aside deferentially. Matucci took Dominique Bosson in. She hadn't spoken a word since they'd left. Ferrand, with a glance at Anders, followed. The Italian waited, gazing back across the courtyard at the

302

front of the building towards the large portal. The great mass of yellow and pink sandstone glowed in the dark, as though stored daylight was being excreted. Ferrand's parked car looked abandoned. No movement, only a cold breeze. He turned and went inside. The caretaker shot home two bolts.

'What is your name?' Anders asked the man.

'Jacques, monsieur.'

'Are you alone?' He could hear echoing steps as the others climbed the staircase. He'd told them where to go. His throat had tightened with nerves, the taste of steel back in his mouth.

'The duty maintenance man is down in the basement, monsieur … the heating's not on I'm afraid.'

And very few electric lights, Anders thought. 'Never mind,' he said. 'Do you have an electric torch I could borrow Monsieur Jacques?'

'Yes, monsieur.' The man's rubber-soled shoes squeaked away on the parquet floor towards a door to the basement stairs. Anders went back to the door they'd entered by. He slid back the two bolts. After a moment's thought, he didn't snib the old-fashioned lock open. It would be nothing to this man. If he came. He went upstairs, each step seeming a great effort. He murmured, 'Get yourself together.'

This suite of rooms, on the first floor overlooking the courtyard of the vast square building, was what had attracted his interest on the previous visit. Specifically, the narrow corridor about twenty metres long and empty of furniture, which was the only approach. It had struck Anders that the original eighteenth-century occupant of the suite had required privacy. And, perhaps, a good warning of persons approaching. The various apartments to which it gave entrance were relatively small, but sumptuously appointed.

Dominique Bosson was no stranger to the Palais Rohan.

When Anders came in, she said, 'Why here?'

He looked at her gravely. 'Is there a safer house in Strasbourg, madame?'

Matucci gave him a look. This was no safe-house: it was an invitation to dance. Was he going to tell her?

Anders went and took the tasselled protective cord off a divan. 'Please make yourself comfortable.'

Her eyes, which had seen so much tonight, regarded him with hard curiosity. 'I think you're setting a trap, Inspector. Am I right?'

Matucci and Ferrand stood by, faces expressionless.

He inclined his head, as though considering this. 'I hope by tomorrow there'll be no further need for safe-houses. Or protection.'

'Do you ever give straight answers?' She turned, and sat down, wrapping herself from head to ankle in the fur coat. 'They're not to smoke,' she said with a succinct nod at the two detectives. She took a second look at the cut of Matucci's suit, as though she was seeing something out of context.

Yes, a remarkable woman, Anders thought again. The vision of her husband's headless torso, spouting gore, must be hot-etched on her brain, but she gave no sign of it. And afterwards – all those phone calls.

He left the room. Outside, he walked up the corridor like a duellist stepping off distance, came back, thinking it through. Large double doors gave access from the corridor to the room where the others waited. One of the doors was locked in place, the other open. He stared through the opening. About five metres into the room was a high-backed chair. He walked back to the end of the corridor, turned, and had his centre-piece. Now about twenty-five metres distant, the chair was framed in the doorway. He returned, and considered the small alcove located in the side of the corridor – about five metres from the double doors. He re-entered the room. Dominique Bosson sat calm and statuesque. Matucci and Ferrand were enduring the uneasy silence.

'Madame, I'm going to ask you to sit in that chair,' Anders said quietly.

She raised her eyebrows. 'Really?'

'It is important.'

'For whom?'

'In the interests of arresting the person responsible for your husband's death.'

'Person? That's new. How much have the police really told us?'

Anders was silent. She studied his serious face, a slight humorous twist to her freshly-painted lips. Suddenly, she shrugged, rose, and walked across to the chair with the air of a rich woman striding through a Parisian house of haute couture.

Anders turned to his colleagues. 'Leave now. Go out, get in your car and drive off.'

'Let's go,' Matucci said to Ferrand.

As he'd told them, he was lowering the odds: luring the bastard in. Matucci stared along the corridor: it was a killing ground – but for whom? He was sweating. He told himself: if the bastard comes, there'll be no prisoner taken.

The detectives each made eye-contact with Anders, and left.

Dominique sat down, arranging the fur around her, one

white hand on the collar, and gazed through the doorway at the long approach. Then she stared at Anders. A new look, acknowledging a fellow ruthless operator. The risk-taker.

'No coffee,' she'd said caustically. 'How do I get through a night like this without coffee?'

He turned his back for a moment while he drew and armed the Beretta.

'No need to be delicate for me, Inspector,' she said. 'I trust this isn't a bad career move for us both.'

'Try to sleep, Madame,' he murmured sardonically.

She smiled.

'I'm going to take up a position in the corridor,' he said. 'In the small alcove just beyond these doors. If any action starts, please throw yourself down on the floor.'

'Inspector, do I really look like a person who'll throw myself on the floor?' She had been down on the floor once tonight; not again.

He smiled tensely. Anton Anders, facing death in the dawnlight of that chilly 1875 morning, would not have had in mind a woman of this kind. He said, 'I urge you to do it.'

The corridor was lit with half a dozen small chandeliers equidistantly positioned. The polished floorboards shone mellow in their light. He held the Beretta at his side. The torch stood on its end within reach of his left hand. Faintly, he heard the car leave.

Had *he* been watching their departure from the apartment? Had he followed them? And even if so, would he step into this jungle clearing? The questions whispered in Anders' brain. Lestang's and his own reading of Bayard's mentality took them only so far. The brain he'd been tracking these ten days was cunning and flexible. Almost certainly it could read the mind of DP Anders. Anders was counting on that; that'd he'd know the playing field had been levelled. That it was winner take all ... he'd come to the Libraire Kleber after all.

Yet nothing could be counted out. That black-humoured maniac, geared to the extravagant, the outrageous, that ego, couldn't, mustn't, have evaporated into anonymity. Anders drew in a long breath. Despite the temperature, moisture had drenched his armpits. Swiftly he went over it: if he came – it could only be down this corridor. And there she was – framed like a picture. He would let him get a third of the way down the shooting gallery then – ambush! Bayard would want to deal with him first. He was counting on that.

*

Bayard sat in the dark thinking. He'd watched Anders and his men take her out of the apartment building. The Italian had anticipated his return. He smiled. It was a set-up. He gazed at the side-door by which they'd entered.

It had opened. Voices. Anders' colleagues came out and walked towards a lone car. He watched them drive away, wound down his window and listened to the engine fade away in the distance. This was no safe-house. It was a challenge – by a desperate man. To a one-on-one encounter. How amazing!

He made up his mind. Anders was a damaged man. Unreliable nerves, unreliable powers. Though sometimes they worked. However, a suggestible candidate; he could have put him under that last time on the phone. He'd done it before – the fountain. Tonight he'd sow confusion, get to close range, then he'd have to be precise and very, very fast.

He left the van. His new clothes were in the Mercedes parked two streets away. Quietly, carrying his tray of tools with care, he crossed the darkened street. He tried the door. With a plastic card he opened the old lock in a couple of seconds. *Ah!* he sighed. The bolts not shot. What've you arranged Inspector? He drew the pistol, checked it by touch.

Then in the space of an exhaled breath he stepped into the Palais Rohan, soundlessly closing the door behind him. He felt strong.

The corridor was mute, empty of the voices of tourists and the habitués of past centuries. Driving here, similarly, the streets had looked as empty and scrubbed-down as a fish-market at the end of the day. The city had totally soaked up the night's drama. She sat now like a statue gazing ahead into the void. Nerveless. *Stay calm* – to himself. Had he over-rated his ability to bring this off? Taken enough account of the way he was? But luck was with you, or it wasn't. *Stop thinking.*

Ah. A breeze had sailed through the airless rooms to strike his cheek. *Him? Is he in?* He whispered into the room, 'Please don't speak. Don't move from this point on, Madame.' Anders stiffened. The chandeliers were going out. Slowly dying like a sunset. In a moment the corridor was black. He listened. Hearing was vital now. His heart was beating fast. Too fast for a fifty-one-year-old.

But he *was* in the palace! The fates had delivered! How long would it take him to come from the power-control point? Maybe three minutes. 'Take it easy, Inspector.' She'd spoken in a stage whisper. He was excreting fear – she'd picked up those vibrations.

A surge of shock. Undisguised footsteps were coming through the large room beyond the corridor. Rubber squeaking loudly. No effort to hide the approach. A rough French voice was calling back to where it had come from. 'It's in the west wing junction box, Jacques. I'll deal with it.' Suddenly a radio was blaring rock music. A flashlight appeared at the end of the corridor directed at the floor. The voice called out. 'Maintenance coming. Everything under control.' The beam lifted, shot ahead and transfixed Dominique. Kept coming. The hard-rock was powering at them, into them. 'Oh, there you are Madame. Nothing to worry about' – practically shouted.

In a great whoosh Anders' world had become a cloud of darting bats, the air filled with their small, sharp cries. Vigorously he was shaking his head, shooting them out of his mind, flight-by-flight. He stepped out from the alcove, fell into a crouch, levelled the torch – the beam went down the corridor and revealed the big figure in workman's uniform fifteen metres away, coming fast and efficient, jingling with equipment.

Anders was aiming the Beretta at the centre of the equipment-harnessed torso. A giant, jittering shadow was cast behind it. He was concentrating fiercely. *What is this? What is this?* The maintenance man from the basement! *Decision. Decision. Mustn't get to close quarters.* The figure's flashlight beam jumped to the side revealing Anders' face. 'Aha!'

The only way he'll ever be taken is to shoot first. 'Down! On the floor,' he yelled to her. They fired together. Bzzzzz. Anders heard, felt the bullet pass.

The figure lurched in Anders' light-beam, the flashlight shattered. Anders fired again. The figure hurled back without exclamation and thumped on the boards. The pounding music was inside Anders' head.

Anders waited, the torch and the Beretta trained on the recumbent figure ten metres distant. What would the next illusion be? The next hallucination? He was aware that Madame Bosson remained seated. Cautiously he moved forward. Closer. His torchlight played on the face, on the maintenance uniform, equipment, the red hair, the steel-rimmed glasses. The Beretta held unwavering · on the recumbent form.

With a commando yell, from the waist it jack-knifed up.

They both fired. Anders' got him in the chest, felt his hat whipped off.

Anders staggered, then the echoes died away and all was quiet.

'Monsieur Gas, Monsieur Bayard, Monsieur Whoever,' he said, loud enough for her to hear. Though it was difficult to articulate the words. He felt as if every one of his muscles had seized up. The white face on the ground seemed to be settling into death as he stared. 'The Judgment Day group, in person.'

He turned, walked back to the door, the torch-beam wavering over her face. 'Madame Bosson,' he said. She was sitting there: rigid. Sharply he drew in his breath and stopped. From the doorway, the beam of light played on the tense, half-amused face. But she was dead: a red wound in one eye.

Anders swayed. Vertigo swooped at him, as the bats had, then swooped away. He stood midway between the two corpses. A clock in the room was striking midnight with brittle chimes. But everything had stopped for Anders, and the faint fist-pounding below of the

310

imprisoned caretakers seemed, to him, to be coming from another world.

XXII

THE TWENTY-FOURTH
OF OCTOBER

IN THE autumn chill Anders crossed Raven Bridge to the Grande Ile. Walking in his life, surviving in it, he mused why Bayard had taken that difficult head-shot at him. It came to him: after the shot at the Libraire Kleber, Bayard had assumed that he wore a bullet-proof vest! He smiled grimly. Without luck, you didn't survive; you didn't solve cases.

Despite his overcoat he shivered. Wherever you were, autumn penetrated your bones. Quicker, once you passed fifty. He sniffed with his cold. It was·his final day in Strasbourg. His chest still ached and his stump was as painful as it'd been for years.

Bayard's elimination, and his story, had caused a world sensation. Congratulations had poured in – to the French government and the police. Dominique Bosson's death had shocked Europe; had been the crowning sensation. Until the authorities had decided how to play it, it had been sticky. After a flurry of conferences, the inconvenient details of the confrontation at the Palais Rohan had been skilfully glossed over. His actions, after all, had got the big result.

But behind the scenes, the authorities were amazed and

appalled at his action. How did they think *he* felt? No-one had asked.

The French Ministry of the Interior had proved as adept as their Italian counterpart in keeping him under wraps. Initially, a rumour had been leaked that he was wounded, and fighting for his life. Frantic questions on this were met with 'no comment'. When he turned up, five days afterwards, the first white-heat of the media furore had passed. Finally, the French government were portraying him as a reticent officer under great personal strain, hinting at a nervous breakdown. This happened to be close to the truth.

Commissaires Rolland and Dubost were able to accept the responsibility of the limelight.

Anders was dealing with the carnage of that ten days in October, and especially Madame Bosson's death, in his own way: withdrawal, and reticence.

Initially he'd been in shock. Then, the despair had fallen on him drugging his mind and body. But the routine of case-closure had got him through these last days. The nightmares and the hallucinations had stopped. For the present ...

He winced as he turned to look for Ferrand. The detective arrived within a few minutes. They drove to the university. Anders was shown into Professor Lestang's room by a sorrowful secretary, and left alone. To the Italian, the room already had a bereft and dusty air.

He'd been there all the time. The man of the dead face, the dead eyes fixed on the corridor ceiling in the Palais Rohan. In that military photograph with Lestang, blowing up the house. Standing there, in profile. Preparing himself for the future: how much was he planning, even then?

Anders lifted the frame off the wall. Captain Bayard, pencilled on the photo's reverse. Carefully, he replaced it. He looked acutely at the teary-eyed, middle-aged secretary, spoke his commiserations, and departed.

Until the early hours this morning, he'd read Bayard's EC competition directorate's file, and his French Ministry of Defence dossier, the latter scarred with blackouts. Enough remained: a poor kid's scholarships, an economics major, an exchange-student in Stuttgart. Anders had paused there. Had he run into Karl-Heinrich Stuckart at that point? Kept in touch? He must have, to have come after the typewriter. Five years in the military, recruited by the Directorate of Counter Intelligence, interesting activities against Greenpeace in the South Pacific (had he swapped sides at that point?), then a change in direction – more university studies, and into the competition directorate. A loner who could be charming, but not a woman in sight. Not a word about hypnotism, either; the secret life within a secret life. What a man

At this point, Anders sat back and thought about Lestang's grand conspiracy theory. Had the professor been on to something? From what Anders knew of the world, it couldn't be discounted, but he knew also that he'd never get anywhere near anything like that. Nor would they know the juncture at which Bayard's brain, or perhaps others' – if Lestang's thinking was followed – had ignited the terrorism.

A lilting breeze in his face, Anders arrived at the restaurant ten minutes before Marguerite. He exchanged greetings with Signor Cantini. The man's respect for Anders was now enormous. He called him 'Dottore' and had collected all the local press cuttings. On a newsstand he'd caught a headline: *Deutsche Rural-Credit – Shock Bad Debts*. He

315

smiled sardonically. He'd heard the merger had been thrown into doubt.

Marguerite came across the place with her erect, no-nonsense walk, the Kammerzell house behind her. Today the black hair had been fixed with an amber crescent. Her face, hauntingly beautiful to Anders' eyes, seemed in a flash to have detached itself from the abundance of carvings on the half-timbered façade. He stared as she came as straight as an arrow.

He helped her out of her tweed coat, and handed it to Cantini. 'This is a gentleman from Verona, the city of Romeo and Juliet,' he said with a strained smile, introducing the proprietor as he hadn't before.

It was a lunch of good food, though Anders had little appetite, and not so good silences. The Veronese fussed over them, as if sensing the need to build bridges. They did talk of Anders' forthcoming book.

He took the bulky little volume from his pocket and held it out. 'I should return this.'

'Please keep it. For good luck.'

He nodded his thanks. Thoughtfully he regarded it in his hands. It came to him, that here was another act of closure.

'What's next for you?' she asked finally, with an upward shift of eyes which again seemed alight with flecks of amber.

She produced a cigarette. His quick-draw lighter flared. He shrugged. Lyon. 'My computer screen is waiting.' His voice was thick with the cold.

She stared at him through her cigarette smoke. That lovely expressive mouth. He remembered what the kissing of it had been like. It had tasted of crushed berries. No-one was an open book to him, but with the women he found in byways, he'd usually caught the drift of their stories. He hadn't picked it up with Marguerite.

'I'll send you my book,' he said. It was all he could find to say. Though would it ever come out?

She smiled tightly, shook her head involuntarily.

Of course, he knew what was troubling her. How could any normal and reasonable man have brought two woman into such danger? One of them killed. What kind of man was he?

He wished he could tell her about that; soften her stark, disbelieving, yet not unkind gaze. He'd brought her to a window, and shown her another world. One that appalled her. That would appall any normal human being. But he could not tell her. Nor anyone. The wear and tear of his life had rendered him inarticulate about some matters.

All this Anders realised, as they parted with a handshake.

He stood watching her until she was lost in a crowd of tourists.

NOTES ON HYPNOSIS

'The hypnotised individual appears to heed only the
communications of the hypnotist. He seems to respond
in an uncritical automatic fashion, ignoring all aspects
of the environment other than those pointed out to
him by the hypnotist. He sees, feels, smells and otherwise perceives in accordance with the hypnotist's
suggestions, even though these suggestions may be in
apparent contradiction to the stimuli that impinge
upon him. Even the subject's memory and awareness
of self may be altered by suggestion, and the effects of
suggestions may be extended (posthypnotically) into
the subject's subsequent waking activity.'

Encyclopaedia Britannica

'A public which does not know of how hypnosis may
be misused is a sitting target for unscrupulous and
criminal abuses.'

Robert Temple, *Open to Suggestion*

'Under hypnotic trance some subjects can be made to
release, unconsciously, information which they have a
prior strong motivation not to divulge.
Under light hypnotic trance some subjects who are
conscious of what they are doing can be "forced" to

319

divulge information they intend to withhold.'
Jack Watkins, Chief Clinical Psychologist,
US Army Hospital, Florida

'All sciences alike have descended from magic and
superstition, but none has been so slow as hypnosis in
shaking off the evil associations of its origin.'
CL Hull in *Hypnosis and Suggestibility*

The Wooden Leg of
Inspector Anders
by Marshall Browne

The first book in the series introduces the Rome detective who lost a leg – and his nerve – in an anarchist explosion fifteen years ago. Asked to cover up the killing of a judge, he decides to redeem his life with one last dramatic action.

The setting is a city in southern Italy.

'Dazzling mystery debut.'
Publishers Weekly